Acknowledgements

FOR MY EDITOR WHO CAN walk into a room of my characters and tell them to pick a number for their turn to speak. She keeps the voices in my head in line. I simply could not publish a book without you. We've a long journey ahead!

For my fans. This adventure of becoming a published author has been surreal. The best part is meeting all the readers who love Dover's Amalgam as much as I love creating it. To all of you around the world, you are the reason I keep going!

For my beta readers: Bessie Whipp, Tanya DuBois, and Jillian Malloy.

For my proofreader: Alaina Hebert. The original Grammar Nazi and Harry Styles lover. Publish that novel, girl. The world wants to read it!

For Trey whose inspiration found the title for Category Jeremy. I'm still waiting on that theme song!

For the English Heritage Foundation and Friends of Dover Castle. They keep Dover's Castle in tip top condition so generations can enjoy the beauty of British culture and heritage. Visit *http://www.english-heritage.org.uk/* or http://www.dover-castle-friends.org/ to see how you can be involved. A special thanks to Graham Hutchison for allowing me to donate a portion of my books for the upkeep and awareness of the castle. I love being a part of such an amazing place.

Dedication

For Terry, Trey, Jillian, Jonah, and Abbey. If not for your obsession with Smallville, Jeremy would not exist. I can still see little, baby Abbey singing the theme song every Thursday night when it played on the CW. I hope that Jeremy meets your expectations of super hero status. I love you all. Being your mom is the greatest honor ever.

Disclaimer

The hero in this book has autism. Any reference to autism was used for creative purposes and is not intended to diagnosis or treat. I am a proud sponsor of #Lift4Autism. A division of Talk About Curing Autism *http://2016ff.tacanow.org/* It is authors and bloggers coming together to raise medical funds for the families of autistic individuals. Visit their website to find out how you can help Autism Awareness. We can all make a difference.

Chapter 1

A guardian may never prevent the life or death of any given person by means of bending time. It is wrong to interfere in the providence and ultimate will of God.

Rule 1: Amalgam of Dover

TORNADOES ARE CLASSED BASED ON how much they 'consume.' It is pretty much the same with hurricanes in that they are classified by the destruction they cause, thus what they 'eat.' Beau was an expert hurricane tracker. She was only nine years old when Hurricane Libby barreled through Wright, Louisiana, the Gulf Coast community where she was born and raised. By that age she was already a professional weather tracker. It was part of her Cajun lineage to be adept at tracking. Her mother once said that instead of crib mobiles, Cajun babies needed a Saffir-Simpson Scale Chart dangling over cribs. With mega storms on the rise, she had plenty of opportunities to track hurricanes. Living in coastal Louisiana made her a fierce storm tracker.

Libby's name would remain on the lips of future generations as they retold the horror of mass destruction she left in her wake. Packing excess winds of two hundred miles per hour, it was the first unclassified mega storm the world had known. Libby became a class all her own and ushered in the dawn of the mega storms. If the Saffir-Simpson Scale were to be applied, she would be an impossible six and a half. In other words, Libby had no category—she was off the charts.

With her destruction she also stole many lives, particularly the life of Jeremy Cameron—Beau's dearest friend. Beau did not know that while expertly tracking with Jeremy at her side, she would lose him to the storm. If she had known, perhaps she would have insisted that her dad let her evacuate instead of staying behind to man the store her family owned. If she had left, Jeremy would never have gone looking for her in the eye of the storm. He would not have snuck out of the Gueydan High School gymnasium, the town's designated shelter. She had told him her family was evacuating, but instead her dad decided to ride out the storm at home. It was not the first time her dad risked everyone's lives for the almighty dollar. When the storm receded—and recede it did—people would need provisions, and Benoit's Grocery Store would be waiting, open for business.

The news of the missing boy spread quickly throughout the state, and then the nation. Search parties were organized and executed. But it was Beau, along with her cousin Elizabet and Elizabet's new husband, Dr. Jareth Tremaine, who found him—dirty, starving, and . . . something. The storm had altered him. He could do things, like speak with his mind. And while Beau was pretty sure he used those strange powers on Elizabet and Jareth too, she learned the hard way that this should be kept to herself. One hundred sessions with a psychiatrist and an extended stay at a psych hospital cured her of sharing Jeremy's newfound abilities. Elizabet and Jareth disappeared, taking Jeremy with them to some exotic island in the Caribbean and then to London, leaving Beau alone to sort out what happened.

No matter what they tried to make her believe, she knew what really happened, but she needed to see Jeremy again to prove to herself that she was not crazy. It did not matter what anyone else thought. She needed affirmation that she was not a lunatic.

Eight years passed before she saw him again, but when he finally appeared, confronting him was the least of her worries.

The metamorphosis from child to adult had occurred in his absence over the years past. Jeremy was not a quiet, biddable boy any longer. He had changed again, and Hurricane Libby had either nothing or everything to do with it.

JEREMY PRESSED HIS FOREHEAD TO the glass of the window. It was a warm August day, but the artificial air took its toll. His energy was seeping out, radiating from his core as the cold glass drained a portion of his strength.

Life had been perfect in the Cayman Islands and Dover, England. It was rare to lose precious energy in these places. Their climates were perfect for him, and when one failed, there was always the other. Living between two glorious areas was a dream. He did not have any complaints. He had a supportive family who loved him, he was smart, and now he could speak easily and freely. He had been told he was handsome. Living with Jareth and Elizabet Tremaine was wonderful. He could not ask for better adoptive parents. They never treated him any differently than their own children. The twins, Solomon and Abigail, were seven. Peter was five. Gideon was three. And there was one in the oven—another boy they were naming Benjamin. Although their brood was large and growing, he was still considered a part of it. Never did he feel like an outsider. He was a Tremaine in all senses other than by physical birthright.

He leaned back with a huff and pressed the button that allowed the car window to slide down. It had been an hour since he pulled up to Benoit's Grocery. Elizabeth had told him to drive into town for milk, but he was stubborn. He did not want to go the local Winn Dixie when he could walk right into this community store and pay triple for a gallon of milk.

After all, Jareth could afford it. And then Jeremy would get to see Beau, the girl he left eight years ago. The very one who probably hated him as much as she hated her cousin Elizabet for abandoning her. Of course, he'd never know how she felt unless he got out of the car and walked into the store instead of gawking like a stalker from across the parking lot. Today she was working the drive thru window, handing out cigarettes and liquor. The line of cars was impressive for a small mom-and-pop shop; Jeremy figured it had to do with the general laziness of people these days. Why go into a store to purchase one's vices when it was easily done with a drive by? Chris Benoit had capitalized on the wildly popular demand in the South. Beau's father had a way of milking money from every avenue possible. There was a sign that boasted they were open till midnight. Jeremy was willing to bet that Chris did not work late hours, but his children did.

From what he could see, Beau was the same as he remembered her. She still wore her brown hair long. Her face had lost the plumpness of youth and was now exquisite, as he knew it would be. The customers did not tarry, so she had obviously remained all business and no small talk. He smiled at that thought. Eight years could change person,but he reckoned it could not change deep-seeded personalities. After all, he was still the same on the inside. What he felt for Beau remained. It was constant and something he could not shake off. He had tried—desperately.

He had tried, and a few girls had helped the feeling dissipate temporarily, but it never worked in the long run. They were not Beau, and Jeremy knew there was something to that. He had to discover the reason why. Elizabet had cautioned him to take it slow. Beau would need time to forgive them for leaving her behind. She would require space to accept that they were back and he was different. Jareth, however, was completely against it. He reasoned that they could not protect a normal human from the world they lived in. It would complicate things, and should Beau prove unfaithful, it could cause their outing. No one could know he was a host to a hurricane. The secret that he had the ability to destroy much of the world was not something they wanted on the five o'clock news. Within his body was a contained weapon of mass destruction, and people did not generally take well to humans infected with a DNA mutation. The exposure of his kind could lead to the end of his freedom. The end to a life led as closely to normal life as possible.

Added to his turbulent insides was the fact they all had the ability to manipulate time. Jareth was guardian to an array of ancient wristbands that allowed them to jump time, particularly time periods surrounding Dover, England, where Jareth reigned as the duke in the fourteenth century. Yeah . . . that pesky detail could cause a problem, as well.

Having access to time manipulation was not something they could chance being leaked. The ability to bend time was crucial in the survival of hundreds of hosts like him. They were expertly hidden throughout time—stored for use when needed, and overseen by a legion of warriors named guardians. The guardians were chosen from different centuries, and each were rescued from a fateful demise. They were saved from death and trained by Jareth to protect the hosts of Dover's Amalgam. What they were could never be revealed to the common world. Society would have a massive problem welcoming warriors who lived and died by ancient creeds deemed barbaric.

Take the Spartan, Gabriel, as a prime example. You could take the warrior out of Sparta, but you couldn't take Sparta out of the warrior. Sparta wasn't their only representation; the league was a motley conglomeration of combatants, each one scarier than the last. Add that they were necessary and indispensable because of who they were protecting, and welcome to a nightmare of cataclysmic proportions. Ancient warriors who jumped time and ruled over DNA mutated hosts created a recipe for mayhem and misunderstandings.

Although Beau could never know what he was, Jeremy liked to think they could pick up from where they left off. Despite what Jareth said, he could never stop Jeremy from making a friend. And while Jeremy's feelings had evolved into something that bordered obsession, he had to be slow and methodic in his approach. Feelings were fickle, and all the hype he had built up may possibly come crashing down if he realized Beau was merely a girl like the rest of them. They had been the sort of friends who finished each other sentences, knew the likes and dislikes of one another as if it were law, but over the years he recognized that there was more. Underneath the basic companionship was attraction. As children, they protected their bond, and now he had come to terms with the fact they were grooming to be made for each other. To belong to one another.

The mind was a tricky, powerful thing. In his imagination, Beau was capable of no wrong. She had always been perfect. He followed her on social media and literally watched her grow up. He would love to say that he watched her morph into a beautiful woman, but that was only partially true, as it were. He had watched her become a social pariah—granted, a beautiful one. She was lovely, as he expected, but she was haunted by circumstances of his doing. To think of her in no other way but positive, Jeremy labelled her an enchanting outcast. Oh yes, he was obsessed. He wanted her as badly as her father wanted a million dollars brought on by no effort.

A breeze blew through the window, bringing the scent of the approaching autumn, and with it came the sense of biting fear. The sensation was familiar to him, although it had been years since he felt it. He sat up and watched as Beau closed the drive thru window and receded into the store until he saw her no more. Closing his eyes, he allowed his senses to pick up what others could not.

Something red and hot with anger bolted through him and he grappled to open the car door with a trembling hand. It was time to get out of the car and purchase some milk. And perhaps, become a hero.

THE BACK OF BEAU'S NECK prickled as she wiped off the counter near the register. It was not dirty, but she always had to be moving or her dad showed up. It worked that way. Murphy's Law, Elizabet used to call it. She could be busy for hours and sit down for ten seconds and that's when her dad walked in.

Like now. Thank you, Murphy.

"Not many customers tonight," Chris Benoit said as he leaned over the counter and grabbed the keys to the ice machine that hung on a nail next to the cash register. It was a deliberate move, not so much to retrieve the keys, but to impose his presence.

"Thirty-four," Beau said, and scrubbed harder at a spot that did not exist. She hated how she jumped when he crept up like that. It was not so much from fear as agitation. He needed to go away before he made a snide remark that seeped into her heart and soul. There were times she wished he smacked her around; that would make it easier to justify how much she loathed him. "We've had thirty-four customers."

"Should be twice as many."

"Maybe they heard you were back," Beau muttered under her breath. He was home from his hitch off-shore, where he was a part-time cook for a national oil company. *Part-time,* meaning when he felt the inclination to work.

"Or maybe you ran them off with that smart mouth of yours," Chris snapped. The bell chimed as the store door opened, and his face turned friendly in an instant. "You've got a customer."

"Lucky me," Beau said. She tossed aside the rag and smiled facetiously at her dad. "I saw you took the cooler keys. Why don't you make sure the beer is stocked? Rixby said he couldn't do it earlier. Football practice."

Chris's knuckles turned white as he gripped the key ring. His lips curled into a snide smile. He hated when females told him what to do.

And Rixby never did as he was told, period—it didn't matter if it was male or female doing the directing. He was her twin, after all. They were in sync with ticking off their dad, even when they weren't trying. That was where their twinship ended, though. They got along about as well as a snake and field mouse.

Beau glanced at the customer who had entered. He stood at the door with his back to her, staring at Chris over in Row One—the candy and Little Debbie aisle. A prickling sensation crept over her as she realized he was a stranger. And while many of their customers were hunters and fishermen from out of town, this one was different. He was dressed way too nicely to be someone passing through looking for bait, ammo, or tackle. "Can I help you?" she asked.

He was big. Tall, broad-shouldered and devilishly handsome from what she could tell. If only he had not turned away so quickly. He glared at Chris as he passed, his large frame eating up the width of the aisle as he strode forward like a man on a mission.

"Milk?" He had an accent. It was barely detectable, though, because he spoke in a guttural tone. She could see his jaw work, grinding his molars, and hear his breathing. His barrel chest sawed in and out methodically as he continued to sweep the area with his gaze, but it stopped at Chris again. His stance widened a fraction, and his body hid Chris from her view.

Beau pointed to the coolers at the back of the store and she noticed that her hair was standing on end. "Over there," she said. She frowned and shook her arm in that general direction. "Against the back wall, next to the fishing nets and crab traps."

"He might like something to go with his milk," Chris added. He moved closer to his daughter. He lifted one blond eyebrow and tilted his head. "Cereal, snack cakes . . ."

"Just the milk," the customer said, his voice forceful. He was right there behind Chris, gallon of milk in hand, overhearing everything that was said.

Beau's eyes narrowed. The guy was quick. The store was small, but she had not detected when he left the cooler. It was weird.

Chris straightened slowly and pasted a smile on his face as he turned. His gaze was even with the stranger's pecs, so he stepped back and tipped his head up. The smile turned faker still. "She can get you right here." He patted the conveyer belt with his palm, but his eyes stayed on the stranger.

Beau switched on the conveyer belt. The sound of Chris' palm squeaking on the rubber made her cringe, but it was worth it. She did not want to stand there privy to their pissing contest, although it was the most entertainment she had enjoyed at her father's expense in a while.

The unknown customer reached around Chris and placed the milk on the conveyer, then looked head on at Beau. "Thank you for your help, Beau."

Beau grabbed the milk as he spoke and made eye contact with her. The stranger's height and nerve was not the only thing that set him apart. His black hair and blue eyes also did. The two were so contrasted it was eerie. She had only known one other person with features like that. The gallon she was holding became wobbly and slammed against the scanner.

No, no, *no*.

"Jeremy." The name tumbled out of her mouth.

He smiled then, eyes crinkling. His shoulders bunched together as he crammed his hands into his front pockets. "Yeah." He nodded. It was a shy gesture and his face flushed to go along with the sweetness of his features that made him uniquely him.

It made her feel better that he was not Mr. Cool while she stood there about to have a panic attack. Her heart was like a feral caged animal in her chest, screaming to escape, banging its body back and forth against the cage. After all these years, Jeremy Cameron stood at her register, buying milk. And a pack of gum that he tossed on the trolley as an afterthought. The walls fell away and it was just them—in the moment.

"You're back." Beau felt her face flush. It was a hot type of flush that she knew was not attractive.

He nodded again, watching her with a slight tilt to his head as if he were curious or expectant. His lips quivered as if he were going to speak, but thought better of it and said nothing.

Chris narrowed his eyes as he looked between them, taking in the tension. His voice erupted the shell they had created, but it did not affect the intensity of the situation. "Well, well, lookit who's come home." Jeremy's smile grew as Beau's face turned the color of ripe persimmon. "You came back with that fancy doctor?"

Beau was aware they were staring openly at one another, sizing up and measuring the changes that had occurred. But the silence was stretching out and he had a question to answer, so out of habit she prodded him. "Talk, Jeremy."

"Yes, ma'am," Jeremy said, his smile nearly blinding now, and all for her. It struck her in that glorious second that he was speaking in full phrases and her prodding hadn't been necessary. His speech was not flawed, and he seemed to enjoy that she was dumbfounded at that. The smile he sported was indeed more mocking than charming at closer inspection. What flowed from his lips could not even be classified as mere words. They were mini songs—lyrics spoken in the dialect of a cultured lord. His accent was British . . . and devastating.

He tore his gaze from Beau to look down at Chris. "Dr. Tremaine and Elizabet are my adoptive parents. Jareth—Dr. Tremaine—has opened a surgery clinic in Vermilion Parish. The location is perfect, because we're also here to help the Presbyterian Church with regulations. Jareth is both surgeon and reformer." He shrugged with one shoulder. "It would seem that the south is a hotbed for something other than mega storms. A doctrinal breach has been identified here in this community. Besides that, this area needs a good surgeon. The last one retired three years ago and has never been replaced. Like I said, it's the perfect location for dual purposes."

"You mean to fight the regulation?" Chris asked, his tone shifting to cocky. Of course, he had honed in on the scandalous part and not the casual small talk of health networks. "Good luck with that."

"We do not require luck." Jeremy's mouth curved at the corners. "We will win. The liberation of Church from State is a matter of technicalities and Dr. Tremaine is here to see justice served. He has much experience in Church reformation and he never loses. You are mistaken if you believe a fight will occur. But if it does, the doctor has never lost when matters of doctrine purity are at stake. To that, sir, you have no idea the tenacious moral implications he follows in the highest regard."

Chris opened his mouth to respond, but the chime sounded as another customer strolled in, thereby saving him. Beau was quite sure he hadn't understood half of what Jeremy just spouted. She hadn't understood all of it, but she cataloged it away to pick apart when he wasn't around to gawk at. Ogling was a much better choice at the present. She was listening, too, and had been caught off guard when Jeremy began speaking in complete sentences with a heart-shattering, bone-melting drawl.

Chris tipped his chin to Jeremy and thrust his hand out. "See that Beau gives you the preacher's discount. We do our part for clergy here at Benoit's Grocery. Regulations be damned."

Jeremy hesitantly stuck his hand out to shake Chris's hand, and his eyes tapered as he watched the older man walk away, zoned in on the next pliable customer.

Beau continued to watch Jeremy whilst he was unaware. The way his dark hair curled at the nape of his expensive Oxford cloth shirt and how his waist was narrow, but the rest of him filled out his designer jeans broadly was simply . . . delicious.

It was not fair that he had changed so drastically while she had stayed relatively the same. Her frumpy shirt and dirty boots were visible; he might make an assessment of her and find her lacking. Of all the dreaming she had done, this was not supposed to happen this way. Jeremy should not be dressed in designer clothes looking more like a fashion model than a red-blooded, all-American boy.

She scowled, coming out of the cloud of yearning she had created. Chris' crass words and her wayward thoughts needed to be reined in. "Bravo," she said. Her voice sounded rusty. She cleared her throat, embarrassed that it had squeaked. She clapped her hands lazily to hide the tremoring.

Jeremy turned to her, his eyes saying that he had known she was sizing him up and liked what he saw. Her clapping ceased as she noticed her inability to hide the slight tremble. "Why didn't I ever notice the similarity between your dad and politicians?"

She glowered and cleared her throat again in case it decided to squeak unbidden. "That was a fine thing you did there," she drawled. She hated that he knew her history. He remembered that she lived in a household where women were . . . well, not equal. Women cooked, cleaned and took care of the men in their lives. He knew her father was a total moron, even though he tended to be slick about it. "Sort of like old times, except you actually said words." Her gaze was hard. "You opened your mouth and something came out." She waved her hand blindly in the air and then propped it on her hip. "When exactly did that start to happen?"

"A while ago." He leaned forward, a grimace on his pretty face. "I guess that wasn't such a good idea. I should've have warned you—or him. Both, maybe?"

"You think?" She let her tone become caustic. Although it obviously didn't bother her dad that Jeremy was speaking now, it made her head mushy, and her tongue would probably say stupid things because of it. She read the price sticker on the milk and viciously punched numbers on the register. Her hands were too weak to pick up the gallon and run it over the scanner. It was taking all her blood supply to feed her brain and she needed to be sharp. It also felt as though her heart was about to explode. But besides all of that, she had to ask the million-dollar question. "So, did your voice change automatically once you were adopted by a British doctor? How does that work? Enlighten me. I need to know these things for when Elizabet decides to talk to me again, too. I want to be prepared for when she sounds like the Queen of England."

He straightened, motioning absently to his mouth. "Oh, this." He shrugged and it was adorable. Beau wanted to kick her own backside for noticing. "Happened after Libby. I lost my voice from the trauma." He smiled, but she did not follow suit. His shoulders slumped and he dug his hands into the front pockets of his jeans. He chewed the corner of his lip when the bell chimed on the door as another customer came into the store. Jeremy lowered his voice. "So, um . . . Jareth employed a voice coach until I learned to speak again. Elizabet sounds the same. I guess. She sounds the same to me, at least."

"It's . . . different," Beau said. She stared at his mouth. He grinned sheepishly, looking every bit like the Jeremy she remembered, but way hotter. Her mouth turned down in the corners; he would not make her forget every transgression that had passed between them just because he went and got attractive. "Do you think you can simply walk in here and start making small talk with me? You think I'll just forget how you left? You never answered any of my letters. Did you even get them?"

The past several years had not been pleasant for Beau. The reason so many teenagers lament over bullying and injustice is because it truly exists—and thrives. She would go as far to assert that every teenager had a degree of misery allotted to them, but hers was a cut above the norm, and on top of that, she had been alone. The two people she counted on abandoned her, and one of them was the cause of her own personal trauma.

"There it is," Jeremy said. He pulled one hand from the confine of his pocket and wafted it in the air. "The large elephant in the room. I wondered when you would call the fellow out for a roundabout."

"Did you get my letters?"

"Yes."

The breath left Beau's lungs at his admission. She shakily pushed the milk aside and reached for the gum. "So, you just ignored me?"

Jeremy's eyes were on the gum as she scanned it. "It was forbidden to me," he murmured.

Beau tossed the gum at him. It hit him square in his chest and tumbled back onto the counter. He blinked owlishly at her. "Forbidden? By whom? Elizabet or that control freak she married?"

Chris peered across the aisles at the rising volume of their voices.

"Beau. Your dad," Jeremy warned. He tipped his head slightly.

She wouldn't even ask how he knew her dad was staring when Jeremy had his *back* to him. Did he have eyes behind his head or was his memory that good? And did she honestly just hit him with the gum he was purchasing? "Do you think I care?" she asked instead. She snapped her hand at him. "You just told me that my letters were forbidden to you. Why would anyone forbid you to read a letter, Jeremy? That's stupid, weird and . . . well, it's just stupid. Let's just leave it at that."

"Not forbidden to *read* them," he clarified. He leaned forward, and his hands came to rest on the counter between them. "I read every single one of them." He tapped his index finger on each syllable. "More than once." Beau stepped back, but Jeremy reached out and grabbed her wrist to stay her. "It tortured me not to respond, you have to believe me. I wouldn't have left you if it hadn't been absolutely necessary."

"You could've fooled me," Beau hissed, then shook her arm until he released her. She looked pointedly at the register and drew in the best calming breath she could muster. "That will be nine dollars and ninety-seven cents."

His mouth dropped open a bit. "Bloody hell, that's expensive!" He shook his head and reached for his wallet. "Is this how you plan on extracting your revenge? By inflation?"

"Buying local keeps small businesses open." She allowed her tone to sound hostile, and his hand paused.

She struggled to maintain her aloofness. His face was the sweetest one she could remember and he was looking at her as though she had just kicked a kitten. It made her feel mean-spirited. She could hardly remember a time when he was angry or upset, but she had to protect her heart or he would think he could walk in here like nothing happened.

"Well, in that case," he said, turning on his heel.

She watched him with her eyes narrowed. Was he planning to walk out of the store? But no. Instead, he loaded his arms full of groceries, mostly fruit, yogurt, and two boxes of Wheat-O cereal. He worked quickly, probably mindful that he was holding up her register—and she hated how she knew that about him. He dumped the contents onto the counter with a lady-killing smile on his face.

"Will that be all?" she asked as she ran the groceries over the scanner. There was a theme to the items. All were healthy and natural. Did he plan to eat all of this himself? At one time his choices would have been candy, soda, and snack cakes. Again, her memory was her enemy. She should forget all the small details that made him humanly Jeremy and not the big bad wolf.

"Is it enough?" he asked.

She looked up at him, her eyebrows raised.

"To keep you in business? I want my local store to stay open. How else will I get the chance to see and speak with my all-time favorite cashier? I bought all of the bananas and apples." He thumbed over his shoulder. "You'll have to restock the cereal. There's only one box left."

"And the yogurt?" she asked sarcastically. Outwardly, she ignored his comment about her being his favorite, while inwardly, she fanned herself for being his favorite anything—and he most certainly did not need to know that.

He held up two fingers.

"Is all of this for you?"

He nodded, his smile showing all of those white teeth. "I'm a growing boy."

Of their own accord, her eyes did an up and down motion from his head to toe. And immediately regrets it. "Thirty-five dollars and sixty-seven cents."

Jeremy held out a fifty dollar bill and Beau snatched it from him.

"Umm," he hummed, looking sheepish as she gathered his change from the register. "You didn't answer me. Was it enough? Because I can get more. I saw that you had a local food section. Is the honey good? I see it's harvested here in Wright."

Beau placed his change in the center of the counter; she didn't want to touch him. "It will never be enough for you," she answered. Jeremy reached out, and the side of his hand brushed hers before she could pull away. "I don't care if you buy the entire store out. You'll never be able to fix what you did."

Jeremy drew back, his eyes trained on her fingers as she cradled the hand he touched in her other hand, massaging it to stop it from tingling.

His eyes smiled as he gathered his groceries. Tipping his head as a goodbye gesture, he walked out of the store.

And out of her life—again. He hadn't answered her ugliness, which was so like him. Because, while the old Jeremy was non-verbal to everyone else, he was always able to talk with her. And always the sweetest person she knew.

Beau looked down at her hand. Something had passed between them. Electricity? Feelings? Thoughts? Perhaps all of the above. She rubbed her hand against her thigh. There was no use dwelling on it. She would get her chance. If he was back, then so was Elizabet. And Elizabet was family, which meant she would eventually see her cousin. Her cousin would probably have her adoptive son along—ergo, Jeremy.

She would be ready next time. Jeremy had questions to answer.

Chapter 2

A host is forbidden to interact with humans during the training period. Once control and safety have been established, the host should be gradually reintroduced to family and familiars.
Paraphrased by Jeremiah Cameron Tremaine

Rule 2: Amalgam of Dover

JEREMY PLOPPED DOWN IN THE grass next to Jareth. "What are you staring at?" He looked up at the blue sky that was riddled with clouds and took a deep breath of fresh, country air. Louisiana had a different scent than Dover, but it was not unpleasant. It was not familiar, either, and this was where he spent most of his childhood. His family had relocated from Oregon when he was five. So while Louisiana wasn't his original birthplace, it was the place he remembered most, and that made it pleasant. His old nature preferred things of habit.

The irony was that they moved south to escape what happened to his father's brother, Uncle Eddie. In 1980, Eddie went on a field trip with the elementary school he attended. It was an excursion to Spirit Lake, located on Mount St. Helens. Needless to say, only Eddie survived the field trip and he was never the same. The mountain made sure of that. The family flipped out and sent him away to a commune on the Cayman Islands, where he had resided ever since. As Jedidiah Cameron, Jeremy's father, matured, he realized that Jeremy was a lot like his brother, Eddie. They both had autism and Jedidiah saw that as a thread. Although being a host was hidden within his family, they had done a bit of research on their own. The irony was that they escaped the volcano only to run into the arms of a hurricane that was more than willing to turn Jeremy. The move to Louisiana had been a precursor to his turning.

"Nothing," Jareth said as he blindly spun the spoon in the ice cream quart that rested on his chest. He shoveled a mouthful into his mouth. "All right, you caught me. I am lying." He took a deep breath and shoved in another heaping spoonful. "I am worrying." His words were mumbled as the frozen confection slid down his throat. "Here is my new spot where I come to worry."

"That was easy." Jeremy laughed. He knew something was up. It wasn't every day that Jareth lay on the ground dressed in a three-piece suit. The tie was undone and draped over his shoulders as if he had tugged it off in a hurry. The man was the captain of the fashion police; his burden had to be great if he was willing to risk grass stains on his new bespoke suit from Saville Row. "What is worry but a reminder that we are faithless creatures?"

Jareth glanced at him, but did not turn his head. "Using my words against me? Do you not have any originality?"

Jeremy reached over and used two fingers as a scoop into the ice cream. The cold shot through his fingers, up his arm, and into his core. He felt his heartbeat decrease instantly. "I'll give you an advantage and eat something cold."

"*Pff!* I am not at a disadvantage. You just want ice cream." Jareth drew the quart away at arm's length. "Are your hands clean?"

"Too late if they weren't," Jeremy said, his mouth full. He sucked his fingers and showed them to Jareth. "All clean now, for sure."

"Juvenile," Jareth said with a sniff, then balanced the bucket on his pectorals again. "And very, very nasty."

Jeremy smiled and brought his hands behind his head. Ice

cream was not worth the price. The day was brisk and he need-ed all the warmth he could maintain. He closed his eyes and let the sun feed him what he had lost from a spoonful of momen-tary self-indulgence. Besides, he had just eaten all of the grocer-ies he had bought at Benoit's Grocery. He should be good until dinner. "I saw Beau when I went to the store earlier."

"I know."

Jeremy frowned. "Is anything sacred in this house?"

"No."

"Since you know it all—tell me what you're worrying about?" Jeremy asked. "So I can know everything too and feel special."

"Elizabet. Her pregnancy." Jareth felt the ground beside him blindly until he recovered the lid of the quart.

"She is quite small, but she has done well all the other times."

"This I know, but that does not stop scenarios of monstrous proportions playing through my mind." Jareth frowned. "We are perhaps the most vain of creatures. I have no control over any of this. Drives me nuts. I keep wondering, 'what if she labors while we are in medieval England?' I do not have fetal monitoring at the castle."

"You've never had this concern before."

"She's getting older." Jeremy passed him a look and Jareth laughed. "I know, Twenty-six is *ancient*." His expression sobered as he placed the ice cream bucket to the side, far from Jeremy. "I am becoming spoiled by technology and want all the latest in the castle, even though I tempt time if I relent. Our time in medieval Dover is increasing as I train Solomon to the duke-dom. The passing of mantles is a serious matter and I want him prepared for the task."

"He's seven years old, Jareth."

"One is never too young. It is essential that being the Duke of Dover be ingrained in his innermost nature. It must be a part of him. Solomon should love the land as I do, and he will not develop that bond in modern England, nor here in Louisiana. Must I remind you that twenty-first century Dover Castle is no longer the residence of the acting duke?"

Jeremy could not help it; he laughed. Jareth's knickers always got twisted when he contemplated modern Dover. "Sounds like you're at an impasse. Just smuggle in a complete OB unit and that should make you happy."

"I have recently been reminded by Harrow that the more I smuggle in, the more I must hide and be ready to destroy." Jareth waved his hand dismissively. Speaking of his surgical mentor often made him testy. Harrow's personality was a menace on the best of days. "But do not trouble yourself over my worries. You are here to talk." He looked at Jeremy. "So, speak. I am all ears."

"Ah, so you know it's not your company I seek."

Jareth laughed ruefully. "My flawless counsel is known worldwide, but you are a teenager and do not care of such lofty guidance and reputable reputations."

"I want to see Beau."

"Ah, straight to it," Jareth said. His smile disappeared. "Brave lad." He crossed his arms over his chest.

Jeremy grinned up at the sky. "I am a Tremaine, after all. Not by birth, but by all that matters." People told him often that he could pass for a Tremaine. He had the same black hair and blue eyes as Jareth; the same build, same mannerisms. Turning into a storm hadn't only altered his DNA. Living with a medieval knight had its kickbacks. It was impossible not to adapt to the way of life that had no shades of gray. People frequently commented it was uncanny how alike they were, and not just in physical appearance.

"Buttering me up shall not work," Jareth replied. They watched the clouds reflectively for a moment before he spoke again, his voice lower and filled with concern. "You think this will end well? Would you care to recall the last time you decided to be amorous?"

"That was Malia. She was like gasoline to fire. And I wouldn't say I was voluntarily amorous. That was stalking on her part, and frankly, I got tired of running from her." Jeremy didn't want to talk about Malia and Beau in the same breath. It was sacrilegious.

"That is how you expect me to see it?" Jareth asked. "I caught you in a compromising position and your excuse it that you were *tired?*" He made a *tsk*ing noise. "I do not believe a word of that, but I digress. We are speaking of Beau, and they are two very different ladies." He glanced at Jeremy. "Do you understand the risk you are asking of me? Of us, the family? What happens when she picks up on things? Clues I know you cannot prevent from spilling? You do remember that she is sensitive to your abilities because you have ties to her."

"I've learned to hide it. It will be different this time. I'm in control."

"It is autumn, Jeremy. You will grow weak as the seasons change. It will become difficult for you to hide your condition. To be in the kind of relationship you are seeking requires total honesty. You cannot conceal who you are when you are romantically involved."

"You had to bring up the word romantic, didn't you?" Jeremy asked. He crossed his arms over his chest and glared at a cumulous cloud roving the sky. "You promised me I would have a normal life. I've done everything you asked of me, now it's my turn."

Jareth rolled up slowly, running his long fingers through his hair. He rested his elbows on his bent knees and sighed.

Jeremy stared at Jareth's bowed head. "Look—you know how I am. I can't get her out of my head. I've tried. Nothing has worked. I want the same chance you had. Is this too much to ask of a man who adores his family to distraction? You and I are alike, Jareth. We find that one person and that's it for us. Beau is my Elizabet. I know it."

"She was just a child then," Jareth said, and then glanced behind him. "She may have changed. She may not be the loyal soul you remember, nor the prized confidant you once knew. *You* are the reason her reputation is in tatters. *You* are the reason she is mocked as a nut case. Have you considered the implications of those facts?" His hair went in every direction from fretting with his hands as he sighed again, this time forcefully. "But as much as I am loath to admit it, you and Beau together would make the duchess immensely happy."

"Did you have to ruin it with all that other drivel? All that rot about her being crazy is my fault? The part about me and Beau being together would've sufficed," Jeremy grumbled. "Even repeating the word romantic would have been welcome."

"I did know this day was coming," Jareth admitted. "Your obsessions are few and far between, but this one remained. Under all of that superhero bull is still just a boy struggling with social norms with an over obsessive disorder that vexes the both of us." He smiled with half his mouth. "Perhaps it will be a good thing? I would rather like getting to know her. Elizabet has missed her and it will be good for the children to know their mother's family."

Jeremy sat up abruptly. "You see? This is a good idea."

"Good idea?" Jareth asked with a grimace. "Bleh! Never a good idea. I said a good *thing*. Big difference. Love involves pain and sacrifice sometimes, and in this instance, I say pain. That is why I ask you to let it happen naturally. Do not seek it out. If it is meant to be—"

"I'll challenge you for it," Jeremy interrupted. Jareth fed on competition. "If I win, I get to go straight for it. I'll walk up to Beau and be like, 'hey, you and me.'" He motioned to himself and a pretend Beau. "'We belong together.' I might even *do* something romantic if so inclined." Jareth rolled his eyes. "If you win, I sit back and watch it happen. Gradually. Boringly. Like the rest of your life."

Jareth crossed his arms and reached up to stroke the neatly trimmed hair on his chin. "I would not say boring." He grinned. "What I do with the duchess is hardly boring."

"Okay, gag." Jeremy mimed, poking his finger down his throat and pretending to wretch. "You can't keep talking like that. We're not in Dover anymore, Toto. People don't make reference to their marital bed while speaking with their kids."

"Technically, you are not my son. You are my friend."

Jeremy shook his head. "Mere technicality. People won't care. They know I'm adopted and I am a mere ten years younger than you are, so technically—"

"I could never be your father. I would have been twelve years old when I sired you." His pointed look bored into Jeremy. "Not impossible from where I hail, but demented to the modern mind. And I have a modern mind where procreation is concerned."

Now it was Jeremy who rolled his eyes. "Where are we going with this conversation?"

"You are giving me a lecture as to why I should not make reference to my virulent marriage bed." Jareth looked smug when Jeremy scowled and shook his head. "Knowing, by example, that children thrive in an environment where their parents exhibit healthy, romantic ideations for one another."

"Still gagging," Jeremy said. He made a chopping motion with his hand. "Look—enough. I haven't got all day. Swords and shield or rapiers? Your choice."

"Rapiers are the best bet here." A diabolical smile curved on Jareth's full mouth as he pointed to the ground. "We cannot have the neighbors thinking we are barbarians with swords and shields." His nose crinkled. "At least, not yet."

"So, rapiers?"

One of Jareth's bushy black eyebrows rose as he lifted his

left hand to inspect the nailbeds. "You shall lose."

"No, I won't," Jeremy said. He leapt to the balls of his feet in one graceful movement. "You taught me that when fighting for issues of the heart, one rarely loses."

Jeremy lost, and Jareth was a liar. One did not automatically win when it was a heart issue.

"Do not look so glum," Jareth said with a grin. He moved the asparagus around his dinner plate and then speared one. Jeremy's jaw tensed. The spearing of the vegetable held the same passion the rapier had against his chest but an hour ago. He knew when he was being taunted. "I do believe that slow and boring have their redeeming traits." Jareth pointed the forked asparagus at Jeremy. "Mark my words, it is for the best."

"What are you fighting over now?" Elizabet asked as she leaned over Jareth to place a bowl of smothered okra on the table. Jareth and Jeremy both grimaced at the added vegetable. Her arm brushed Jareth's shoulder and he turned instinctively toward her. The besotted expression that appeared on his face always made Jeremy feel awkward. But when he glanced at his siblings, he saw they were oblivious. Perhaps there was healthiness in romantic displays after all, as Jareth claimed. "Is this about Beau?"

"It is all settled, love," Jareth said before he crammed the asparagus into this mouth. "Jeremy will take the Tremaine approach." He shrugged, and chewed viciously with his mouth closed. "Suave, debonaire—"

"Ugh," Jeremy and Elizabet said in unison. They glanced at each other and Jeremy motioned for her to take the conversation over. She had a better chance at making Jareth see reason.

"I've been thinking." Elizabet wiped her hands on the pink cupcake printed apron she wore stretched over her slightly rounded belly and stood back. Jareth laid his fork down, and slowed his chewing. "Since Beau won't talk to me, maybe Jeremy can get through to her. She had a whole conversation with him at the store while she hung up on me when I tried to call. Twice."

"She threw him out of the store," Jareth said after he swallowed. He reached for the glass near his plate. "The girl needs time to adjust before he throws himself at her." He gave Jeremy a severe look. "You broke the code. We settled this over rapiers. Did you forget how it works?"

"Spare me the man codes and testosterone flying around everywhere," Elizabet said. She turned to Gideon's high chair and rearranged the asparagus that had fallen off his plate. "Jeremy shouldn't have to wait for anything. It's not as if they are getting married tomorrow."

Jeremy choked. Elizabet hit his back without looking at him, but kept her gaze fixed on her husband.

"We know how this will end," Jareth muttered over the rim of his glass. He gulped down a hearty portion of apple juice. "Someone is liable to get hurt. Namely, Jeremy."

"Daddy," Abigail said suddenly. "Mummy said we would have a guest for dinner tonight. It is rather nasty of you to be so cross when we shall have company."

Jeremy looked up from his plate. The children were all freaks of nature of a different sort than him. They were child prodigies like their father and spoke with the vocabularies of adults. It was creepy at times, but he was glad for the interruption. He could tell when Elizabet was losing and she was, most definitely.

"Whatever are you speaking of, princess," Jareth asked with a pasted smile on his face. "Daddy is on call tonight." He passed Elizabet a heated glance. "Mummy knows not to have guests when I might be called away."

"Unless I wished it that way," Elizabet murmured. Jareth's left eyebrow rose. She smiled facetiously. "Well, you're being such an unreasonable—"

"Do not say it," Jareth warned. He looked at Elizabet

sideways. "You would not dare. The children." He motioned to whom he spoke of.

"*Jackass*," Elizabet mouthed over the twins' heads as she made her way to her seat at the opposing head of the massive table. She tucked her apron primly as she took her seat.

"I believe my man card may be revoked after all." Jareth sounded exasperated. He looked down at his plate and frowned. "I halfway expect my food to accuse me of being unreasonable as well." He passed Elizabet a disgusted look. "Ah, I see you have slipped okra onto my plate unaware. It is known to deplete testosterone significantly. Mrs. Wheatley," he turned to the kitchen and shouted for the servant. "Hurry, bring the trash bin. Elizabet is attempting to emasculate me in front of the children."

Abigail and Solomon giggled, which made Peter do so as well. Even Gideon had a belly laugh from his high chair. Jareth had his way with disarming a feud by getting the children's funny bones involved. It always worked. The case was closed.

But then the doorbell chimed and Elizabet sprang up as if she had been bitten. Jareth turned to Jeremy, who had dug back into his meal, while the children's giggles died down to lower volume.

"I'll get that," Elizabet chirped.

Jareth narrowed his eyes and looked to his oldest child. "Solomon," he said in a low voice. "Who is this mystery guest Mummy's invited?"

Solomon placed his fork next to his plate methodically and sat up straight as if he were ready to conjugate Latin. "Cousin Beau, of course."

Jeremy's stomach took a nosedive as he bussed the carrots around the steak on his plate. He was wrong. Elizabet was not losing. She held the ace card—a whole bloody hand of aces. How blessedly sneaky she was. His mouth could not help but smile in triumph.

Jareth ground his jaw. "But of course."

BEAU KNEW BEFORE SHE ARRIVED that she would not be eating. Her stomach was unsettled each time she thought of what she would say or how she would act when face to face with Jeremy. It had been so long. She had been invited for dinner, but there was no way she planned on staying long enough for a meal. Between the two times she had hung up on Elizabet, she had managed to say that *maybe* she would drop by for dinner.

Yet, here she was ringing the doorbell at a home that should be in a magazine. It was newly built, way out in the country, standing alone in the middle of a field. The driveway was two miles long. She knew because she had clocked it. Things the Tremaine's owned were extravagant; she had expected all of it.

It was not basic curiosity that brought her here, nor was it the invitation from Elizabet. Although her strained, absent relationship with her cousin needed to be addressed, it was her incessant urge to get into Jeremy's mind and find out what happened that intrigued her enough to pass by. Elizabet had an excuse. She got married and went away with her husband. Whatever. Stuff like that happened. People getting lost in storms and performing mind tricks did not.

She tipped her head back to admire the large home that was fashioned after a classic antebellum manor. It held both classic features and something that was uniquely Elizabet, like the cupola off to the right of the house. That medieval gothic element looked odd added to the overall architectural design, but it strangely fit. Had her aunt, Elizabet's mother, been alive, she would have loved it.

The door swung open, causing her to step back at the suddenness. She was twice as shocked that it was Elizabet answering the door. Her heart contracted painfully to see the likeness of their mothers, who had been twins, in this new, older Elizabet. Twins ran wildly in their family. There were their mothers, herself and Rixby, and then her mom threw another set, Amos and Aries. Elizabeth's firstborns were the latest installment.

"You came," Elizabet said. Her hands twisted in her apron as she used it to dry her hands.

Beau pursed her lips together in an effort to stave off saying something hurtful. She tamped down the alarm gnawing in her belly and focused on why she was here. It was on the tip of her tongue to tell her cousin that she wasn't here to see her, but in the end, a nod was all she managed.

Elizabet swept her arm open. "Please, come in." She stepped aside. "Welcome."

Beau breached the threshold, keeping her cousin within her vision as she tried to take in the décor without seeming like a poor relation. She grimaced at the thought. She was, in fact, a poor relation. Her home was a metal building attached to a grocery store that boasted a cigarette drive-thru.

"We started dinner," Elizabet said. She closed the door behind them. "When you weren't here at six, I assumed you were held up or something."

"Rixby's doing part of my shift," Beau said, her eyes on the large oil painting in the foyer. It covered almost half of a wall. She stepped further inside. The interior was huge; tall ceilings, fancy, antique knick knacks, and a suit of armor in the corner. She had to do a double take. "I was late because I had to jump start the minivan."

"Oh," was all Elizabet said.

Beau swung to face her. She looked her up and down; the silver knight's armor was forgotten when she heard the pity in her cousin's tone.

Elizabet wore a pair of navy blue scrubs under the cutesy apron. "You didn't forget what it was like to work, did you?"

Beau smirked as her gaze landed on the distended girth beneath the apron. "I see that you're working in a different kind of way now."

Elizabet's hospitable demeanor vanished. "How dare you speak to me that way in my own house." Her voice lowered, became fierce. "Jareth is a good man. It's a privilege to be his wife and the mother of his children. I've made my own decisions. I'm not your mother, Beau. I don't get beaten. Not physically or verbally." Beau looked away as her face heated. Elizabet blew out a loud breath. "I didn't invite you over to fight, but I refuse to act as if I haven't wronged you." Beau snapped back to attention. Elizabet pointed menacingly; she still moved around while she spoke. It was a habit she owned since a child. At one time, Beau had thought it was cute, but today it aggravated her. It was another reminder that their closeness had been ignored and trampled. "Stop being mean. We have never walked on eggshells before and I won't start now, but for the sake of my young children, I ask that you behave until we can clear the air between us."

"I'm not here for dinner with your family," Beau said, her voice low. "I'm here to talk to Jeremy. That's it. I'm not ready to hash it out with you. I'm sure there will be plenty of time for that later."

Elizabet stood straighter, obviously insulted that her invitation was being sidestepped. "You'll say hello to my family before I let you talk to Jeremy." Beau shrugged and crammed her hands into the back pockets of her jeans. "And you'll be nice."

Beau took a step back instead of forward. When had Elizabet become so loyal to this family? It was like a slap in the face. Once upon a time, it had been her that Elizabet championed, and now it was reversed. She did not like it at all. It made her remorseful, however. She may act as if she did not care, but she did. She still loved Elizabet. What she was doing was grandstanding, plain and simple. She had to protect what was left of her heart.

"Of course," Beau stammered, her pretense slipping. "I would never hurt your kids, Lizabet. I know what that's like. Remember?"

"I remember." Elizabet kept eye contact with her for a while before motioning her forward. "I can't just call him out. He's in the dining room with the rest of us. We don't do dysfunctional. It's poor form and Jareth won't allow it. I'll introduce you and then you can speak with him in the den." She put her hand on Beau's arm and they stopped walking. "This isn't how I planned things to happen, but I get it. It's a lot to stomach all at one time." Beau pulled away, but Elizabet followed, keeping a hold on her. "Don't ask too much of him. There are questions he can't answer—ever. You'll have to live with that if you want to be in his life again." Elizabet's eyes shadowed. "He's different. He's vulnerable. After Libby, he was never the same."

"I just want to talk to him without everyone around." Beau schooled her face to not give her satisfaction away. It was good to know that Jeremy's defenses were down. Hers were down, too, and that made them even. She did not know what to expect. That made her susceptible to groveling, or worse. Begging him to never leave again was not an option she wanted to explore. She had to stay strong and the best way was not to have an audience. Besides, no matter what Elizabet warned, Beau was going to be asking Jeremy the hard questions.

"You'll get your wish, but there is a catch. I must warn you that Jareth is old fashioned. You'll have to be chaperoned. The doors must stay open."

Beau's eyes widened. "You don't do dysfunctional, but you'll do freaking weird? Really, Lizabet? Chaperoned?"

Elizabet held up her hand. "I'll ignore that and leave it to that I've explained Jareth is old school." She smirked. "And British. Believe me when I say there's a whole 'nother way of doing things across the pond."

"Whatever." Beau sniffed, insulted that she was being treated like a child. Was chaperoning even a word? "Just get Jeremy already. Rixby isn't doing my whole shift. I still have to close, you know."

"Beau," Elizabet said, gripping her arm when she went to turn away. Beau looked down to where she was held and then back up to stare at her cousin's intense brown eyes. "Don't make me regret this."

Beau's stomach bottomed out. Once Elizabet had protected her this way. How times had changed. She shook her arm free. "Don't be so dramatic. Introduce me to your family and then show me where I can talk to Jeremy. In private. Otherwise, release me so I can get the hell out of here." Elizabet let her go so suddenly that her arm jerked away and knocked into her torso.

Elizabet winced. "Don't be so nasty," she said. "I don't expect you to understand our family dynamics, but I do expect you to respect them." She tipped her chin toward the door. "Or you can leave, if that's what you really want. You can't stay if you want to act like that. I'll not tolerate it. Just know that if you leave, Jareth isn't likely to allow second chances. He is very protective of Jeremy, much more than I am."

Beau rubbed her stomach. "Look, I won't cause a scene and I don't plan to hurt him. Is that good enough for you?"

The sounds of laughter wafted into the foyer. Elizabet looked over her shoulder, then turned to Beau, her lips twisting. "For now, I guess it'll have to do. You may have a short memory, but I do not. We're family and we'll get through this. I believe once you get it through your thick skull that I love you and I did what I did to protect you, we'll be all right. We have to be. We're family and families stick together."

DR. JARETH TREMAINE WAS JUST as good-looking as Beau remembered. In fact, describing him as good-looking was like saying the Sistine Chapel was nice. It was universal knowledge that the Sistine Chapel was remarkable, beautiful, awe-inspiring, life-changing . . . Saying that Jareth Tremaine was good-looking was an understatement. She took the chance at being caught and stared longer than necessary, because he was that handsome. The children Elizabet had with the doctor were extraordinary, as well. Meeting them made her sad that she entered their house with a chip on her shoulder. The twins ran into her arms as if they had known her all of their lives. It was evident that someone had spoken highly of her, and that someone could only be Elizabet.

Jeremy said nothing during the introductions and stayed relatively silent even as he led them to the den where they would be allowed thirty minutes on their own. Beau watched him as he walked ahead of her, his socked feet silent against the wide, rug-covered hallway. She did not bother to look at the art that she was sure was exceptional, but took in everything about this grown-up boy.

He was wearing jeans and a navy blue sweater. It was the end of summer and still hot, but he did not seem to mind. He was taller than any boy his age and had filled out like a tree trunk. He used to be lanky and gangly, but now he moved with confidence and purpose—as though he knew he was easy on the eyes. If Jareth was exceptional, Jeremy was extraordinary. They grew them differently in the UK, obviously.

"We can talk privately in the den," Jeremy said over his shoulder. "But he'll be timing us."

Beau jumped at the sound of his voice bouncing off the walls. It was rich and deep and although she had spoken with him the other day, the changes in it still shocked her. "I figured he'd do something weird like that." She muttered the word "chaperone" under her breath and rolled her eyes.

Jeremy stopped and opened a set of double doors, then turned to face her. "And if he heard you call him weird, he would say that he is merely eccentric." He grinned. He still had that one slightly crooked upper tooth. She remembered teasing him, calling it his fang. His mouth had been one of her favorite things about him. His top lip was just as full as the bottom. "Wealthy people aren't weird, they're eccentric. Although you should know that we are not exceedingly rich. Jareth is a surgeon, but he has secondary focuses such as church reform. That brings in zero dollars. A lot of what we have is family money. Jareth's family is old English aristocracy. Most of his money is tied up in estates and such."

Beau blinked as Jeremy stood waiting. She could not, for the life of her, form words to speak. Everything she had planned to say went out the window. This was not the Jeremy she knew. He was someone else who had been replaced with a fully confident dreamboat. This guy would laugh at her. What was she doing here? There may still be time to run. Jeremy waved his hand before her staring eyes. "Earth to Beau, are you there? Hellooooo?"

Beau frowned and swatted his hand away. "Is he really timing us?"

"Probably."

"Wow. He really is weird."

"Eccentric," Jeremy corrected, and then smiled. "And desperately old fashioned without any remorse whatsoever."

She brushed past him. "This is the den?" It was all she could come up with besides standing there gawking at him like some fool or running away screaming. The walls of the room were dark blue, accented with white ceiling and moldings. She looked around, taking in the piano and media area with a massive flat screen covering the wall. There were various musical instruments everywhere: a half dozen guitars, music sheet stands, and a harp near the bay window. It was intimidating, otherworldly, and it had an aura of museum-like authenticity.

"This is where we spend most of our active semesters."

Beau looked back at him. He was still in the doorway, watching her as she turned around to absorb the grandness that he was accustomed to. "You're a senior this year, right? Like me?"

Jeremy's head tilted a fraction, but he held her gaze. "I help teach the children. Mostly music and English classes, some logic, a little Latin and American History. I finished what you would call high school four years ago."

Despite her trying to suppress it, her eyes bugged. "You're only what? Seventeen now?"

"And?" Jeremy slid his hands into the front pockets of his jeans and stood taller.

Beau opened her mouth to say something, then thought better of it. She knew a dare when she saw one. Perhaps they did things differently in England or on those islands where he had lived. She had never been outside Louisiana unless you counted the one time she went to Beaumont, Texas for a field trip.

"Look, Beau, time's ticking." He tilted his head again. "I'm sure you're not here to discuss my education or church regulation." He reached back and slid the pocket doors shut, his eyes on her the entire time. The panels closed with a faint tick. "You want to know where you fit into the scheme of things." His voice was alluringly soft and gentle. "You want to know what I think of you and if I noticed that you've grown up quite like I have."

Beau's mouth opened again, but snapped shut when the truth of his words—and the embarrassment of them—swept over her. He weaved a trance over her. The web of it reached out and blanketed her seductively. She was totally susceptible to it. He jumped into the whys with both feet, because she was a chicken—she knew he knew that! It was Jeremy, for goodness' sake. He was calling her out on her grandstanding the way he always did. "You want to know if I've missed you. And you're wondering if . . ." His eyes traced her body from head to toe as a smile curved on his mouth and his eyes sparkled with sudden moisture. Leisurely, he did it again, in reverse.

Was he *laughing* at her?

"Are you reading my mind or something?" Beau said, her voice rising. Her hands curled into fists at her sides. How did he do that? He managed to go back to exactly where they left off. This kind of behavior was why they were here now, squaring off and tiptoeing at the same time. She mentally cast off the blanket of apathy he'd thrown over her. She would not accept his mind games this time.

"I'm intuitive. I've still got most of the idiosyncrasies you no doubt remember." He tapped his temple.

"Well, it's creepy," Beau said. Jeremy rocked back, his shoulders squared off as if she had struck him. She shook her finger at him. She would waste no time; after all, he started it. "I remember the humming noise when we found you. The field of dead animals. The way you had this . . ." She widened her hands to show a span of measurement. " . . . Force field around you. I remember us speaking to each other without words. I could hear your thoughts and you could hear mine. That's what you're doing now. I can feel it."

Jeremy averted his eyes. "I don't know what you're talking about." He shouldered away from the door and pushed past her into the heart of the room where he made a spectacle of arranging music sheets on the podium nearest to them. "You're imagining things."

"I know your doctor had all the evidence removed," she said. Her lip trembled as memories flooded back. "They thought I was crazy," she hissed. Jeremy's lips twisted as he stared at the sheet music as if something on the page was not right. He gripped his hands into fists and shoved them into his pockets again. "Look at me," she said. "Damn you, look at me!" She sliced her hand through the air and hit the podium. The papers took flight. "I've had to live with being called the crazy one, while you left—you ran away. *You left me!*"

"Beau—" He sounded tired. His body drooped.

"No!" She stepped back when he started toward her. She shook her head. "You asked for this. I planned to ease into it, but since you insisted on bringing it up, why the hell not? Let's talk about it. You're the one who's in my head!"

"You need to calm down," Jeremy said. He advanced another step. His hands came out of his pockets.

"Calm down?" Beau cried. A tear slipped down her cheek. "You left me with no explanation. You *left* me to deal with what I saw and nothing to explain it. You *left* me to be mind-probed by the government and quacks and you never once called or wrote to me." She swiped angrily at the tears streaming down her face. "Excuse me if I'm not all happy that you're back and doing it all over again. I just started to forget what I saw and was finally starting to believe that I'm not crazy after all." A curt, self-deprecating laugh popped out of her mouth. "But here you are to bring it all back and you want me to roll out the welcome wagon? You and my cousin. Here to make things all better and you want me to *calm down*? Excuse me, but stay out of my mind, Jeremy. I don't want you there."

JEREMY WATCHED AS BEAU FOUGHT to gain control of her feelings. He did what he could to stay out of it, but it was always hard for him when he cared deeply for someone. His nature wanted to share some of the pain with her. He wanted to reach out and touch her, siphon the hurt from her so she could rest a moment. She didn't want him to see her cry and it broke his heart to watch it. But she did not want him to and even if she did, he could not. He could never let her know what he was. This was the proof that she couldn't handle it.

He had made a mistake to speak plainly to her about why she was here. The miscalculation had them at this point—her crying and hurt and him at a total loss as to what to say to make it better. So he stuck his hands back in his pockets, looked down at the floor, and closed his eyes. He concentrated on his breathing and tried not to allow the winds within him to flow toward her. It was overwhelmingly tempting because he felt so strongly for her and the closer he got to her, the more at her mercy he became.

Suddenly, he felt like the lost boy again. The non-verbal freak whose emotions ate him up on the inside, but never bubbled out. Being a host was similar to being the boy he was before Libby. What was on the inside had to stay bottled up and capped under pressure or an explosion would occur. It had been that way when he was mentally unable to verbalize his feelings. There were the obsessive talents that had been outlets, and there was Beau. She was the only person he conversed with. There was something unique in their previous relationship and that was the ability for her to tear down any barrier between them—including his autism. She had been an uncommon denominator, breaching every wall he erected to protect himself from shame and scorn. In that moment he realized their roles were now reversed. He was the breach and she was the scorned.

"What . . ." Beau's voice choked on the word. Her voice jarred him from his meditative breathing. Her strangled tone had him opening his eyes.

Jeremy looked up to see the lights blinking. Somewhere in the house, a light bulb busted with a loud pop.

Beau narrowed her eyes accusingly and he knew he could never hide who he was from her. The raw emotions he felt were all tied to the girl standing in front of him. It was only a matter of time before she figured it out, and then what would he do?

"LUST," JEREMY SAID. "I FELT lust."

Jareth rolled his eyes as he scraped a chair across the floor and placed it at Jeremy's bedside. "Try again. The truth this time." He waved his hand in the air. "Why not 'I'm stupid.' That would suffice."

"You said you wanted my confession. I'm confessing that I had unwholesome thoughts toward our guest." Jeremy smiled. "That makes me normal—right?"

"That makes me want to run you through with my sword." Jareth smiled, too, but it had a wicked bend to it. "This is Elizabet's cousin we are speaking of, and I am bound to demand her honor even if she is causing near blackouts in my home."

Jeremy's smile wobbled. "You're so horrid, but so forgiving at the same time. I messed it up pretty bad, didn't I?"

"In the nature of the flesh?" Jareth nodded. "Yes. Most definitely." He motioned to the clock at the bedside. "But you cause me to digress. Speak. Tell me what is on your mind. I am on call, remember?"

"I've said my confession. I'm full of lustful desire. I must be chastised. What is my penance?"

"I am tired, Jeremy," Jareth said. Seriousness overtook the tone of his voice. "Speak plainly with me and quit this jesting. I know it was not lust that burst the light bulbs in the foyer. It was anger. Or fear. I need to know what it is so we can move on with a plan. I make lists—strategies. It is what I do with this brilliant mind of mine. I wrangle hosts." He reached up and rubbed his eyes with his thumb and index finger, pinching slightly. "I confessed to you that I worry about my wife. Often. Now, give me the same confidence and tell me what it is you want from me."

"What do you mean?" Jeremy asked tentatively. He was the emotion siphon, not Jareth. He would never understand the discernment the knight had. It was incomparable. It also needed to be said that he could not conduit any of Jareth's feelings. That had always been an odd factor in their relationship. Jareth was the only person he could not manipulate. "I don't know what you're talking about."

"Do not be coy," Jareth said with a sigh. "I have the unearthly feeling that Mr. Marceaux's gallbladder will not hold out until morning and I will find myself in surgery shortly, so make haste. Tell me what you must or I will sneak you in with me and have you scrubbing as surgical assistant at an ungodly hour. I would love a full night's sleep, but alas, I chose the life of a surgeon and a guardian. Do I regret my choices? Yes, each and every day I question my sanity."

"I like her," Jeremy said with a shrug.

Jareth's hand fell heavily into his lap, and then he made a circle around his head with his index finger. "Your boomerang emotions are giving me whiplash." He looked up at the ceiling. "Please, tell me something I do not know. You have liked the girl since we met. Tell me what you want from me, because settling it with rapiers did not work." Jeremy began to say something but Jareth stopped him with a chop of his hand. "Do not take me for ignorant. Tread lightly. I repeat, to my everlasting annoyance, tell me what you want from me."

"Now you're asking what I want after you had me fight for the chance to move things along?" Jeremy accused. Jareth waved his hand dismissively. Jeremy pulled the covers up under his arms and sank further into his soft bed as if he could hide. He wanted to hide. Speaking of this made him uncomfortable because he knew what was coming. Jareth did have a special ability. It was called wisdom, and as he so loved to brag, discernment. "She suffered because of us and that's not fair. Her feelings caught me off guard. They were raw, as if the wounds were fresh. I could practically taste the hate she holds for how we abandoned her."

"Life is not fair."

"You're using clichés?" Jeremy shook his head against the pillow. "Oh, this is rich. The almighty Jareth Tremaine is reduced to trite phrases."

"We have gone through this multiple times," Jareth said, the weariness in his voice replaced with an edge of annoyance. "You cannot change what has been done. I made excellent decisions and I would make the same again if I had to do it over. We could not bring the girl with us. She was a liability."

"She's Elizabet's family," Jeremy pointed out. "It could have been handled differently, but it wasn't." He knew when to back off. Jareth's jaw was as rigid as if he had tetanus. "Geez, Jareth. I'm not asking to breed with her," he grumbled. When Jareth looked appalled, he added, "For what it's worth, I don't just like her, I love her, you know."

"You love her," Jareth repeated. Jeremy briskly nodded once. "Oh, this is charming. Whether or not you admit *breeding* will occur, if things progress in the natural course, that is highly likely. She is your Elizabet—" Jeremy opened his mouth to speak, but Jareth pointed at him. "Your words, not mine." He ran his hand through his hair as he flopped back against the seat. "Breeding aside, you run the risk of exposing the Amalgam. Have you considered that? That you could exploit your family of fellow hosts? You do have an allegiance to them and it would behoove you to remember that vow. Tonight, you broke code by siphoning from her. She knew you were in her mind, Jeremy. I watched her run from my home as though the devil himself was at her heels."

"That won't happen again. Next time I'll be ready for her feelings. I'll know what I'm up against."

"First you talk about explosive feelings, then about breeding, and then you bring in love . . ." Jareth's hands flipped over in his lap. "I surrender. Run me through with your sword, because this is equivalent to losing a duel. You do understand that the course of love is marriage and then fruitfulness, right?"

Jeremy rolled his eyes, but nodded.

"Jeremy, as a host you are volatile. You are wired to be sensuous and you conquer things. It is what you do, quite frankly.

Nature ravishes, it simply does not play by the rules of love and war."

Jeremy nodded again. "Tonight, when I realized that I loved her, I felt something I never felt before. It was the insistent urge to make things right for her. After feeling the malaise within her, I understood that the cause and pain were mine to heal. And I can do it, Jareth. Only me. That's what she needs. She needs me to make this right for her. Can you understand this? Make sense of any of it, because now I think I sound addle-brained. I know we were just children back then, but I've carried something more with me. Something about her makes me feel things I know is more." He was frustrated trying to explain things he didn't understand himself. "Ugh, I don't know. I just want . . . no, I *need* to make things right with her. I want her back in my life. I want her the way she used be—happy, whole, and Beau. I messed her up, but I can be the one who puts her back together."

Jareth slumped in the chair. "You want to fix her," he said softly. A smile tugged at half his mouth and a dazed expression crossed his face as if he were thinking of something or someone else. A short laugh escaped. "Perhaps it is love."

Jeremy looked up at the ceiling. He blinked back something that felt oddly like tears welling up. He was so confused yet saw with clarity at the same time. What a glorious mess he was in. "Perhaps."

"You do realize that this has only one way to end, right? If Beau discovers the secrets of the Amalgam, she will be hunted. Stalked by our enemies. If Gyula discovers you have a weakness, he will hunt and kill her. I do not make rules to make you miserable. They exist because this is not a game. These are our lives and this is Beau's life. If she comes into our fold, I cannot allow her leave. She will be stuck in this muck we call the Amalgam."

"Do I hear resolution in your voice? Because it sounds an

awful lot like you're caving in."

Jareth pulled back a fraction. "Was there ever a question that I would not allow you to give court to the lady who holds your heart? Have I ever been a stickler for titles and dowries? Do I care who a person is other than the moral fiber they hold to?" He shook his head, answering his own question. "No. I was quite clear that you are free to love whomever your heart chooses. I asked you to be patient instead of barreling toward waters like a bull in heat."

"Eloquently stated, your grace," Jeremy drawled.

Jareth snorted. "Not likely eloquent, but rightly spoken." He frowned when Jeremy's grin widened. "Rightly spoken, indeed." He tipped his head to the ceiling and laced his fingers behind his neck. "Just see that your . . . breeding inclinations stay well harnessed around the delicate constitution of my wife's cousin. We do not know the dynamics of a non-host and host together. It must be monitored closely. I would hate to have to kill you over this. You are the best trained host I have."

Chapter 3

All host who dissipate must make provision for home base return.
It is also requested that host learn to carry a change of clothes so their
allotted guardian is not subject to any of their wobbling bits.
Paraphrased by Gabriel Morton—guardian in first command

Rule 3: Amalgam of Dover

"THEY HAVE A DISTURBANCE IN Michigan," Gabriel said. He stuck a toothpick between his teeth. "I can check it out on my way home."

Gabriel and Minh, Jareth's two best guardians, stood in the kitchen at his home in South Louisiana. They had traveled by wormhole, something Jareth did not altogether agree with, but it was a regulated jump. It was necessary that they stay in touch, and sometimes cell phones, email, or plane trips simply did not suffice. Wormholes had horrible reception.

Gabriel was a Spartan by birth; Minh was a former Minister of War for the Ming Dynasty. Both had been rescued by Jareth and trained to be guardians. He had saved their lives and given them new ones. For that, they were grateful and served Jareth with fierce loyalty. They were also brothers-in-law. Gabriel was married to Minh's sister, Liang. Minh tended to hold that against Gabriel.

"I will send one of the guardians to see to it," Jareth responded as he polished an apple on the front of his scrub top. "I need you close to home. We can classify this mission as proper orientation as long as you bring along one of the new hosts.

The chances that a host located in Michigan as anything but benign is low." He looked at Minh. "Did you get the stats on the last tsunami in Sri Lanka?"

Minh chewed vigorously at the fresh piece of gum in his mouth before he answered. "Malia is on it. I sent Ezra after her. She tried to scare him off—again."

Jareth scoffed and tossed the uneaten apple back into the fruit bowl. His appetite was gone and he was starving at the same time. He had spent half the night in surgery and now his head felt as if it was stuffed with rocks from lack of rest. One surgery in modern time and one in medieval Dover and then he spent the day at the office. He had seen twenty new patients. Twenty, when ten was the accepted norm. He leaned against the cabinet, suppressing the urge to cry like a little girl. Ezra was his weakest guardian, an army sergeant he rescued from the Vietnam War Era. "How is it that a host is allowed to scare off a guardian?" It both flabbergasted and annoyed him.

Minh looked away sheepishly. He glanced at Gabriel before he shrugged almost unnoticeably. "PTSD?"

"Or Malia's a freak of nature," Gabriel suggested. "Hell, Jareth, she scares me sometimes. I think you need to consider terminating her. She's unstable. I don't trust her. In fact, is there anyone who trusts her? You said it yourself—she's a ticking time bomb."

"And she's still pining over Jeremy," Minh added. He blew a miserable bubble and sucked the gum back into his mouth. "Ezra's PTSD aside, I caught her trying to contact Jeremy. I intercepted the email."

Jareth's jaw ticked. "Jeremy is a big lad. Ezra can handle her along with his personal issues. I shall contact him and be sure he is clear that termination is an option. I do not care that she is the only tsunami we employ. I would rather send Eddie underground if we need." Eddie was a better choice anyway. Volcanoes were more stable than tsunamis, especially ones that were older and exerted control over their abilities.

Gabriel grinned. "That's a good option," he said. "Too bad all of your guardians cannot be Spartans, eh? Things would go effortlessly." His hands made a waving motion. "Smoothly."

Jareth smirked. "Oh, definitely. I so enjoy how you heathens operate. You are all hearts and laughter."

Gabriel pressed his hand against his chest. "I've converted."

"By the hardest," Jareth murmured, turning to Minh. "Have you had any new development with Darian? Has he spoken yet?"

Minh's new host, Darian, was a tornado—on his best days. They found him in Oklahoma, locked in his parents' cellar. He had been in seclusion there for three years. The boy was dangerous. "He doesn't like me."

"I don't like you," Jareth said in a rare usage of contractions to mimic Minh's casual speech. He shrugged. "And yet, you live. And while you live, you train." He pointed at him. "See that he is trained in combat. Soon. We will need his strength in the coming months while Jeremy is weak. As long as it stays warm here, we are safe." He looked at Gabriel. "Bring Darian with you on the run to Michigan. It will be good to get him out. He needs to adjust to traveling by wormhole, but do not allow him to dissipate. For now, he is still too unstable to trust in host form."

"Gyula is quiet," Gabriel said. "Perhaps you should let me breach the past and future to see what we are dealing with. I think that's more important than a potential host formation. I could still use Darian. The new recruits need to understand what we are up against. All island life teaches them is how to surf around with their awesome talents while getting a wicked Caribbean tan."

"No," Jareth said. "You think to move me by pissing me off? By claiming that the Cayman Island base is merely a tropical vacation spot for the physically elite?" His eyes traveled to

Elizabet, who entered the kitchen from the hallway. His body tensed, which let his company know to keep information to a minimum. She smiled at him as she walked to the refrigerator and opened it to take out the milk. Her back was bowed with the increasing weight of her pregnancy; her steps were slow and careful. Jareth returned her smile, but his expression became shuttered when her back was to him. Worry etched his face. "The law is that no time shall be breached other than what is necessary."

"And keeping your family safe isn't necessary?" Gabriel asked. He tipped his chin to Elizabet.

Jareth's eyes narrowed. "I know how to keep my family safe. Do not think I require your instruction, Gabriel."

"*Wah, wah, wah,*" Gabriel made a gesture of yapping with his hand. "It's all words until you are standing over them with swords run through—"

"Gabriel," Minh interrupted. "This is not wise, brother."

Jareth watched the interaction between his two best guardians. They had dealt with Gyula and his pack of Mongolian warriors for years now. It was not fear that had them tangled up, but sincere concern. Gyula had been the original bearer of the time bands. Eight years prior, he had given them to Jareth in lieu of payment for saving his son's life. The travel stones for a life. Jareth cured the boy of meningitis and afterward, Gyula went back on his word. He returned for the bands when Dover Castle was vulnerable and stole two back. He nearly killed Elizabet in the process. It was a miracle they retained the five they had now. If Elizabet had not thought quickly and hid most of them, time would not be the luxury it was. They would not have been able to find and protect hosts. It was ghastly to even speculate what would have happened had Gyula succeeded in stealing them all.

Gabriel's expression hardened. "I've a family, too, Jareth. A wife. Children. Let's not be stupid. We know they're on the move. These weather disturbances aren't natural and you know it. It's the Huns. They will attack and we'll be screwed, especially with our ace in the hole stuck in a winter wonderland down south so you can have your precious church reform. Isn't it enough that you spark the Protestant Church in the beginning of Church history? Are you so vain and ambitious that you want this century, too?"

"I will have your head, Spartan, if you do not stand down," Jareth said in a voice that was deceptively quiet.

Gabriel growled low in his throat. Elizabet spun around to eye the trio suspiciously. "I don't like your tone, Jareth," he said.

"And I do not like your disrespect. Remember to whom you speak. I am the head of this amalgam."

"Jareth," Elizabet said. She looked at Minh, who looked away as soon as they made eye contact. "This isn't a normal meeting, is it? What's going on?"

"Listen to your wife, *Magister*," Gabriel said. He flipped his hand out toward the den. "And to the innocent voices of your children playing in the other room. Would you sacrifice them for the sake of a league of hormonal teenagers with super powers and angry Huns with a vendetta to destroy us?"

"That is enough," Jareth said, his voice becoming louder. He jerked his head to beckon Elizabet to his side. Her comfort took precedence over soothing Gabriel's paranoia. She placed the milk on the counter, walked to him, and placed her hand on his arm. Her gaze was wide and questioning. "I know how to take care of what is mine," he repeated. He ran his hand under Elizabet's hair and rested it over the back of her neck; his thumb found the pulse point in her neck with a soft caress. How he loved his wife. Simply touching her made his world right. It was physically painful to imagine someone hurting her. Gabriel was not paranoid, but overzealous. There was a time to strike. When the opportunity came, he would be prepared. He was ardent when it came to defending his family. "My question to you, Gabriel, is do you have that same skill?"

A bubble of manly laughter erupted from Minh. He quickly covered his mouth as if he had belched. Gabriel shot Minh a warning glance before looking back at Jareth. "So help me, Jareth. If anything happens to Liang or our children, I'm coming for you and no wormhole will be able to hide you then. Mark this day as the day I warned you. Gyula is on the move and he's packing an army of his own hosts. The only evidence you need is written all over the skies."

JEREMY PLUCKED AT THE PIANO keys. He was at his father's church, the place he was raised and where he learned his love for music. If he looked hard enough, he could see the blood stains on the keys. There had been a time when music was an obsession of his. He would play until his body was incapable of going on. With the piano, his fingers bled from the repeated force he used to strike the keys. He had been playing Mozart at the time and had played for over twelve consecutive hours before his mother realized he was not in the house with the rest of the family.

His disappearing acts were normal to them. One time his brother, Joel, locked him in the cellar when they lived in Oregon. No one realized he was missing for an entire day. This could be quite traumatic to an average six-year-old. Jeremy had never been normal, but he did remember crying a good deal that night. There were rats in the cellar. To this day he hated rats and spiders with a vengeance.

"Jeremy?" a deep, masculine voice ricocheted in the small church.

Jeremy turned, expecting to see Joel. "Caesar," he said. His voice revealed his shock. "What are you doing? And in church?"

Caesar laughed. "Half expecting the roof to cave in, huh?" He lifted one shoulder. "Your girl has me here, man." He leaned against the pew nearest him and rubbed his chin with his thumb. "How you been, mate?" he said with a feigned British accent.

Jeremy frowned. He was growing tired of everyone pointing out his change in dialect. It was not as if he had a choice in the matter. "What girl would that be? My sister isn't here. I just saw her back at the rectory."

He had not seen Caesar since his fate filled day of Hurricane Libby. Caesar Randolph II had been the closest thing he had to a friend besides Beau. He was the only person, in fact, who even talked to him. It was probably due to the fact Caesar was an outcast, as well. His name alone was unusual in a place where if your last name was not Hebert, Broussard, or Romero, you were just weird. Cajuns were territorial, and Caesar's family was from somewhere in Alaska. They had relocated with the oil field boom. His mother was richer than Midas. As for his father, no one had ever seen the elusive Caesar Randolph I.

Jeremy knew all about not fitting in. If it wasn't his autism that had him ostracized, it was that he had been a transplant, too. They were the odd ones out and had bonded over their random fate when they were boys.

"Oh, you have a girl, believe me, and it ain't Valerie," Caesar said with a grin. "You just don't know it yet. You've had her for some time now. Remember? Mousy brown hair, big blue eyes, about yay tall?" He held his hand at his chest level.

"Beau?" Jeremy asked. No use playing stupid. Jareth knew what he was about now. The rest of the world might as well, too.

Caesar's thumb traced up his cheek until it pressed against the navy blue paisley bandanna that held his long red hair out his eyes. He moved it up a notch before he nodded. "You know she'll be pissed that you are here. She thought you hated your parents, otherwise she wouldn't have come."

Jeremy's body stiffened and his fingers curled, haphazardly

hitting an off tune key. "Watch your mouth, Caesar. You shouldn't speak that way. This is a church, remember?"

Caesar laughed. His hands dove into his front pockets as he leaned fully against the pew. "Oh, I remember that stick up your butt. Still get stiff like a board and righteously offended. But let's mention the obvious and stop this chit chat. We were never ones to hold anything back. I'm downright scared that you talk like a normal person." His eyes narrowed. "You're even looking me right in the eye and I think I see murder there."

Jeremy closed his eyes and looked away. He could feel the anger stirring in his core and that was never good. It had been a long time since he had been unable to control his beast, but something about Caesar was setting him off. He stared down at the piano keys, concentrated on the stains he had left behind long ago, and forced his breathing to remain within the bounds of his chest cavity. Tricky that—not morphing when there was an evident threat in the air.

"Whoa, buddy," Caesar said, his voice skipping. "I didn't mean to get you all riled up. It's just weird, man. Beau was right. You've changed, and it's not just the British invasion."

Jeremy looked up and leveled his gaze on him. Caesar smiled; his face had a patchy beard. It was amazing that they allowed him in the public school looking like that—assuming he was still in school and had not quit. Not finishing high school was common in this area, but he was from a wealthy family. Jeremy would bet Caesar was at the top of the class, both in grades and in pecking order. Even though he looked like a biker-rocker or whatever, he wore it like a tailored suit. Caesar was money and confidence on a stick.

"Don't dig, Caesar," Jeremy said. "I can't promise I'll be all PK like. I've been away for a while. I'm not the same preacher's kid you remember."

Caesar laughed again and it rankled Jeremy that he sincerely didn't seem rattled or threatened. But there was something holding him back from reading Caesar. They had been friends once and he remembered trusting him. For that reason, he would not probe. Siphoning was like being a lord; it brought great responsibility. To go around feeling out people emotionally seemed intrusive, so he limited using the ability to when it was necessary or unavoidable.

Jeremy would respect this distance and accept it without being the siphon for once. In all probability, this was the normal territorial male ritual. He was accustomed to it. Medieval England made him a straight A student on the subject.

"Remember that? I never would've figured you listened to that after all these years." His eyes sparkled with laughter. "Good ol' preacher's kid. PK." He pointed to Jeremy with both index fingers. "That's all you. I still see the same kid. He just talks now. I bet you're the type who's just rebelling on the inside instead of the outside like the rest of us sinners."

"Caesar," Beau said as she came into the sanctuary with a smile on her face. "Who're you talking to?" Her face fell when she noticed Jeremy, who stood at her approach. "I didn't know you'd be here."

"Neither did I," Jeremy said. He was glad she showed up, though. Otherwise he ran the risk of saying something stupid to Caesar. "I came to see if the old piano needed tuning." He motioned to it beside him. "I'll be leading worship on Wednesday. Jareth is speaking on church reform."

"Oh, nice to know that," Beau said. She turned to Caesar. "You ready? I'm ready. Let's leave. Now."

"Beau," Caesar said. He draped an arm lazily over her shoulders and gave her a slight squeeze. "Play nice."

She stiffened. "I'm playing nice. Let's go before I decide not to." She tried to turn him, but he stayed put.

Caesar's lips twisted as he patted his chest with his hand until he found what he was looking for. Reaching into the front pocket of his red flannel shirt, he removed a smashed pack of cigarettes. "I'm gonna go burn one before we take off." He looked at Jeremy over her head. "Gives you two time to do whatever needs to happen before y'all kill each other." He shrugged. "Makes me no difference either way, but it is church. Repent, make amends and all that stuff you Christians believe in." He held up his pack of smokes and flashed it before Beau's face. "And your delicate nose won't let me smoke in my own car, so—"

"I'll go with you," Beau muttered. She grabbed Caesar's forearm and attempted to steer him.

"Oh, no, princess," Caesar said. He jerked his arm from her hold. "You finish what you started here. I'm not listening to you whine the whole way home."

Beau grimaced. "Can you just stop already?" she whispered.

Caesar smiled as he put a cigarette in his mouth. "What kind of friend would I be if I didn't run this intervention? Obviously, you two are stubborn. Someone has to help you or you'll make everybody miserable. One particular 'everybody' being me." He touched his bandanna in a mock salute. "Happy trails." And then, to Jeremy, "She's all yours, bro. Good luck with that."

"HOW LONG HAVE YOU BEEN hanging out with Caesar?" Jeremy asked after the church doors clanged shut.

Beau still had her back to him, standing in the aisle watching after Caesar. Unbelievable—he abandoned her. Her shoulders slumped. "We've been friends since you left." She turned to him, and allowed her eyes to snap with anger. "He was the only person who didn't think I was crazy. He was your friend too, re-member? I wasn't the only person you left behind." She crossed her arms. "Caesar kept me sane. In short, he's all I've got in the friend department. Happy?"

"Ecstatic." It sounded as though he was lying through his teeth. "I'm grateful to him."

"It's none of your business who my friends are," Beau retorted. "You have no right to be grateful one way or the other."

"Caesar understands," Jeremy said. He covered the piano keys and walked down the wide, shallow steps of the altar. "He understands that we have things we need to work out." He walked up the aisle until he stood in front of her. "So, you're Pres now? I thought your dad didn't allow anything but Catholicism."

"Things change," she bit out. "I do what I want and I want to attend a church that isn't regulated. I like the gospel to be undiluted, you know what I mean?"

Jeremy smiled. "I guess this is the time to change the subject. Jareth says to never discuss religion or politics unless prompted. You know what I mean isn't really an open-ended question when you're shooting lasers with your eyeballs while saying it. You're definitely not prompting me to comment, so what do you want to talk about instead?"

"What happened to the lights the other night, Jeremy?" she asked baldly.

Jeremy's jaw tensed.

"Exactly. You aren't interested in what I want to talk about." She shook her head and turned on her heel. "I've got nothing to say to you."

Jeremy grabbed her, preventing her escape. "Don't go, Beau. Please."

She looked at where he held her. Her arm thrummed with some sort of invisible energy, but it was not uncomfortable. "Why is it every time we are together lights bust out and I get practically electrocuted or my mind read?" Jeremy released her instantly and stepped back. "Geez, I knew that would work. You're the king of secrets and that will obviously never change."

"I can't stay away from you," Jeremy said. He shoved his hands under his armpits as if that was the only way he could keep his hands to himself. "I've tried and it doesn't work."

"Do you think that line will work with me? You sound like a bad romance novel," she scoffed. "News flash, Jeremy. You did stay away. Eight long years, to be exact, and not once did you answer any of my letters."

"I couldn't."

"Oh, that's right. It was forbidden."

"Not like that," Jeremy said. Something that felt like misery in his heart was evident in his tone. "I wanted to answer. I did," he said when she shook her head. "I even wrote some, but I never sent them." He hunched down to catch her gaze when she lowered her gaze to the floor between them. "I kept all of your letters. Read them nearly every day." She looked up at him. "I have secrets, but doesn't everyone?"

"Your secrets are like boulders, Jeremy," Beau clipped. Whatever fleeting tenderness she had was gone. "They are everywhere, reaching out and shocking me every time you come around me. They're the kind that land people in psych wards."

Thunder rolled outside then, rattling the windows. The suddenness of it startled both of them. Jeremy tipped his head and perked his ear as if he were listening attentively to the weather. "Can't you just be happy that I'm home? Haven't I told you I'm here to stay?" Beau tried to hide her surprise but failed. Jeremy stepped toward her. "I'm staying, Beau. Right here, with you. You won't get rid of me easily this time. I plan on fighting for you."

"You can't mean what I think you mean."

"I do," Jeremy said. He stepped as close to her as possible without embracing her. "But to clarify things—would you like me to be clear? I can speak plainly, if you'd like. I can even sound like a bad romance novel. Would you like that? For there to be no more walls between us?"

"The walls between us are cinder block, Jeremy. An explosion couldn't remove them." Her voice sounded breathy, as though she had been running, and *she hated it*. He was unbelievably beautiful and could make her forget all the reasons he was bad for her. All of his facial features were engraved in her memory, but she gazed at them from this short distance in total awe all over again. He had some sort of power over her that she was helpless to overcome. She was practically drooling and leaning toward him. She felt that invisible web close over her; she couldn't resist his charm. He was too close for her to clear her head. He was surrounding her with his energy and tempting her to remember what was between them. "But please," she heard her voice saying, "Tell me anyway. Be clear on why I should listen to anything you have to say."

A smile played on Jeremy's mouth.

The church doors opened and Caesar poked his head inside. "Sorry to cut this little love fest short, but we got rain about to come down hard. I got the top off the Jeep, remember? We're gonna get soaked if we don't leave now."

Beau shook her head as if trying to come out of a fog. She frowned and pushed Jeremy away. "What are you doing to me?" It was obvious that Beau could not think straight when he was around; he was like heroine to her. One minute, her resolve was firm, the next she was babbling, begging him to make everything better. Her pathetic ways made her want to vomit.

Jeremy glanced at Caesar, who jerked his head upward when thunder boomed again. "Can I come over? Tomorrow?" he asked. He sounded desperate as he grabbed Beau's arms when she pushed away. "We can talk more then—please."

"I have school." She flopped her arms to be released.

"I can pick you up. What time?" He squeezed her arms.

Beau looked at Caesar for help. He merely shrugged and turned on his heel to leave. She looked back up at Jeremy to find his eyes pleading with her. She had heard . . . something. Something he had not spoken with his mouth. Had he asked her to please say yes? She didn't hear that with her ears.

At once, she had a choice to make.

"Three." She heard her voice, but could hardly believe it. She was going to test the theory and see if it worked. Oh, she was stupid. She knew it, but she didn't care. "You can pick me up at three o'clock. I have a band meeting."

"I'll be there."

She nodded, looked into his eyes, and concentrated hard. *"Gueydan High School,"* she said in her mind. His eyes widened a fraction. They stood so close that she saw his pupils dilate. Thunder shook the windows again, so she turned to leave, disappointed that her experiment hadn't worked.

For a beat he said nothing, even though she walked at a snail's pace, waiting for a sign. Her pace increased, and mentally she shook herself for being so stupid. Perhaps she was crazy, and now she would be stuck spending time alone with him tomorrow.

"I remember," Jeremy murmured. His voice was so faint she barely heard it. "Gueydan High School at three o'clock."

Her shoulders stiffened and a smile carved her face, but she did not look back. He realized what he'd done, she could sense it, but it was too late. He had already answered her thought.

She had him now, and she was ready to play his game.

MINH THREW HIS CIGARETTE ON the ground when Jeremy ran out of the church. Beau had left and Jeremy had been smart to wait until the coast was clear. He put two fingers into his mouth and whistled.

Jeremy did not look his way, but threw a thought into his head. *"I'm on it."*

Minh smiled and looked at Gabriel, who was on his cell phone checking for weather updates. The local station had yet to pick up the isolated thunderstorm that was nearly on top of them. That's what happened when it was not nature, but a host. They could literally drop right on you without warning.

Jeremy dissipated, leaving his clothes in a heap on the church steps. As the only host who had mastered taking his britches along with him, he left all but his boxers behind.

"He didn't even fuss that we were tailing him. I do say, our baby is growing up," Minh commented. He scooped up the discarded clothing.

Gabriel frowned and slid his cell phone into the back pocket of his jeans. "Poor lad knows it won't do any good." He gave a curt laugh that held no humor. "God knows I'd rather be home than be assigned to teenage drama duty."

Minh squatted to shove the clothes into the backpack he carried. "This is better than being on the island any day. You don't know what it's like having a battalion of teenagers whining over unrequited love and all that rot. I'll take Jeremy's brand of drama over that any day."

Gabriel ignored his comment and instead looked up into the sky where Jeremy was breaching the host that had been causing all the commotion. "We better head out. Jareth will meet us in Dover. He will want to question the host. A cell will need to be prepared. One that can hold—what is this? A passing thunderstorm?" His lip curled in disgust.

"If Jeremy lets him live." Minh secured the button closed on his backpack and stood. He, too, glanced up and grimaced when he saw the flash of lightening as Jeremy hit his target dead on. The sky lit up with white light, and instantly there was a loud clap of thunder. The ground shook.

"We couldn't be that lucky," Gabriel drawled. "I'm sure he'll allow him to live. He always does." He snapped his wrist toward the lightening display. "He's all bark. We never get to kill anybody these days."

Medieval Dover, Year 1320, Reign of Edward II

JARETH BARELY HAD TIME TO change from his work clothes. Half in scrubs from the waist down and half in medieval wear, he made his way through the tunnels of Dover Castle. It was good to be home. He just wished the circumstances were different.

"Make it quick," Jareth said when he caught sight of Gabriel near the holding cell. Minh jumped up from the small wooden table where they were having dinner. He bowed as Jareth passed and then regained his seat. Jeremy did not flinch, but remained seated peeling an apple.

"Newly turned," Gabriel said. "Name is Silas Moore." Gabriel leaned against the cell, watching the host. "From Newport, Rhode Island. Turned with that Category One storm last year."

"Pathetic," Jeremy said under his breath.

Jareth looked sideways at Jeremy, but did not address his lack of manners. "Where does his allegiance lie?"

Gabriel peered into the dark cell. "With the flavor of the month," he said with a sneer.

"And the flavor of the month is Mongolian Mint Chocolate Chip," Minh said between bites of his food.

"Pathetic," Jeremy repeated.

"Is he stable?" Jareth asked.

"He is now," Gabriel said. He thumbed toward Jeremy. "Little bugger is terrified of Jeremy. He squealed big time. Gyula is on the move." He smirked before continuing, "Told you so. He sent Silas as a spy."

Jeremy scoffed and placed an apple slice in his mouth, then continued to pare the apple intently. "You do not like him," Jareth said to Jeremy. "He has surrendered and we need to give him a chance to make recompense. Hopefully, he will reform and understand our cause."

"I don't trust him," Jeremy said. He looked up. "He reeks. There is something on him that smells funny and it is not because he's a Mongolian recruit. I don't like it."

"Noted," Jareth said with a nod. "But he did surrender, did he not? He came willingly?"

Jeremy placed another apple slice into his mouth and chewed slowly. He gave a faint nod as if it rankled him to admit it.

"Well, then," Jareth said. He motioned to the cell. "I will question him later. I was just informed that we are under siege by the French. In about an hour, the castle will be under attack." He looked irritated. "I am beginning to see the need for an app that informs one of what is happening in history on whatever day it currently is. It would save me a great deal of effort. Elizabet does not like us to be separated. I had to send her and the children back to Louisiana."

"Can we join in the fight?" Minh asked.

"Pretty please," Gabriel added. A grin broke across his face. It was lost on no one present that he said please and meant it.

"That would be acceptable," Jareth said. "I am on call and must be home before nightfall. Elizabet will skin me alive if she has to play doctor for me . . . again."

"Goody," Minh said gleefully. He reached for the quiver he had stashed under the table.

Jareth paused in the doorway of the cell and looked over his shoulder. "No firearms. So help me, if I see one spark from anywhere near you, there will not be any of your remains to carry home to your families. Understood?"

Gabriel smirked and unsheathed his sword. "Who needs to cheat? It's Frenchmen, not Vikings. Bring on the amateurs. I haven't killed anyone in months."

BEAU MET JEREMY AT THREE o'clock only to tell him that

he could drop her off a block from the school. She had work at the town snowball stand, a place called "The Sneaux Shack." in true Cajun form. It peeved him that she thwarted his plans, but when he insisted on picking her up after her shift, she did not refuse. He was aware that she was running him on a chase, but he did not care. The chance was his to take, and while her motive seemed to be to wear him down, he was in it to win. While she waited to pounce on him about his little slip up at the church, he was biding his time and trying to get her to see that he was a man in love—not some side show that she needed to interpret.

He was left with three hours to burn, so he went to visit his parents. Big mistake. Valerie treated him like a stranger, and his parents were barely better. They sat around the kitchen table in awkward silence. Thankfully, Joel was at football practice or hostility may have been thrown into the mix. It was difficult to acknowledge that his own flesh and blood despised him for something he had no control over. Even before his turning, his autism did a pretty good job of making him the least popular member of the family.

In fact, they stared at him as if they were waiting for him to have an outburst. It had been a daily occurrence in his old life—the frustrated tantrums that came when he couldn't contain them any longer. Somehow, his emotions always erupted and he would flail about and throw things—hit things. If he were to do that now, he would kill everyone in the room with him. It wasn't that he was healed. He was altered in another way. The boy they once knew was still there, but he was kept under the influence of a storm that owned his body. He wanted to tell them that he was still their son, but what would that accomplish? His mother kept far away. He felt the fear streaming from her and it made it difficult to keep up with the meaningless chatter his dad offered.

On the other hand, his dad looked at him as he would any parishioner. A guest in the home of his youth. The china plate with playful kittens that he gave his mom for Mother's Day was still hanging where he had last seen it. One of his watercolor paintings still hung in the foyer, but he reckoned it wasn't for sentimental value, but rather that it was pleasing to the eye. It served a purpose, but his purpose was gone. He didn't belong here. They had moved on without him.

They served him Lipton tea—it was ghastly. He managed to get a single cup down before he broke the awkwardness and took his leave. It didn't take any siphoning technique to know how relieved they were at his departure. It was time for him to move on as well and leave behind broken memories of being their son. He had a family who loved and accepted him.

He drove around the city of Gueydan, reminiscing, and then continued onward to the community of Wright, where he visited the bridge where he was found after the storm. He stayed there for two hours, sitting against the old water pump shed, nearly weeping because the memories were so strong. It took a good bit of cheer to get out of the funk he had put himself into, and he wished that the drive back to Gueydan was longer than five minutes.

"Can you drop me off at the softball field? My coach called practice," Beau said as soon as Jeremy took his place behind the wheel. She did not like him getting the door for her, but he did it anyway. He had the impression that he embarrassed her when he did it at the school earlier. This time she hopped in the car quickly and did not say a word. "One of my teammates called just now. I won't be able to hang out after all. Sorry. Maybe some other day. We have a good chance at making State this year and I can't miss a practice."

"And they called this practice today? Right now?" he asked. He eyed the T-shirt and shorts she had changed into. He glanced down at her feet and saw she was wearing cleats, as well. This was not the attire of someone who wasn't prepared for practice.

"I knew there was a possibility. Like I said, we made the parish finals." She reached into the side pocket of her backpack and took out two bread ties. "I'm always prepared."

Jeremy's mouth twitched, despite the fact she was deliberately running him in circles again. He turned to her and reached for the neon yellow ties. "Let me help you."

Beau moved her pony tail aside so he could scrunch the first sleeve. She moved so fluidly that he was reminded how often they had done this before. "You remember," she said, smiling. Jeremy had the ties between his teeth as he bunched the sleeve up to the collar. He smiled and she laughed. "You're cute. It reminds me of the time you almost choked on them." He motioned for her to give him her other shoulder. She turned in the seat, which put them face to face in the tight space.

Jeremy secured the tie, then checked his handiwork of both sleeves. They were equally tight, both sleeves held off her arms. He slid his index finger under her chin and turned her face. "All done."

Their faces were two inches apart. Her gaze popped to his, eyes wide. "Thanks," she said, then slammed back against the seat. His hand fell between them to rest on the console. She motioned to the road. "We better get going. I can't be late." She glanced at him, flushing when she saw he had not moved. "I'm the pitcher, you know. They can't start without me." She snapped her fingers in rapid fire. "Chop, chop. Let's go."

Jeremy waited for a few seconds to see if she would look at him again, but when she did not, he sighed and righted his body in his seat, then reached for the ignition. "Will you let me stay to watch you practice?"

Beau laughed, a nervous chuckle that sounded forced. "I'll need a ride home. So yeah, please." She did look at him then. "I don't know if Rixby will remember to pick me up."

Jeremy reached over and squeezed her knee, his eyes on the road as he pulled out of The Sneaux Shack. The anxiety rolled off her in waves. "Does he still give you trouble?"

"He barely admits we're related, much less twins," she sneered. She wiped the condensation that had formed on the window with the heel of her hand. "I have a better bond with Amos and Aries. They're ten now."

"The family of fraternal twins," Jeremy said, reciting what he had heard Elizabet say over and over when speaking of her aunt's brood. "They come in twos."

"There is Andre," she said. "He's three."

"You have another brother?" Jeremy asked.

"Yeah," she said, and then pointed across him. "Turn here. They moved the parks. This one's the softball field." Jeremy frowned, partially from not knowing that her family had grown and partially because he recognized at least two of the vehicles in the parking lot. "You can't be expected to know that my mom had whelped another kid." She unbuckled her seat belt. "Well, well, Rixby must have found out that Natalie made the parish team." She tipped her chin toward a beat-up white minivan. Jeremy was appalled that it was the same van her family drove eight years ago. He eyed Caesar's Jeep that was parked next to his dad's small family coupe. Joel was here too—oh, joy. And he thought he had lucked out earlier by missing brother dear. His day just kept getting better and better.

"You still want to stay?" she asked. "He probably won't give me too much flack." She shrugged. "And if he does, Caesar will bring me home."

That made up Jeremy's mind. "No. I'm good. I'll stay and take you home after."

Chapter 4

Amorous relationships should be avoided until the host is able to adequately contain the mutation he has been dealt. Otherwise, one might cause a complete black-out for neighboring villages—just saying.

Paraphrased rule by Jeremiah Cameron

Rule 4: Amalgam of Dover

"JERM." CAESAR TIPPED HIS CHIN in greeting as Jeremy took a seat next to him on the bleachers.

Jeremy had never liked the nickname Caesar used for him. It sounded just like germ and he did not care to be likened to something that made people sick. "Hey," he replied. He tilted his head and greeted the girl whose legs Caesar was leaning against seated one row behind them. "Jeremy Tremaine."

"Mandy Broussard," she said with a smile.

"Blimey," Jeremy said. He pulled back a fraction to get a good look at her. "Mandy, you've grown up." It was an understatement. She was gorgeous and had the body of a woman. A body that was rather on display. His eyes bounced away immediately when his brain made that connection.

"I remember you as Jeremy Cameron." Mandy giggled and shoved at Caesar. "He does sound like those boys on that reality show." She dimpled a smile for Jeremy. "Can I say that you have grown up, too? Joel said you were back, but he didn't tell us you weren't—"

"Mandy," Caesar grated. He yanked the cigarette from his

mouth. "Keep a lid on it."

Jeremy could feel the undercurrents that Mandy was sending him and he did not like it, but he must press on. If things were to be made right for Beau, the way had to be paved. "I speak," he said to Mandy. "Well." She nodded, and her long blonde hair glided over her shoulders with the movement. It was a practiced movement that he recognized. Why did girls think fidgeting was alluring? It must have something to do with all the jiggling body parts they had going on. He averted his eyes again. "And the accent. It can't be helped. After Hurricane Libby I was unable to speak. My voice had to be retrained and we lived in London, so . . ."

"Yada-yada-yada," Caesar drawled. He folded his arms over his chest and thrust his chin toward the field. "I'll tell you all about Jeremy later, Dee, just keep your panties on. He's here to see his little pitcher play ball."

Mandy shoved at Caesar again and gave an indignant huff. Her face flushed a deep red all the way to her hairline. She watched as Beau took the pitcher's mound. She turned to Jeremy, her lip curled slightly. "You've got to be kidding me? Her?" She looked at Caesar. "What is it with the little cray-cray girl? She's not even pretty."

Jeremy shrugged, his mouth curled in an entirely different way. "She's my angel." It had been a long time since he used the nickname, but it seemed the time. Beau's mother had a propensity to give her kids Cajun names. Beau Angelle meant beautiful angel in Cajun French. It was only fitting that Jeremy had always called her angel as an endearment. It sounded different coming out of an eighteen-year old's mouth, though. When he said it as a nine-year-old, it had been cute. Today, it was a declaration. The word sounded possessive. It made him want to cringe because it sounded so ridiculous.

So be it. He did not care. Girls like Mandy ate stuff like this up. This was for Beau. He would give her that edge. She would be envied by all of those who had tormented her for something that had been real. Something she had no control over. He knew all about what that was like.

And perhaps it was partly vanity, but he knew what girls thought of him. He was quite the male specimen. He hadn't asked for the bone, muscle, and sinew to be distributed the way it was on his body. It had just happened, and good for Beau, because it was all hers. He didn't care if he'd been made ugly, but for her—he was glad he was considered such a fine catch.

A bark of laughter came from Caesar. He looked over his shoulder, and took note of how many other girls were gawking.

Mandy huffed again and frowned at Jeremy. "You do know that she's crazy, don't you?"

"He said she's his *angel*," Caesar enunciated each word clearly. He reached into his pocket and tossed a ten-dollar bill at Mandy when she gave him a blank stare. "Go get me a cup of ice." The bill hit the front of her shirt; she caught it before it tumbled to the ground under the bleachers. A little indignant huff passed her glossy lips. "Come back with a better 'tude and your mouth closed. Capeesh?"

Mandy stood with a girlish shriek and jostled Caesar's head before storming off. The hostile gesture did not seem to faze Caesar. He watched the field as if nothing had happened to disturb his attention on the game.

Jeremy watched her leave. "Thanks," he said. "I guess."

"No problem." Caesar leaned back and hooked his elbows on the bench behind him. "I've been listening to the talk about you. I figured it would be bad."

"My voice," Jeremy grimaced. "Yeah, there's nothing—"

"Seriously?" Caesar asked, his expression shocked. He tipped down his sunglasses to the end of his nose.

"It freaks everyone out, here at least." Jeremy shook his head. "I don't get this back in Kent, and the Cayman Islands is a British Colony, so—"

"Dude, I'm talking about *you*." He used his index finger in an up and down motion. He used the same finger to press his glasses back into place. "You're like the freaking dude who wears his Speedo on a dingy in remote Italy for that perfume commercial. Do you spend *all* your free time in the gym?"

"Oh, that," Jeremy said. He turned and noticed his brother glaring at him from a few seats above. Joel gave him the middle finger. In return, Jeremy tipped his chin in greeting; he refused to be baited. "Joel looks a lot like me. What's the big deal?"

"You're an enigma," Caesar said as he pulled a cigarette from the front pocket of his flannel shirt. "You open your mouth and sound like a chick's wet dream. Joel ain't got nothing on you, man."

"We could be twins," Jeremy pointed out. "We both have black hair, blue eyes, our father's mouth and nose."

"And?" Caesar asked before he paused to light his cigarette. "He's hateful, you're sweet. Girls dig that. But don't worry, I've got your back. Although if you keep saying things like "blimey," you're on your own. Dude, that even freaked me out a little."

"Thanks," Jeremy said. "I guess." He smiled as he turned away and saw that the concession was serving actual food. "Hey, want some nachos?" He hadn't had those in years. Jareth said the cheese would clog his arteries in a second flat. The likes of nacho cheese could never hope to find itself inside the Tremaine pantry.

"With peppers?" Caesar asked.

A good memory of playing little league with Caesar and the lunches of nachos galore popped into his mind. How he had missed Caesar after all. "Is there any other way?"

Beau was going to have a panic attack. It was bad enough that Jeremy insisted on staying for practice. It seemed everyone from Gueydan was present. Usually, the park was empty for a late practice, but with football season on the heels of summer's end, she had not counted on it being packed with students procrastinating about going home. Now everyone had seen them—together. Old questions were bound to circulate. She hadn't thought that through. She was trying to shake her past, not dig it up and parade it through town.

"Is that Jeremy Cameron?" yet another girl asked.

Beau frowned, glared up where Jeremy was seated, and let someone else answer. Yes, it was Jeremy Cameron and he belonged to her—sort of. For today. Well, he was here with her anyway.

"It's Jeremy Tremaine now," Natalie Schexnider, Rixby's ultimate crush, corrected. "I saw him drop off Beau in a *Land Rover*."

Was that what it was called? Beau smiled. It was a good thing Natalie was nice or she would have ignited on the spot. "He's an old friend," she explained when everyone listening turned expectant eyes on her.

"He's cute," Natalie said, elbowing Beau. "Does he really sound like a foreigner?"

"Who cares what he sounds like," the shortstop muttered as she passed.

Natalie rolled her eyes and smiled at Beau. "So, what's he like, really?"

"I don't know what you mean," Beau said as she reached for the oil. Her glove was new and stiff. She could not look like a fool in front of Jeremy. Pitching was her greatest gift. Elizabet sang *and* she pitched. It was the way of things, and it was what he remembered, so she wanted to be on point. Besides, she wanted to hit something, and warming her glove was a good option. Meanwhile, everyone was eyeballing Jeremy.

"Everyone remembers that it was you who found him after the hurricane. You guys have history. You said so yourself: you're old friends."

Natalie left out the part that everyone called her crazy because of him, but she could hear it in her voice. Beau pasted on a smile. "His mom and my mom cleaned houses together, so yeah, we've sort known each other since we were kids."

"He sure isn't a kid now," Natalie said, her eyes popping suggestively.

Beau looked up into the bleachers where Jeremy sat and found him staring at her. He waved sheepishly and made a sign. Their sign. When he used to help her pitch, they had developed a sign language. Jeremy would watch the game and signal her how to pitch. He was better than a coach and freakishly accurate.

She smiled like a dopey fool and lifted her glove to salute. Jeremy gave her the "okay" sign and turned to Caesar, who was talking and hadn't seemed to notice that Jeremy was no longer attentive. Jeremy picked up the conversation as if he had not been distracted.

So, he wanted her to pitch a curve ball. She looked at the batter and grinned wider. The girl up to bat could not hit a curve ball to save her life. How did he know that?

That's what she thought after she threw three perfect curve balls and put the girl out. But that was not the only thing on her mind. She was also wondering how she would get into the car without Jeremy holding the door open and how she would make it back home without declaring her undying love for him. Embarrassment was certain either way, and both ended with her wanting the earth to swallow her whole. There was also the fact he was hiding something from her, and that could cancel out all of the above. She loved and hated him at the same time. It was complicated.

"Why do you seem . . . off?" Jeremy asked as he started the vehicle.

Beau snapped her seat belt and tried to ignore the legion of people staring. She had barely gotten to the car in time to hop in before Jeremy did his little chivalrous stunt. Caesar had managed to keep him occupied while she snatched the keys and made a break for it. There was nothing she could say. He had her totally off track and confused. It maddened her that he stalked back into her life and proceeded to act as if nothing happened. He wanted to ignore that he could accomplish things like answering her thoughts.

Jeremy leaned over, draped his arm over the steering wheel, and turned. "Are you ashamed of me?"

Beau snapped to attention. "Of course not, no. How could you think that?" she sputtered and pulled a face. "Where did that come from?"

Jeremy's eyes tapered. "You're jumpy. You practically ran to the car ahead of me, as though you didn't want to be seen with me. Your plans keep changing, and I think it's because you hope I won't press the issue and leave you alone. You went from pushing me away to agreeing to see me, to letting me carry you around everywhere. And you're being halfway nice to me."

He was so wrong and so right at the same time. Being with him amplified everything. It brought it all back. "Can we just get out of here?" she asked. She looked out the window as a group passed, making obnoxious sounds. Someone rocked the vehicle and the crowd busted out in raucous laughter. She turned to Jeremy. She knew she looked as miserable as she felt. "Please."

Jeremy's eyes followed the crowd. "They made fun of you," he said. He looked at her. "When I was gone, these are the ones who made fun of you."

Beau shut her eyes briefly. "Let's just go. We can talk about this later."

"All right," he replied. He leaned back and shifted the car into reverse. "Have it your way." He glanced in the rearview mirror so he would not back into the crowd who lingered. "One question now, though." He put the car into drive and looked at her. "Did they make fun of you because we were friends or because of what happened to me after the storm?"

He stared at her so fiercely that she didn't answer right away. Her eyes circled his face, and took in the way his cheeks were pink at the apples and his nose was flared, but it was always his mouth that fascinated her. Right now, it had a stern bend to it. She chewed the inside of her lip, making her eyes water. "After." She looked away, jutted her chin forward, and swallowed down the emotion that she did not want him or anyone else see. "They said I was crazy."

Jeremy muttered something under his breath before driving off, but she did not hear. The sound of her heart beating was caging her. It was in her ears, in her throat. And the rush stayed that way until she was safe at home. But even then he followed her, and she knew the time for running was gone.

"It all looks the same," Jeremy said in awe. He reached out and touched her music box. It twinkled with its tune. "You bought this at a church garage sale."

"I did," Beau answered. She wrapped her arms around herself to shrug off the internalized chill she felt. It was surreal to see Jeremy circle her small bedroom, touching things and looking around as if he would uncover something important. He only paused to bite the pear she had gotten for him in the kitchen. The boy was a human garbage disposal. She saw him order and eat five plates of nachos while watching her practice, and he still claimed to be starving. "It was Labor Day weekend. The week before the regulations became permanent."

It was one memory that flooded her mind. Having him here was dangerous. It sparked remembrances of yesterday when a shy boy gazed at her as though she held his world in her hands. When his handsomeness was unnoticed by everyone but her. When he was unloved and shunned by all because he was the non-verbal, timid kid who sometimes chose to use hand gestures rather than speak.

Jeremy was the youngster who was always polite, but no one acknowledged the fact because it was uncomfortable to communicate with him. He was the boy who—even though she was only nine years old—stole her heart. It was physically painful to watch him now. To stand there like a fool, wishing he would spill his secrets so she could run into his arms and forgive him for everything. Instead, he reopened a concealed wound that had never healed.

She always knew it was him. And now that he was here, touching her things and digging up the past, she was not sure it was a good thing. He was no longer her introverted Clark Kent. The guy who stood only inches from her was beautiful, confident and well-spoken. He had the ability to shatter her into millions of pieces that no one could fix.

"I remember," he murmured. He stopped before a poster on her wall. His head tilted as he surveyed the boy band she loved. He looked over his shoulder. "Cute." He thumbed toward the poster. "They're British."

Beau's lips twisted. "The fact I like them has nothing to do with you."

"Undoubtedly," he said with a grin. "How would you know I'd pick up the dialect like a pro? But I am a British citizen . . . just sayin'." Beau rolled her eyes, to which Jeremy laughed. He pointed to the poster. "The one with the big mouth and curly hair had a ruptured appendix last May. Jareth was the surgeon who removed it."

"He does not have a big mouth," Beau countered, but smiled too. She shook her head, her arms relaxing at her sides. It was too easy to revert back to their bantering like when they were friends, when she was the only person he spoke in whole sentences to. "Don't hate. It's not nice."

"Cheeky lad," Jeremy said. "He made a pass at Elizabet." Glancing around, he spotted the trash can and pitched the pear core into it. Of course, it was a perfect shot.

"Wait. You're serious? You really met them?" He nodded and she gasped dramatically. "I thought you were joking."

"People from England aren't like Americans. They maintain their humility even though they become famous. I sit next to the blond one on the underground all the time. At least twice a week. He goes to university in London."

"Take me to London." She clasped her hands together in a prayer pose.

"Oh, no," Jeremy said while shaking his head and smiling ruefully. "You might like them more than you like me. Can't have that."

Beau's smile faltered as something in the air shifted nostalgically. Their eyes held for a beat before warmth flooded her face and she looked away. "What are we doing here, Jeremy?" She touched her forehead with the back of her hand. "You've been gone a while." It was an understatement. She cleared her throat because her voice sounded gravelly. "We can't just jump back to where we left off."

"We could try," he said. "I thought we were doing pretty well until you brought up the past."

"No, Jeremy." She shook off the sensation that electricity was riding on her skin. Instead of being frightened, it made her angry. How dare he pretend nothing strange was happening? She motioned at the space between them. "You know, I thought I could give you a chance, but I just can't. Not as long as this hangs between us."

Jeremy took a step toward her and she stepped back. "What are you talking about?"

"This," she said. She motioned madly with her hands, her arms flailing outward. "Why can't you just say it and be done with it? Admit what I already know is real. Don't try to tell me there isn't something in here with us, something happening all around us. I can feel it." She pointed to him. "You're causing it. I know it and I won't stop until I find out what it is."

Her mother called her name from the living room.

"Beau, calm down," Jeremy said. "You're not making things

any better. Your mum will come in here and toss me out."

"I will not calm down! You stole everything from me. My childhood. Years of peace. My sanity." She took another step further and lowered her voice. It had to come out or she would explode. "My heart." And there it was.

Before she could protest, he was next to her, pulling her into his arms.

"Quiet," he whispered into her hair as he tucked her closer. She fought against him, but he buried her face in his chest. "Be still," he said, and kissed the top of her head with his arms wrapped around her. He brought her body flush against his, molding her smaller frame to his large one. "I'm not leaving you again. I'm here to stay. I promise. You have to trust me. Please, angel, I want to help you. Let me."

It was strange. The tilt in their perpetual friendship had shifted. She was in his arms, leaning into him and he had kissed a part of her body. If he had any doubts that what he felt was anything but romantic love, it had just been obliterated. Beau was soft, pliable and warm. She was heaven in his arms.

"I shouldn't have let you in," she sobbed. "I was getting better. Why did you have to come back? I'm not strong, Jeremy. I can't fight you."

"I know," he crooned. "Ssshhh, it's okay. I've got you. You've got me. You don't have to fight anyone."

She did not fight him; she went limp. Leaned into him and cried like a baby. "You were my friend. I . . . I—"

"Trusted me?" His hands skimmed her back to soothe them both. He rested his cheek atop her head and hugged her closer.

She nodded and gripped the front of his crisp shirt into her fist. "But I hated you, too. After you left."

"I know," he said. He pulled back, ran his hands down her arms, and grabbed her hands into his. "I promise that won't happen again. I'm here, Beau, and I'm yours." She looked up at him through teary eyes. He pressed his forehead to hers. "I

might as well put us both out of our misery and say it first."
He pulled his breath in raggedly. "I love, *love*, love you. I'm not
going anywhere unless you send me away, and even then . . . I
don't know if I could go. Please, don't ask it of me."

She pulled away and remained in the circle of his arms as
her hands traveled up to his face. Her fingertips skimmed his
cheeks, over his mouth. She touched him as if it would be the
last time. He had a sinking feeling in the pit of his stomach because he knew what was coming next. "Then tell me, Jeremy.
Tell me what happened to you. Tell me so we can make this
work. Tell me what happened to you. Why can I hear your
thoughts in my head? How can you hear mine?"

"There is nothing to say," Jeremy said tightly. "I don't know
what you're talking about. What you're saying is impossible."
The lie hung between them, the gauntlet tossed right next to
it. It tasted bad in his mouth. Like he drank acid when seconds
before he almost kissed her mouth, and he was sure that would
have tasted sweeter than anything he ever sampled. Even as the
words left him, he knew they were wrong. But it was a script
he was playing, diverting the truth so he could be with her and
have her close, in his arms.

A sad expression took over Beau's countenance. He stared
into her eyes and let his gaze linger as if it was the first time
they had seen each other—or maybe the last. She shook her
head slightly before she leaned up and pressed her lips to his.
Her hands bracketed his face and she held him there. Their first
kiss was bittersweet and short. He would remember it forever.
"Then you have to go," she said against his lips. She drew back,
looked at him, and then tilted up to kiss him again. This time
he was ready and held the kiss longer, taking more than she
was willing to give—desperate to have her hold on to him and
not care about his secret.

He willed it, but still she drew back. Her mind held her
own thoughts and not the ones he wanted her to have. "Go

and don't come back until you are ready to tell me everything."
She pulled away and stepped back. He felt the shift in her as
she steeled her spine. Jeremy knew he looked as if she had just
killed his entire family and carved his heart out. "I don't want
to see you until you understand that loving someone is trusting
them. Something happened to you, and it wasn't just getting
caught in a storm."

He opened his mouth, but she put her hand up to stop him.
"No more lies, Jeremy. I don't think I can take any more from
you." She waved her hand toward the door. "Go. Please. I can't
stand the sight of you as long as you want to lie. You have no
idea what I endured because of you and your lies. I thought I
could try, but I can't. If we move on, I want all of it. The truth
or nothing at all, because so help me, I love you, too, and love
doesn't lie."

The trouble was that he did know what she had endured.
Her emotions were tangled with memories and he had seen
them all. Instead of sweetness, what he tasted on her lips was
the pain she bore on his behalf. She might as well have carved
his heart out, because he was leaving it with her. He could not
stay, because if he did, he was at risk to give her whatever she
asked.

When Jeremy arrived home, Jareth was in the garage, tin-
kering under his car. He had a passion for remodeling classic
cars and this was his newest project. It would take months to
restore. Jeremy rounded the black car that sported an animal on
the hood in a pounce stance and kicked Jareth's leg.

"I need to talk," he said over the blaring rock music.

Jareth slid out from under the car, his face flushed. His hands
and face were smudged with grease, his expression dazed. He
was such a petrolhead that Jeremy wanted to laugh at the picture before him, but he had a bone to pick and he had left his
heart behind with Beau. There was no laughter left in him.
"If it has to do with Beau—I know already. She called Elizabet

crying."

Jeremy frowned and put his hands on his hips. "Nothing is sacred in this house."

"Look at it this way: I wanted you to build a bridge between Elizabet and Beau and you have succeeded. Mission accomplished. Not all is lost. It's a small step, but a step nonetheless. It wasn't a long conversation and it ended badly when Beau decided she should not have called, but the duchess is exceedingly glad. My thanks." Jareth pushed to slide back under the car, but Jeremy put his foot on the creeper to stay him.

"I suppose she hates me now." Jeremy waved his hand in the air. "I refused to tell her what she wanted to know. I guess they were re-bonding over what a douchebag I am to her."

Jareth smiled and reached for a rag to wipe his face. "Yeah, it was something like that."

"This isn't funny."

"I think it is hysterical."

"You're the douchebag," Jeremy muttered.

Jareth threw the filthy cloth at him. "Watch your mouth."

Jeremy grabbed the cloth and tossed it into the nearby aluminum trashcan. "What are you going to do about it?"

In one smooth movement, Jareth hopped up to stand in front of Jeremy. They were equal in size. "Absolutely nothing." He put his hand on Jeremy's shoulder and squeezed. "Look, being who you are is a privilege. To have your abilities, and every possibility of helping mankind from evil is an honor you should be proud to protect. I know it is hard, but you have been taught to accomplish hard things. I am proud of you."

"Living my life for the sake of others grows tiring, Jareth. What about me? What about what I want? You speak of this and then you go into a home where your wife waits for you. Your life is freaking perfect." Jeremy shook his head. "You don't understand."

"Said every teenager," Jareth said. He squeezed Jeremy's

shoulder again before he let go. "You forget that I am afflicted with my own vices." He motioned to the car behind him. "It is a struggle every day not to obsess over trivial matters. Part of me wants to tear this car apart and do nothing else until I solve all of its riddles and secrets. I know you struggle with this as well, but you have your abilities that help you overcome it. Just because your DNA mutation makes things manageable, it does not mean you are free. You are who you are. Your obsessions remain, but you must preserve the code. Beau cannot know what you are or we risk the safety of everyone involved. You do not want to admit it, but look at what she did after your turning." Jeremy wanted to say something in Beau's defense, but Jareth stayed him with a simple glare. "She was scared, and I get that. But she talked to the wrong people. People I had to remove from our trail to protect the Amalgam. Do you know what it takes to get government officials off your back? The trail I left behind is riddled with blood."

"I remember," Jeremy admitted reluctantly. He remembered because he was the main henchman who carried out the orders given.

"By adopting you, I protected you. The American government cannot touch an English citizen, but we are in this country on visas. Do not muck it up or I will remove you."

"It is torture to be here," Jeremy admitted, his voice rough. They had come because southern Louisiana was a hotbed for host formation. It was their mission to prevent the turning of any more hosts by defusing any mega storm that approached. Gabriel had been to the future and reported five hosts, two of which were stronger than Jeremy and had rebellious hearts.

Those turnings, which occurred roughly every three to four years, had to be thwarted. That put them in Louisiana for at least the next twenty years. Jeremy would be sent into the mega storms to diffuse them to mere tropical disturbances, and they would never have the opportunity to turn anyone.

The first storm reported was arriving in the next hurricane season. It gave them a year to establish roots in Vermilion Parish and set things into motion. Jeremy couldn't simply go shooting into storms from any coast. He needed to learn the lay of the land all over again, so his body adjusted to the seasonal changes. He was strongest when he was adapted.

"I understand," Jareth replied. "The food here is awful."

"Don't joke, please," Jeremy said. "You know I'm speaking of this . . . romantic inclination I have for Beau. You've so graciously agreed to allow me my leisure, but she won't let me within an inch of her. She hates me."

Jareth shrugged. "Have it your way. Brood all the time for all I care."

"It might make me feel better if I get you into trouble, too. That way I'm not alone in my brooding." He thumbed over his shoulder. "I could tell the duchess about your secret love for rock music."

"It is a game we play," Jareth said, not looking threatened whatsoever. "I pretend I do not know how the station was changed from classical, or else I blame it on you." He grinned. "Besides, she is quite aware of my musical taste and she likes it. I would say she even approves."

"Of all the time-jumping knights to get adopted by, I get the petrolhead, head-banging doctor with a moral chip on his shoulder."

"What can I say? I am close to perfect," Jareth said as his beeper went off. He looked down at the number scrolling across the display and frowned. "Finish up here." He tipped his chin toward the car. "Make sure I tightened things up, then get ready. That was Gabriel. We are needed in Dover. The host you wrangled the other day is ready for release to the Caymans for training." He turned to leave, then spun back with a shy smile on his face. "And turn off the radio on your way out. Elizabet thinks I only listen to soft rock. I am easing her into the heavier stuff."

Jeremy smirked. "Just what I want to do. Cover up for you, then travel back in time where I'll likely freeze my bits off. Or," He pointedly eyed the classic Jaguar as he passed it on his way to shut off the radio. "Stay here and muck up your beautiful disaster that you love as much as your wife. Probably get punished for ruining the interior or some rot like that." He did a fist pump with no enthusiasm. "Yay. It's so fun being me."

Chapter 5

"Sometimes, you have to go with your gut—screw Jareth. He doesn't know everything, even though he acts as though he's omnipresent. You have to be true to yourself or you've got nothing."

—*Gabriel Morton on the day he married Minh's sister, Liang, against Jareth's counsel.*

BEAU COULD NOT STOP THINKING about Jeremy. What was he doing? Why did he listen to her and leave her alone after he promised he would never leave her again?

It was her fault. Jeremy was a gentleman and he was doing what he thought she wanted—what she asked for. A month had gone by since that fated day in her bedroom without a word from him. It was as though he disappeared all over again, but she knew he was around. Elizabet would not leave her alone. Sometimes she received five phone calls in a week. The only comfort in this was that Jeremy was still in the general vicinity. It should not make a difference to her, but it did.

"We'll be back tomorrow," her mom said as she buckled Andre's car seat into the minivan. Her parents were going to Lake Charles for a conference on how new regulations would affect stores that accepted food stamps.

"I'll be here," Beau sniped. She was grateful they were taking the baby and the twins. Aries and Amos were ten, but still could be an obnoxious handful. Andre was just bad. "Getting acne, eating Blue Bell and Ramen. Having no life."

She waved as they backed out. Good riddance. Now she could be depressed on her own . . . save Rixby, but if he was telling the truth, he was staying at a friend's duck camp over-night. Beau could only hope he wouldn't show up and spoil her pity party. She was due a good cry and with no one to witness it, this was opportunity knocking on her door. There would be hours of staring at her phone, willing herself not to cave and dial Elizabet's number with the hope that Jeremy would an-swer. The rest of the time she planned to shove food in her face until she went into a carb coma.

"Really?" she hollered, exactly an hour later when the lights flickered as she stood over a simmering pot of Ramen noodles. She switched off the stove and moved the pan off the heat. What a lousy time to have an electric stove. She kept her hand on the pot's handle and listened attentively to the pounding of the raindrops on the tin roof and the howling of the wind as it picked up outdoors.

One Mississippi. Two Mississippi. Three Mississippi.

Boom! The thunder crashed.

Beau blew a breath she did not realize she had been holding. The storm was three miles away, but it was loud and causing an electricity failure. She found her cell phone and pulled up the weather app, but the radar showed nothing but clear skies. That was weird. A flash of lightening lit up the room when she drew back the window curtain. *"Mais-la,"* she breathed and stepped back. "Come on, really?" she grumbled again, in English this time.

This parish needed a new meteorologist. She could not re-lax with that storm barreling forward, so she grabbed a carton of Blue Bell ice cream and headed for her bedroom. Painting her toenails while watching Netflix was always an option. To not paint her whole foot while being scared to death—that was the trick. Beau and bad weather did not get along. It went back to the time people went missing during Libby. She was grate-ful that mega tornadoes hadn't gotten this far south and there were no hurricanes in sight. She would just have to ride this one out with her ear buds firmly in place and pray it was just a passing thunderstorm.

Jeremy pulled his body along on the creeper and slid out from under the car. It was quiet in the garage other than the sound of Jareth rotating a wrench and an 80's rock tune on the radio. He was still until the thunder boomed again. The back of his neck prickled with the voice that rode the wind. "Do you hear that?"

"Thunder?" Jareth asked with a slight pause in his work. "Only you can tell me if I should hear something else."

Jeremy walked around the car. "Where's your phone?"

"You need a weather update? Is this a joke?" Jareth pushed away from under the hood and grabbed the oilcan when his elbow struck it. He barely caught it before it sloshed over the side.

"I'm a bit off," Jeremy admitted. His eyes bounced around for the phone. Saying he was "off" was an understatement. He was downright depressed since Beau brushed him off, but he would give her space to figure out where he fit in—*if* he fit in.

The duchess and her brood of children filtered in. "Gabriel just called," she said. The twins flanked her sides, Peter hung around her neck and dangled down her back, and Gideon lay in her arms. She spoke rapidly. "Jareth, the host Jeremy contained last month has escaped the island. He killed two hosts on his way out. Eddie put the Amalgam on high alert. He believes he's headed this way."

Jareth grabbed a towel for his hands and hit the remote button to open the garage doors. He tilted his head, one eye on his wife as she hushed Gideon when he began to cry.

Wind and a widening shaft of light swept inside as the doors angled open.

"I knew it was a message," Jeremy said as he made his way out to have a look at the weather. "He's using the undercurrent. It's why I'm off." He made a circle by his ear. "Too many voices at once."

Jareth turned off the radio and wiped his hands of grime. "What did Gabriel say, exactly?" he asked Elizabet. Jeremy gazed up into the oddly shaped cloud formation that hung ominously low.

Elizabet walked up to Jareth. "It's a super cell, packing twin tornadoes," she explained. Jareth grabbed Peter from her back. "He said that Jeremy can diffuse him, but he must be quick. It's an F5." She delivered the last announcement with awe in her voice. "Both of them. I thought Silas was a category one hurricane?"

Gideon was in a good wail now. Jareth kissed the top of Elizabet's head and bussed the baby's cheek. "He is able to spawn killer tornadoes, like Jeremy. No worries, love." His voice said something different, though, when he addressed Jeremy. "It is just one host, though he is twisting two cyclones to incite fear. You got this . . . right?"

"You won't like hearing this, but I'm going to say it anyway." Jeremy's expression was stark. He stood in the wind current and looked over his shoulder. The wind blew his hair wildly. "Silas allegiance to Dover was false. He never intended to serve in the Amalgam. Gyula intends to kill him if he fails, so he never really had a choice in the matter. He agreed with us to be transferred to the island where escape would be easier. And get this . . . someone on the inside helped him. Someone in Cayman is aiding Gyula, but I can't figure out who. There is too much artifact feeding through the currents. Anyway, he is using code, sort of like Morse code, to speak between what he is allowing me to siphon." He shook his head. "On the flip side, it's only me they want. They will leave your family alone if you turn over control of the Amalgam."

"How absurd," Jareth said. "There is no such thing as 'only you.'" He put his arm around Elizabet and tucked her to his side. Gideon had settled down and was sucking his thumb.

"What does Gyula think he will accomplish with this tactic? You are the stronger host. There is no contest of strength here. He is sending his boy on a suicide mission."

"And Silas knows this. He's terrified that if he aborts this mission, Gyula will kill not only him, but his family as well. There is so much fear riding the wind," Jeremy said. "I'm having difficulty siphoning Silas alone. He's spinning high wind gusts and dropping lightening in his wake. It's scaring people, and you know how loudly they think when they're frightened." He ran his hand over his mouth as he listened to the currents in the wind. "What I don't understand is why he is dropping down ten miles from here. If it's me he's after, why is his trajectory to the west of us?"

Jareth and Elizabet shared a passing look of concern.

"And you're getting all of this from him *now*?" Elizabet asked.

"He can't keep his thoughts to himself," Jeremy muttered, his face serious as his head inclined into the wind. He raked his hand through his hair and over his mouth again. "Oh, no. No . . . no . . ."

"Jeremy," Jareth said, releasing Elizabet and untangling Peter from his neck. The boy slid to the floor and ran for his mother's leg, where he pushed his sister aside to wrap his arms around her. Jareth went to Jeremy, placing his hand on his shoulder. "Son, what is it?"

A gasp puffed from his mouth. "They're going for Beau." His fingers popped away as if he did not believe the words he was about to speak. His eyes went wide. "He's planning to drop those twisters right on her, Jareth." He gripped Jareth's arm. Anger coursed through his body as he felt the magnitude of the situation. "They mean to kill her to flush me out. They think I'll be too angry to fight if my emotions are involved because I'm a siphon. They know I'm a siphon."

"It does not work that way, not with you," Jareth said, his

voice low. "If it were Malia, yes, but you are a siphon of a different sort." His gaze leveled. "Go. Now. Do not tarry any longer. You must diffuse him." Jeremy let his eyes rove to Elizabet and his siblings. "No, Jeremy," Jareth snapped his fingers in his line of vision and called his attention back. "I protect them. You are not responsible for the lot of us. I am more than capable of breaking medieval over this quaint community if I must. And you forget that I know how to kill a host even when they are at their strongest."

"I'll have to dissipate," Jeremy said. He glanced around. His eyes blindly searched, then landed on the vehicles. "Unless you want me to take the Land Rover?"

Jareth looked horrified. "Gads, no. Are you barking mad? We just detailed it. You will ruin the leather and I will not even consider the wreckage the debris would cause to the exterior." His face became stern. "Better for you to dissipate."

Jeremy nodded even as he stripped off his shirt and shed his shoes. His movements were robotic; he had done this countless times before. He passed Jareth his watch. "There will be a fight." He gave Jareth a pointed look. "It will get nasty. I will have to protect Beau and fight."

"I can send Gabriel or Minh. Will you need help?"

"I can take this host. He's an idiot," Jeremy sneered. He tugged his jeans off and tossed them on the floor of the garage. "I tracked his strength while he was blabbing. F5 indeed."

"So, what you are really asking is whether you are allowed to take a life?"

Jeremy's hand paused on the waistband of his boxers. There was a slight tremble in his wrist while he considered the question, but he didn't allow a break in his response. "Yes."

"You are at leisure to execute," Jareth said. A cell phone went off, the ring tone the "Ride of the Valkyries." It was Gabriel. "Are you sure you want to do this? I can send Gabriel, and we have Eddie on standby. They can take this host down and we can perform a thorough wipe out. No one involved will remember the incident except the Amalgam."

It was a loaded question with much unsaid. Was he ready to expose who he was to Beau? Was he prepared for the changes that would have to be made to bring someone else into the complexity of the Amalgam family? Beau would never have to know he was involved. She could believe she was lucky to survive a tornado outbreak.

"She's frightened, Jareth," he said. "I feel her fear on the wind. I can't sit here listening to her tears and that bastard tormenting her. I must go to her." His features contorted with his agony. "I'm *compelled* to go. It should be me, not anyone else."

"Gabriel is five minutes out," Elizabet said, the phone to her ear. "Minh is with him. They were able to flash in a mile away. I gave them directions."

"Go," Jareth told Jeremy. "Minh will monitor the host and signal if you need help. He will have what is needed to dismantle the host if you are unable." Jeremy walked to the edge of the garage. There was a light drizzle along with the wind. That they were ten full miles from Beau's home was a testament to how large this host could expand. The closer to the core, the stronger it would become, and he was sure it was getting ugly on Beau's end right about now, but Jeremy was not impressed. He could fill the entire Gulf of Mexico with devastating portions of wind and rain. This host was an amateur compared to him. Jareth would not have to break medieval over Wright. Jeremy would do it for him. No one threatened his family.

Beau had just irrevocably become a part of the inner circle of the Tremaines . . . and Dover's Amalgam.

Beau had waited too long. The weather severity had escalated suddenly and there was no time to run next door to the neighbors' sturdier brick home. There had been no warning, no sirens. The storm literally dropped out of nowhere and there was no place to hide. Her home was nothing more than a tin can. They didn't have a cellar or special closet. She would be killed or maimed—if she even made it out alive.

The rumble of a freight train surrounded her as she hunkered in the narrow gap between her bed and the wall. She pressed the heels of her hands over her ears and screamed. She didn't want to die, especially not like this, terrified and alone. Hot tears spilled onto her cheeks as she sucked in another breath to scream. The screaming gave her a sense that she was doing something other than sitting like a bull's eye waiting to be annihilated.

"Beau." Someone called her name through the mayhem. She looked up and the door to her room exploded open, leaving a gaping hole that exposed the outside elements. She gripped the bedspread and pulled it and the mattress toward her. Then she watched, dumbfounded, as Jeremy suddenly filled the splintered doorway. His eyes searched the room until he saw her. A strangled sob left his mouth when he looked into her eyes.

He held out his hand as he approached. "Take my hand. We have to be fast. It's right on top of us."

Beau blinked up at him, unable to do as she was told. She held on to the bed for dear life. Jeremy was soaking wet, his hair plastered to his skull like a black cap. Wearing only a pair of boxers, he was a wall of muscle and cut sinew. She shook her head. "I can't," she sobbed.

He seized her under the arms and hauled her to her feet. She grimaced as he handled her so roughly. "Can and you will," he growled. He kicked the scattered mess out of his way as he half dragged, half forced her to walk toward the rear hallway. The hall window bowed and was sucked out as if the outdoors were a giant vacuum. Jeremy put his body between Beau and the flying debris. He tucked her close and used his body as a shield. Her knees buckled as she felt the aftershock of the blows he took to his bare back.

She imagined it would not be long before they were dead.

Jeremy had just been beaten by debris, and she mentally gave in to the idea that this was it. She didn't know how he remained standing other than if maybe he had experienced an adrenaline rush. She had seen films in the past depicting sickening images of wreckage becoming flying missiles, and they played in her mind today. Jeremy's back must be shredded. She expected to be impaled any moment by a fence post or roof shingle. There was no getting out of this alive.

"The bathtub," Jeremy shouted as he proceeded to move them again, this time toward what was left of the bathroom. A twin-size mattress flew against the door frame as they entered. His arm darted out and grabbed it.

She allowed her hands to run over his back. She expected to feel warm, sticky blood and protruding splinters of wood. Hysteria bubbled up within her, making her shake and clouding her judgement. Her mind screamed at her, ordered her to get into the tub, but her emotions were convinced that Jeremy was hurt.

But there was nothing other than smooth muscle and warm, intact skin beneath her palms. Through the chaos she looked up at him as if in a dream. He peered down at her, his mouth a hard line, and she knew he was aware of her thoughts.

"I'm impermeable," he shouted.

She swallowed roughly. Her eyes travelled to his chest, which was heaving. The skin there was perfect, too. Not a scratch on him. Her own hands that were clutching him and searching for injuries were riddled with fresh bruises and blood-ied scratches. Three of her nails were jagged, bloody messes. Her mind refused to process what he claimed, but the evidence was there.

"I can protect you, but you have to trust me," he yelled. He was doing it again. His lips had not moved, but she clearly heard his voice. Beau nodded owlishly as she obeyed. She trusted him, even though it was happening again the way it did the day she found him after the hurricane. But this trust had nothing to do with secrets. She would go anywhere with Jeremiah Cameron.

He would protect her, so she climbed into the porcelain tub and hunkered down. "Lay down!" he commanded. This time he spoke out loud, but sounded like thunder and wind. The sound surrounded her and pressed against her like a sonic boom. It sent a shiver through her body. She smelled the distinct scent of the beach—saltwater spray. It struck her as odd that she would notice this, but it was so strong that it bathed the air.

Beau lay down, her arms stiff at her sides. The lights strobed above her, flickering on and off and giving an eerie backdrop for what was happening. It was hard to imagine that any light fixtures still had juice to them. The light over the bathroom mirror swung from the wall like a restless pendulum.

Jeremy climbed in and lay on top of her, then brought the mattress with the Hello Kitty bedsheets over them. She thought of Aries, the owner of the sheets. Her sister was safe, and she was glad. Jeremy held it in place over them as a monster wind sucked the air from around them and the house heaved.

Beau reached around and settled for gripping the elastic of his boxers when her hands could not find purchase on his hard body. The house sighed as the tornado sucked them upward into the heavens and all at once she could not breathe. She thrashed her head from side to side trying to breathe, but the air would not come. Her fingers dug into Jeremy's side as she fought. The soft tissue of her lungs refused to inflate. The garish crunch of metal ripping surrounded them as the house folded into itself. The blunt force of the roof collapsing hit the mattress. Jeremy's body bowed and conformed to hers, then became a barrier and the weight was gone.

Silence. That brief pause right before havoc is unleashed. That slight ray of hope that has one thinking they will escape, when in fact the worst is still to come.

A loud crack of thunder, a flash of light, moaning, and a

keening wail rent the air around them. She vaguely noticed Jeremy tuck his left arm back into the tub. The sensation of falling filled her gut.

Jeremy cursed a word Beau never thought to hear him say. He called her name, begged her to breathe. His voice was far away, and the smell of the beach washed over her. Numbness settled over her as her breaths became shallow gasps and for a while she blacked out, only to be awoken by a startling truth that would change the course of her life forever.

Jeremy slipped his hand between them, groped in the tight space until he found Beau's face and felt the last shards of her breath expel. *"No!"* he said through clenched teeth. *"No!"*

Tipping her chin up, he pressed his mouth to hers, opened her lips with his, and breathed into her. It was more than life support; it was a kiss and a siphon of all he was—his memories, his hope. He emptied into her all of his secrets, every missing gap from the time they spent apart. He gave her everything, surrounded her with the love he had for her. It was impossible to know where he ended and she began as he breathed into her a promise of their future.

Beau gasped beneath him as her breaths became her own; her lungs heaved and panted. He felt part of the tension leave her when she realized she was breathing of her own accord. Jeremy tapered off the breaths he was giving, but his lips slid over hers and changed direction as he deepened their joining in a kiss. She was stiff as her body recovered, but then her hands curled around his back and she pulled him closer, returning his kiss, meeting his ferocity. He continued to feed her memories and secrets like water through a sieve. There would be nothing between them now, and he felt her utter and complete acceptance.

He was wrong to think it merely a kiss. It was a benediction, a promise. It was the beginning of them.

He moaned before ending the kiss, and placed a series of

kisses along her chin before he nuzzled her neck. "Now you know," he whispered in her ear before he kissed her there as well.

Beau drew in a sharp breath and turned her head side to side. They were packed like sardines and there was roof on Jeremy's back. "You're a hurricane." She sounded winded, as if she had run a mile at top speed.

There was a slight jolt as the tub landed amid the debris that used to be Beau's home. Jeremy had steered the tub to the ground the best he could without dissipating any part of his body. "Beau," he breathed in warning, a rushed, frantic sound as he braced his forearms on either side of her, planking his body above her as a cage. He braced for the worst as the roof came crashing down on top of them and flattened the mattress over them like a lid. Nails and splintered wood dug into his back and thighs. He rotated his shoulders to dislodge the bigger chunks.

"Was that what I think it was?" Beau asked, her voice breathless. It was pitch black in the tub, but he felt her hands rubbing over him wherever she could cram them in the tight space.

"That would be what's left of your house," he confirmed. He flexed upward and the creak of shifting metal filled the air. He let out an exasperated huff as he rested over Beau again. Roughly ten tons rested on him. If there were bystanders, this could go badly. "Can you hold still while I work?"

Her hands paused over the backs of his thighs and he realized then how close they were; his body was cradled against hers intimately. He turned his head and her mouth slid over his face until it rested on his cheek. She nodded.

Jareth would kill him if he found out all the details of this mission; this was highly irregular. He cleared his throat and levered his body away from hers. "Promise me you won't move? I will try to do it in my natural form, but if you move, I can't promise you won't be frightened."

"You don't scare me, Jeremy."

A jolt of bittersweet pain went through him. She made that seemingly small statement with such conviction that *he* almost stopped breathing. Years had separated them for nothing, because this girl would keep his secret or lose her life trying.

"Wanna hurry up in there?" Minh's voice filtered through the rubble. Jeremy could hear the debris giving and cracking as he tested it for weak spots above them. Gabriel would already be searching for an out to make a quick exit. "The neighbor just phoned the sheriff. We got about fifteen before I have to tell Barney Fife a bunch of lies, then give him a trip through a wormhole to mind wipe. Messy business, and I was watching the Saints kick some Bronco butt before this happened." He made an irritated noise. "Although, on a lighter note, this did get us out of having to eat that gumbo Liang cooked."

Gabriel snorted. They would bicker for hours if allowed and Beau would have no idea what to think. Jeremy lowered his body over hers again and lined his face up with hers to talk against her mouth. "This will work faster if I explain first," he said, and then he kissed her in an open mouthed kiss. Her hands clutched at his sides as she lifted her head to meet him. A hum sounded in her throat as she assimilated all the information he was feeding her in the form of an erotic kiss. They could not get close enough to one another. She hitched her foot over his calf and pressed up against him. Her hands were in his hair, tugging as if she dared him to break contact. It felt greedy and desperate, but so good that he didn't want to stop.

But break the kiss he did. A boy only had so much self-control. "Any questions?" Now it was he who was breathless.

"You have the coolest friends *ever*."

Jeremy stared down at her, aware that she could not see him in the darkness, but he could see her perfectly. Not only was he impermeable, he had 20/20 vision whether it was day or night. "You're not afraid of any of this?"

Her expression turned peeved. "I want to get this house off your back so we can have a little privacy and do that again." She wagged her eyebrows.

A slow rumble of laughter worked out of him. "Kiss?"

"*Oui, oui*," she said and he felt his face blush. "Now get moving before those crazy men start moving stuff and I get impaled after all." She was mad because they could not kiss, and not because her boyfriend was a hurricane and about to bench press a roof off of his back?

Boyfriend?

"I'm pretty sure I'll have to partially dissipate. I can't get us out of this and stay in my natural body. You might not like it."

Beau pressed her lips to his. It was a short, sweet kiss. "I like everything about you. Always have. I have you and I want it all. Now, show me what you can do."

Beau waited while Jeremy shredded rubble to erase that they had been caught under it. Though she was not sure how she felt about that part, or the part that decreed someone had to die so she could be safe. The host who came to attack her was dead. But in this tragedy, Jeremy had told her the truth. She was not crazy.

Of course she wasn't crazy. Jeremy was a host for a hurricane. Duh! She should have guessed.

He had diffused the bystanders—her mom's nosy BFF and her husband who lived next door—with a blast of wind while he heaved out rubble like he was the Hulk. It was wild, but exciting at the same time. The memories he gave her filled the holes and answered the questions she had. It was as if she had walked side by side with him for the last eight years—that was how complete his filtering was.

She watched him looking adorably bashful in his boxers, bare chested and soaking wet, grumbling to Minh and Gabriel while they worked out the details of how this would go. She knew he was uncomfortable with so little clothing, but she reckoned it was something she could get used to. No hardship in being rescued by a host. She considered it a bonus.

"Was the disposal complete?" Gabriel asked Jeremy.

"Silas is dead," Jeremy answered flatly. He motioned to the pile of twisted metal and splintered wood. "His body is either somewhere in there or in an adjacent field. Sorry, I didn't bother to track his fall. I was busy."

"Busy?" Minh asked, one of his thin black brows going north. He was looking at Beau.

Both Gabriel and Jeremy ignored him and Beau was so embarrassed that she looked away.

"We will have to backtrack time a bit and watch to see where he fell. Otherwise, we could be searching for hours," Gabriel said. "We can't have his body found by the cops."

"Come on, Beau." Jeremy frowned as his eyes raked over her waterlogged clothing. "I'm gonna carry you back home. I need to get you dry. You'll get sick standing out here." He turned around. "Hop on."

"It's ten miles," she said, even as she grabbed his shoulders and pressed her front to his back. The heat from his body seeped into her, or the other way around, because a cold flash startled her body. He bent his knees and hoisted her onto his back. His hands gripped the backs of her knees. "How are they getting back?"

"They'll walk or catch a wormhole. Ten miles is nothing for them."

"For a Spartan warrior and Minister of War," she said, her teeth chattering. She hugged him, folded her arms over his shoulders, and nuzzled the side of his neck. "You smell of the beach. I wondered why I kept smelling saltwater."

"It's essence of the Gulf of Mexico." He snickered and looked over at her. "My memory transferral comes in handy sometimes, eh? Filled in all those gaps. Now you understand where everyone fits."

She hugged him again. She would never get tired of being close to him. The newness of knowing she could touch and kiss him whenever she wanted was sublime. "What you are is amazing. You can walk through my mind anytime you'd like."

"Well, thank you, Miss Beau. Are you ready for this part, because I think you might be a little scared." He hefted her higher on his hips, jiggling her a bit.

She giggled and it sounded silly, but she did not care. Even when Minh looked at her as if she were crazy. It was a little off that she was laughing while standing in the rubble that had been her home, but she was *on Jeremy's back*. And she knew everything about him. Part of her life was over and a new chapter was beginning. She had waited a long time for this. "I'll say it again. I'm not scared of you." She spurred his sides like one would a horse. "Now, let's go. I want to see what you can do."

"You do realize he's about to lift off like a helicopter, but then his body will vanish and you'll feel like you're dangling in midair," Minh stated matter-of-factly. He studied an oddly twisted piece of metal, frowned, and tossed it over his shoulder.

Gabriel pulled a face. "Are all of the women in this family soft in the head?" he asked.

Beau smirked. If they were talking about Elizabet she wanted to resound a deafening *yes* to that question. How could her cousin hide from her something as important as being a duchess from the fourteenth century? How could she not know her little cousin was a baby duke? Cute little Solomon was practically a prince. You couldn't withhold something like that from family.

She hid her face in the crook of Jeremy's shoulder and neck. "Let's go, baby. I want to see you fly."

They arrived at the Tremaine house where Dr. Tremaine greeted them with warm towels and a spread of food that would rival Thanksgiving dinner. Beau leaned against the counter in the kitchen with her arms crossed and watched

Elizabet bustle around, pouring this, serving that. She worried over Jeremy as he shoveled food into his mouth, shivering under an electric blanket. Beau sipped at the hot chocolate given her and bided her time, saying nothing, being asked nothing. It was all about Jeremy and getting his heat and energy up.

She stood there, silently seething that Elizabet allowed this to happen. For eight long years she had been a social pariah and it had all been in vain. Her eyes and ears had not been the ones to deceive her, Elizabet had. She tried not to dwell on the fact that Jeremy had a hand in the deception as well, but he had been a child, terrified of what had happened to his body. All of this could have been prevented with a little truth and trust.

It was thirty minutes before the children were ushered to bed by Mrs. Wheatley, the housemaid. Beau wasted no time.

She walked up to Elizabet and slapped her face.

It all happened so quickly. One minute Jareth was across the room and the next, he was right in front of Beau. He placed his hand firmly on her breastbone and gave her a shove. Her body lifted off the floor and she sailed backward into the china cabinet. It tilted and rattled.

"You're a duchess!" Beau hollered despite Jareth's murderous expression. She grimaced and stepped away from the cabinet, her hand going to her lower back. Damn, that man was fast—and a bigger jerk than she first thought. Who pushes a girl like that? What happened to chivalry and the knight life? "A fricking duchess from the fourteenth century."

Jeremy rushed to her side, wiping his mouth with the back of his hand. "What the heck, Beau?"

"Out!" Jareth bellowed. He pointed in the general direction of the front door. "Get her out of my house."

Elizabet blinked, her eyes wide as her hand cradled her cheek. She shook her head and faced Jareth. "No!" She glanced at Beau, a pleading look on her face. "This isn't what I want."

Jeremy grabbed Beau's arm. "Let's go."

"You talking to me?" she asked. She looked at where his hand gripped her so tightly it was sure to leave a mark. "Where are we going?"

Jeremy sneered, "Anywhere but here."

"I don't have a home," Beau sputtered. She was ticked that he would side with Elizabet. She thought he would understand that this would take time. They lied to her. *Lied.* Huge, nasty lies. Theirs made mafia testimony sound like little white lies.

"You think I care?" Jeremy asked.

Beau was confused. "You love me." She motioned between them. "We're together now."

"That doesn't give you the right to hurt my family." Jeremy's voice was thick. He jerked her toward the foyer. "She's my mother. No one strikes her. No one." He yanked her body closer to his. "Not even you."

"He practically hit me," Beau accused, passing Jareth a heated look. She pointed at him for extra measure. "Didn't you see that? He threw me up against the furniture."

"You're bloody lucky he didn't kill you," Jeremy snarled.

Jareth paced the kitchen like a panther circling its prey. His big hands flexed as if his palms itched for a weapon. He passed a thoughtful glance to the butcher block that housed the knives, and then back to Beau. She swallowed the panic that rose up in her throat.

"Did you see him hit me?" she asked, her voice growing louder, nearly hysterical now.

"That was not a strike," Jareth said, his voice rough. "I was merely putting space between you, my wife, and unborn child!"

"Jareth," Elizabet pleaded. "Please, stop. This doesn't have to go this way. Beau doesn't have anywhere to go." Her hands spread. "Please. This is new to her. It will take time. I'm fine. It's fine. No one was hurt."

"She struck you," Jareth growled. "And has the nerve to blame *me* for defending you?" He turned to Jeremy. "Get her out of my sight." He leaned forward and gripped the counter, his knuckles white. "Get her out before I go for my sword and show her how things are done where I come from."

"Jareth," Elizabet pleaded. "Please. She didn't mean it. Not really."

"I don't have any place to go," Beau said. Suddenly she felt remorse, and not only because her house was gone. Elizabet's cheek was red and swelling. She had hit her cousin, and somewhere in the house were kids she really liked and wanted to get to know. What type of monster was she to hit a mother in her own home? They weren't kids any longer. Elizabet was a mother and wife. A darn good one by the look of things.

And Beau was playing the poor relation again to the tee.

"She can sleep with the pigs for all I care," Jareth snarled, his lip curled in disgust.

"*Magister*," Jeremy said. He glanced at Beau. "Elizabet is right. This is new to Beau. If Elizabet is willing to forgive, then maybe you could, as well." Beau sensed that he was doing the mind thing again and he had felt the repentance within her.

"No one hits my wife," Jareth rumbled. He truly was intimidating—and also huge, tall, and handsome. He made the scrubs he was wearing seem like a million-dollar suit. But Beau had no doubt that however civilized he appeared, he really would kill her on the spot if given the opportunity. His threats were not idle.

Elizabet placed her hand softly on Jareth's shoulder after she approached him with timid steps. "Listen, my love, it's all right. Let it go."

"I'm letting go of the fact he practically hit me," Beau inserted. She looked at Jeremy who shot her a scowl and shook his head in warning.

"Really?" Jeremy asked. "Did you really have to say that?" Beau took the chance and slid behind Jeremy.

Jareth growled—again. It appeared as though the counter's granite would crumble under his grip at any second.

"Listen," Elizabet said. She briefly closed her eyes as if it was all too much for her to bear. She ran her hand down Jareth's back and put her arm around him. He straightened and hung his arm over her shoulders while he glowered at Beau. "This night has been trying. We all need to process everything that has happened." She looked at Beau. "You've lost your home and discovered what my family is. I know it's hard, but we are here to help you." She peered up at Jareth. "We have to protect her, not send her away. Our enemies know about her now. It would be a death sentence to send her off." Jareth opened his mouth to say something, but Elizabet put her fingers over his lips. "Don't. You'll break my heart."

Jareth's expression waned soft and something cracked in Beau. This man loved her cousin. This man who aggravated the bejeezus out of her was who made Elizabet a happy woman. She had to be happy to have popped out a herd a babies by the tender age of . . . twenty-six? Obviously, she was crazy over this guy. There was no fear in her cousin's actions, only comfort. It was evident that Elizabet held the key to Jareth's heart by the way he melted into her touch. One look at Jeremy assured her that Elizabet wasn't the only person under his spell. This was Jeremy's father for all that mattered and he loved him, too.

"You do not know what you ask of me, wife." Jareth kissed Elizabet's fingertips before removing them from his mouth. "She struck you." His eyes traveled to her belly, letting unsaid words hang between them.

"Benjamin is fine," she said, her hands cradling her abdomen. "I ask for mercy for my cousin. You're such a merciful lord. I trust you with my heart. Please, don't break it."

Jeremy's hold loosened on Beau's arm and at first she thought it was because of Elizabet's awe inspiring words and that all was forgiven. But then she felt him slipping.

She watched with horror as Jeremy hit the floor, his head striking the tile with a dull thud. All she remembered then was screaming.

Chapter 6

"I am responsible for host who arc under my care. If he falls, I shall fall with him."
Jareth Tremaine, speaking of his adoptive son.

BEAU PRESSED THE TIPS OF her fingers to her forehead. "I can't believe this is what you've been hiding from me." She looked pointedly at Elizabet. "You could've trusted me."

"You say that and yet almost gave Jeremy away eight years ago," Elizabet said, her voice low as she placed heating pads under Jeremy's arms. "We could only go by what we knew, and we knew that you didn't handle the basics very well. If you couldn't handle the way Jeremy communicated, how could you handle something as substantial as Jareth being a duke and that we had wormholes wrapped around our wrists?"

Beau allowed her tone to become rough. "I was nine." She cast a look to where the children were seated in a circle. The brood had refused to stay in the nursery when they heard the ruckus with their older brother. They adored Jeremy. The oldest boy was reading to his siblings, but even though the book was open, he was miming the story from memory. His eyes kept wandering to the bed where Jeremy lay. "Am I freaking out now? Jeremy practically downloaded eight years of info into my micro brain."

"He's pretty incredible," Elizabet said. Beau heard the sentiment in her voice and looked up. "He calls me Mom just to confuse people." Her hands twisted together as she glanced down at Jeremy. "Heaven knows he's like one of my own. It doesn't matter that our ages make that genetically impossible."

Jareth blindly searched for his wife's hand until he found it. The gesture caused a turbulent feeling in the pit of Beau's stomach. They were obviously in love and she had misjudged. It was time she got over grievances that happened years ago. She would have to get used to the idea that Jareth, the first Duke of Dover, was family and he was a time traveling knight from another century. He would have ways that were foreign to her, but that didn't make him a bad person. The memories Jeremy gave her made Jareth a candidate for sainthood—literally. The man's accomplishments were legendary. She had chosen to ignore the information because he was so aggravatingly male. The males in her family were pigs.

"Well, for what it's worth, I'm sorry for hitting you." Beau meant it. She couldn't believe she had stooped so low. "Must be in my genes to be violent, eh? I just sort of snapped." Dear old Dad might be the reason she had a hard time liking Jareth. Although, while Jareth was domineering, he was nothing like her dad.

"Don't you say such a thing," Elizabet chastised. "You're nothing like Uncle Chris. *Nothing*. I probably would've wanted to smack you around too if you had kept a big ol' lie like that one."

"You mean if I was the duchess and your boyfriend was the human hurricane?" Beau asked.

"Boyfriend?" Elizabet squeaked.

"Boyfriend?" Jareth echoed. He reached for the stethoscope that was on the bedside table. "Have you discussed this?" He motioned between her and Jeremy.

"Uh, yeah." Heat rose in her face and she flicked her gaze to her feet. "We sort of figured it out while he was bench pressing my roof off his back."

"If anything, the boy is decisive." Jareth grinned. It was that type of smile that confirmed Jeremy was a chip off the adoptive dad's block. "He can be tenacious. Irritating and inspiring at the same time."

Disbelief coursed through Beau. They had forgiven her quickly. The tone they used to speak with her was gentle and accepting. It amazed her that they received her back into the fold just like that. She was in and she was glad. It would take getting used to, but that started now.

Beau cleared her throat when Elizabet would not stop smirking at her. "How long does this take?" She pointed at Jeremy. "It looks like he has more color."

"He is coming around," Jareth said. He used a stethoscope to listen to Jeremy's heart. "This is nothing." He glanced over his shoulder. "You should see him after he plays in the snow back home in England. He pays hours of hibernation for it."

"It's dreadful," a small voice said. Beau jumped from the close proximity of that quiet statement and saw it was the girl named Abigail. "When Jeremy is tired, the day can get rather nasty. It's no fun at all."

Solomon laughed and flipped the hair that hung low on his brow from his face. "Yeah, but when he is in top form, he makes the best snowmen. He's lightning fast and we win all of the snowball fights in our neighborhood." His head tilted. "You will see, Cousin Beau, how hard it is to stay mad at Jeremy when he's cold and cross." A tremendous smile spread on his face, but his words were cut off when Jeremy spoke.

"What's this guttersnipe in my room?"

The children leapt up and bounded upon Jeremy. Their excited voices tinkled like chimes in the room. Beau had to step aside to not be run down. The smallest one could not climb on the bed, so he leaned and grabbed a fist full of covers closest to Jeremy.

"Easy," Jareth said, but his voice was soft and there was a hint of laughter to it. "There will be no building of snowmen any time soon for your brother."

"Snowmen?" Jeremy asked as he ruffled Peter's hair.

Abigail hopped on Jeremy's chest and stuck her fingers in his mouth, thereby preventing him any other questions. "I made sure not to lick off all the taffy," she whispered in conspiracy.

Jeremy removed her fingers from his mouth and placed a kiss on her open palm. "Um, caramel?" Abigail nodded and Jeremy smiled tremendously. "Atta girl. Did Mrs. Wheatley take notice?"

A smile curved on Abigail's wide mouth. "She says I take the mickey." Her face became stern as her voice mimicked their nursemaid. She shook her sticky finger in Jeremy's face. "That one takes the mickey, I swear it. Can't have any peace around here. Her teeth will rot out of her head before we can marry her off." She became serious, her face drooping. "Daddy fired her."

"For two minutes," Jareth grumbled, and then muttered something unintelligible about proper hand hygiene and child-hood diseases.

"Cousin Beau will build snowmen with us. In England," Solomon announced.

"She's not his cousin," Abigail said with a toss of her curls. She sniffed and regarded her twin with an air of superiority. "Jeremy's adopted, remember?"

Jeremy peered at Beau over the children. A crooked smile tugged on his mouth. "She's most definitely not my relation."

"Thank God," Beau mouthed, her eyes wide.

Jeremy's smile grew.

"Okay," Elizabet said, clapping her hands. "Children, that's our cue." She waved her hands toward the door. "Your brother and Beau have lots to catch up on. Let's go help Mrs. Wheatley finish dessert for dinner." She eyed Abigail. "Well, maybe not you. Why don't you find your godfather and go prac-tice . . . something."

Abigail stuck her lip out. "But I want brownies, too. Uncle

Minh will have me on the archery fields for hours and there won't be any left."

Peter stood on the bed and put his arms out to be picked up. His mother complied. "Dover," his tiny voice said as he flattened his hands on Elizabet's cheeks to get her attention. "Can we go home?"

"After dinner," Elizabet said, and kissed Peter's lips. She jerked her head toward the door. "Come along, Solomon. Jareth, grab Gideon and steer your daughter in the right direction." She rolled her eyes. "Lord knows someone has to."

"We're gonna miss the good parts." Abigail pouted, but moved off of Jeremy and into her father's waiting arms.

Jareth cast a look at Jeremy over Abigail's head. "There are no good parts, pumpkin." His eyes narrowed and one brow rose as he bent to scoop up Gideon. He balanced each child efficiently on his hips. Abigail looked ridiculously big there, but one could tell that her father habitually doted on her, including toting her around when she was more than capable of walking. "Besides, it is more fun to learn how to skewer your enemy in battle. Has not Uncle Minh taught you anything?"

Beau was not sure how he accomplished that look, but she was impressed . . . and embarrassed. Was he suggesting that Abigail skewer *her* if she did not behave? She made a show of straightening out the lampshade that was crooked.

"And remember, Romeo," Jareth said. "You are hardly clothed for company."

Jeremy gripped the covers and pooled them over his lap. His face flushed a healthy pink. He grimaced and passed Beau an embarrassed look. "Deuced complicated, that disintegrating thingy."

"Ummm," Jareth hummed with no humor. He faced Beau. "Feet on the floor, hands to yourself."

Beau wanted to defend herself, but Elizabet reached out and grabbed Jareth's arm and tugged him to the exit. "Really, Jareth?

Sometimes I wonder how we have children."

Jareth ignored his wife. "You are in this family whether I like it or not. Just see that you do not cause me reason to do you any bodily harm. Our home is rated PG, got it? Feet on the floor, hands to yourself, and the door remains open."

"I understand," Beau said, a touch of annoyance in her voice. She understood now that Jeremy had siphoned the particulars to her brain. Jareth was some kind of holy man from another time. She turned to Elizabet. "Can you please tell him I'm not Jezebel?"

"You know of Jezebel?" Jareth asked, his eyes narrowing.

"Of course she knows about Jezebel. She loved Sunday school growing up almost as much as I did." Elizabet grinned and tugged again at Jareth. "Come on, your grace. I'll let you lick the brownie bowl if you behave."

Jareth held his stance, staring at Beau. "If you need absolution, you have it. I forgive you. We start new here."

Beau nodded. "Thanks."

Jeremy motioned to the side of the bed once the room was clear. "You've got it wrong. Jareth isn't religious at all. He's an anti-regulator in this time and a church reformer in the past. Distinctly, the duke is a man of the truth and very picky about what goes into the faith we follow." His lips became tight as she sat on the edge of the bed. He was sore from healing. He'd explained that he underwent trauma, and his body healed instantaneously—but it was not without its drawbacks. "Don't let him get to you. Once you see him with Elizabet, you will see the double standard." He lifted his brow. "PG indeed. He believes it's healthy to display physical affection in a marriage—at all times. I, on the other hand, think he's so whipped he just can't keep his hands off his wife."

Beau glanced at the open door with seeming unease. "There you go. You're in my head again." She pulled a face, her hands waving. "And TMI. I can understand why this guy wedged himself into Lizabet's life, but seeing her all loved up might take a while. It's weird."

"Noted." He made a mime of locking his lips, tossing the key over his shoulder. "We are in one accord about them being weird."

"So, what am I thinking now?"

"I can't read your actual thoughts when I'm not touching you," Jeremy admitted. Her eyes narrowed and he let his smile go lopsided. "That would be sweet, but it doesn't work like that." He pressed back into the pillows. "If you give me your hand, I can transfer memories to you and I can steal your memories. When I'm not touching you, I only feel what emotion you are churning and I'm rather good at interpreting where your thoughts are leading, but when I touch you, I can siphon your thoughts."

"Did this ability come with the storm?"

Jeremy shrugged and stretched out his hand to her. "Yeah. I wouldn't be like this otherwise. It's a package deal. I'm a siphon."

"What else?" she asked. "I mean, you've pretty much downloaded all the good stuff into my brain, but I want more. Tell me again. I want to hear it with my own ears."

"Like what I can do?" he asked. He looked away, his cheeks flushing and his outstretched hand curled slightly.

Beau knew he was shy about having abilities that weren't common. He had always wanted to be just Jeremy and now he was . . . *this*. How could he reveal anything more than what he had already? It was scary.

She placed her hand in his. "Are all hosts siphons?"

"No. Does it bother you that I can rob your privacy?"

Beau shook her head slowly. "I don't have anything to hide from you."

"I know." His voice a whisper. He closed his eyes. "Beau, I'm so sorry for leaving you to those government mind quacks." He squeezed her hand.

Beau chewed the corner of her lip as she ran her free hand over his chest. Her palm was smooth and tempting over his bare skin. "It's all okay now." She smiled when he forced his eyes open. He must still be exhausted. "Let's talk about something else. Will I be able to time travel, too?"

"Would you like that?" She nodded eagerly and that made him laugh. "I think Elizabet said we were going to Dover after dinner. It's what we normally do, and I feel up to it."

"I can't believe I get to see England. A castle." She smoothed her hand over his chest again. "I want to go everywhere with you."

Jeremy covered her hand with his. He tilted his head to the side. "We are really doing this, aren't we?"

"I waited for you Jeremy." Her face warmed, and probably turned rosy. "You honestly don't think for one second that now that I know all about you, you can get rid of me? That is, unless you have something you need to tell me."

He studied her features. Her tight expression matched the worry in her mind. *Bleh!* If only he had good news to share with her. "There were others," he admitted softly.

Beau grimaced and pried both of her hands from his.

"Were there none for you?" he asked when silence stretched, but he knew the answer already. "How did someone like you go so long without a boyfriend? You are a great girl. Pretty, real, and compassionate." He reached for her hand again, but she pulled away and stood, crossing her arms in a hug.

"Don't, Jeremy. Don't feel sorry for me. I was only asking. It's what a new girlfriend does. She likes to know the competition."

"I was running from the thought of you with the others. There is no competition. There never has been and there never will be. It's always been you and me since we were kids."

Beau's lips twisted and she glared at him.

He put his hands up and laughed. "Okay. How's this—I'm rather like Georgie Porgy. Kissed the girls and made them cry, but that's it. I swear it. Is that what you want to hear? There was nothing else to do on the island but kiss girls. But that was all. I have all this pent up energy constantly surging inside me. I was never serious about any of them. Well, perhaps one, but she was mental . . . seriously." He crossed his heart. "You've met my guardian, the big bastard with a chip on his shoulder? Do you honestly think I could go around breaking hearts worldwide? Mr. PG would faint."

That made Beau smile again. It was reluctant, but it was real. "I'd rather not fight about this right this second. I shouldn't have asked that so soon. Today, I just want to enjoy that you're mine." She touched her fingertips to her chest. "Mine. I'll be the last girl you ever kiss, Jeremiah Cameron Tremaine."

"Ah, there she is," Jeremy said. He grinned like a fool. "My beautiful angel."

"What will I do with you?" she murmured.

"Kiss me?"

Beau tilted her head and looked at him. "After admitting you kissed legions of girls, you want me to put my mouth on you again?" She laughed ruefully. "Maybe later when it's not so fresh in my mind."

He motioned with his hand. "Tally-ho, girl. I haven't got all night. We've got a wormhole to catch."

Beau smiled and shook her head. "What the heck? You're so fine, I can barely help myself." She leaned over and pressed her lips to his.

Within moments, the lights flickered and made a cracking noise. Beau tried to pull away, but he caught her face with his hand, cupped her chin with his fingers, and held her there. He tipped his head and covered her mouth with his. "You are *mine*." With a loud pop, everything went black. "Bloody hell, that sounded a lot like a transformer. I haven't blown one of those since I was ten and out of control."

Beau jerked away, her hands braced on his chest as she shoved at him. His chest rose and fell under her fingertips, heaving as he fought to reclaim command. Somewhere in that kiss he had draped her over him like a sheet. Their breaths mingled in the darkness, their lips an inch apart.

"*Jeremyyy!*" Jareth's voice rumbled from somewhere downstairs.

"Oops," Jeremy said sheepishly. He pushed Beau off him. "Feet on the floor, hands to yourself. We're about to get it. I'll bet he's tempted to use a wormhole to get to us faster. I think I just blew out the entire community's electrical supply."

"That was so worth it." Her voice was breathy and faint. "Georgie Porgy."

Even though she couldn't see it, she imagined Jeremy smiled.

ELIZABET OBSERVED BEAU'S REACTION TO medieval life. There were times it still took her breath away, and she remembered being overwhelmed by all of it when it was new. Beau had never been farther than Texas, so this had to be crushing.

"How do you wear this?" Beau asked. She scratched at the stiff collar of the dress she had been given to wear. "And what exactly is it?"

"Wool," Elizabet replied. She passed Mrs. Wheatley a basket filled with bread and preserves to bring to the village orphanage. "We have sheep on the property. It helps if you wear an undershirt."

"Yuck," Beau muttered, and shoved a morsel of bread into her mouth. It was hot, so she puffed her cheeks out and tossed the bread back and between them. "But this," her eyes closed and her face held a rapturous expression. "This is delicious. Who would have thought homemade bread tasted so good?"

Elizabet smiled, and remembered thinking the same. Mrs. Wheatley was magical when baking. "You can stay here while the children and I ride into Kent. Jeremy is in the north tower." She doubted Beau would enjoy the trip. Sometimes they were gone for hours. It was work, not a leisure errand.

"Gotcha," Beau said. She reached for a can of soda. "I think I remember how to get there."

Elizabet laughed. "I remember the days of needing a map to get around here. Who lives in a castle, right?"

"You do," Beau said. She popped the can open and took a swig. Mrs. Wheatley frowned. She did not like when they brought modern food into her kitchens. "I think it's great. Like a vacation." She tilted her head. "How often do I get to come here? I want to see as much of England as I can."

"Every day," Elizabet retorted. She picked up the smaller basket. "Although Jeremy can take you to other places in modern time—wherever you want to go. He can dissipate with cargo. He rarely takes airplanes any longer."

Beau set down the soda. "Wow. Like having my own personal jet. I'll have to think about that."

"Still afraid of heights?"

"You know it," Beau said. "I almost chucked the other night over Gueydan." She shivered with the thought.

"And you're dating a hurricane," Elizabet said with a chuckle. "You might want to re-think this."

"Never," Beau said, smiling. "Bring on the weirdness. I'm ready for the challenge."

"We'll see if you sing that tune when you're flying over London with your body dangling on nothing but thin air. There's something intimidating about seeing Big Ben up close and personal. It's different than seeing it from the seat of a plane, I'll guarantee that."

"Wife," Jareth greeted as he strode into the kitchen. He dipped his head and kissed the top of Elizabet's head. He smiled at Beau. "Cousin."

"Lord Jackass," Beau answered with a teasing light in her eyes. She even bowed.

One of Jareth's brows lifted, but he said nothing. Elizabet passed the basket to him. "You've got ink on your cheek." She licked her finger and worked at the smudge. "Honestly, you should just use a ballpoint pen and be done with it."

"With advanced dating systems' accuracy?" He grimaced. "No, no, and no again. I will not have my documents come into question by future scholars. My work will stand as legitimate. This is scripture, woman. I will not have it defrauded. Not *my* documents."

Elizabet turned to Beau. "Reformer problems," she muttered as Abigail strolled into the kitchen.

Jareth chucked the underneath of Abigail's chin. "Where are your brothers?

"Solomon is in the stable," Abigail said. She lifted her arms and Jareth swooped her up and perched her on his shoulders, all the while maintaining his hold on the basket.

"Peter and Gideon are with Jeremy. It's late." Elizabet passed another basket up to Abigail. "I thought since Beau was here, she could help Jeremy get them to bed and we could take Mrs. Wheatley with us. I didn't count on so much food to be carried. It's been a while since we have been to the village. We could use the extra help."

Jareth nodded and turned to Beau. Elizabet bit her lip so she would not laugh at the severe expression he gave her. But when he opened his mouth to give orders, Beau spoke.

"I know, I know. Feet on the floor, hands to myself, doors open." She bowed at the waist again. "Anything else, your grace?"

Abigail giggled.

"That's cute," Jareth drawled. "Much better than Lord Jackass, although it does have a certain ring to it. But I must insist you call me your majesty. My subjects will not take well to Lord Jackass—in fact, it may offend some. Imagine that." He turned to leave, but then glanced over his shoulder in parting. "Did you not get the memo that I am also a prince of England? I would not want to have to banish you from Dover due to treason or worse."

Elizabet tucked her lips into her mouth so she would not bust out laughing at Beau's perplexed expression. Obviously, Jeremy had left one small detail of Jareth's lineage out. Poor Beau; things kept getting more and more complicated in her new world.

THE CASTLE WAS RIDDLED WITH art. Beau stopped in the banquet room to admire a large painting of Jareth and Elizabet. It was supremely beautiful and contained great detail. The play with lights and dust gave it a surreal look, as if it were real time and not a painting. The subjects seemed tangible. In the lower corner was a scribble of letters. She squinted, but they were partially hidden by the frame.

She pulled a bench close and stood on it, careful to keep her skirts from the great fireplace beneath the painting.

The letters J and C and T, all capitals, were intertwined, an obvious signature of the artist. Of course the talented painter was Jeremy. How could she forget that he dabbled in art? He had painted the mural on the side of her parents' store years ago. He was quite good then, and a genius now.

After a quick study, she realized that all of the art had been done by Jeremy. Portraits of the children, of the family . . . one included him among the Tremaines and that made her want to weep with joy. Jeremy had a family who loved him. His blood family had rejected him, but this adopted family fully embraced him.

She made her way up to the north wing and as she

approached, she heard children's laughter. Pressing the heavy door, it opened into the solar. "Who's having fun without me?" she chanted.

Gideon looked up from where he played before the hearth and Peter momentarily stopped jumping on the tufted stool near Jeremy.

Jeremy, bless him, passed her a look of such relief she almost laughed. His hair was a mess and he had paint all over his arms and shirt.

"Help," he mouthed.

Beau smiled and motioned to the papers he was working over. "What are you working on?"

"Illuminated manuscript," he answered, and pushed away from the desk. He motioned to the children. "Or I should say I'm working on my patience. I've gotten nothing done since Peter took to singing and jumping."

Peter smiled at Beau and took a defiant jump on the stool.

"What's an illuminated manuscript?" She walked over to Gideon and lifted him from the stool and into her arms. He took that opportunity to wrap himself around her like an octopus.

"A tedious process that makes Jareth's biblical translations look like art."

"Can I see?" She pulled the candied apple from Gideon's hand and placed it on the plate on Jeremy's desk, then grabbed a handful of wipes.

Jeremy turned the book he was working on for her to see.

"Ooh," she crooned. She looked up at him with wide eyes. "It's like those ancient prayer books from medieval times."

"Precisely. What I do is use the text Jareth has translated and make a storybook of sorts out of it. We distribute it, but we have to be careful. The Church in these times is corrupt. They don't want common people having scripture, so we must go through the Church for distribution. It's a mess, really. Mostly,

Elizabet keeps the books for the children."

"Sounds like home," Beau said. She let her fingers graze the page. "Regulations started early. It's a miracle we still have the Bible in print." She looked up at him. "It's beautiful, Jeremy. You're an artist."

"I wouldn't say that," he muttered. He slid the book from her reach.

"I saw the paintings. JCT. Ring a bell? I know someone with those initials."

"And?" He tucked the book into a leather satchel and placed it in a drawer that he locked.

Beau bounced Gideon on her hip. He was a heavy toddler—probably too big to be carrying around. "So, we won't talk about your artist genius." She motioned to her clothing. "What do you think of my dress, then?"

"Uhhh," Jeremy stammered.

"It's ugly," she stated baldly. Jeremy grinned and nodded. She chuckled. "I know."

"Then why did you ask?"

"The subject needed changing and I wanted to see if you'd lie."

"My lying days are over." He sat back, linked his feet in the chair rungs, and tipped the chair on its back legs. He motioned to the children. "And welcome to my lair, by the way. Want to see freaks of nature of a different sort? I can make your grand appearance memorable—something you'll never forget. Something besides my artistic genius."

Beau looked at Elizabet's angelic children and wondered how she ever thought she would be able to stay away. And she wondered what Jeremy was talking about.

"They're not like me." Jeremy crossed his arms and appeared smug. "But never underestimate the power of progeny genes."

"I'm intrigued." Beau grinned.

"Peter," Jeremy said and the boy looked up attentively. "Play something for Beau." He motioned to the guitar in the corner.

Beau's lips twisted. "He's how old? Six?"

Jeremy held up his hand to display five fingers. "He's big for his age."

"This should be interesting," Beau murmured. She scanned the room for a chair and when she found none, folded down to sit on the floor. Gideon sat in her lap. He reached up for his apple that she had put away.

Peter grabbed the guitar, but only after sticking his fingers in his mouth and sucking off the sticky caramel from the candied apple he had been eating. He sat across from Beau, the guitar in his lap, and reached for a box that contained a cord that he plugged into the guitar.

"You've got to be kidding me." Beau said in wonder.

Jeremy shrugged with one shoulder. "We're a modern family. We improvise. Besides, it gets boringly quiet out here without modern conveniences."

"What would you like me to play?" Peter asked.

Beau could not help it, her lips twisted again. "Anything. You pick." She glanced at Jeremy, who wore an amused expression. Her heart skipped a beat. She had the impression he was deflecting his own abilities and it bothered her that a small part of the insecure boy remained in this capable man. He did not want her to know what an amazing artist he was because he felt inadequate. She didn't need to read minds to figure that out.

Peter's face screwed up, he was concentrating so hard. It looked as if he may ignite on the spot from using too much gray matter.

"Play Hendrix," Jeremy suggested.

Peter smiled, looked up from his intense thoughts. "Too easy."

A bark of laughter left Beau's mouth. "You've got to be kidding me! He can't play Hendrix." She looked down at Gideon, who only smiled up at her and licked the apple he clung to. His face was a sticky mess.

Jeremy made a gesture with his hand. "Are you gonna let this girl talk about you like that?" He pointed at Beau. "And stop saying 'are you kidding me?'" He used a high falsetto voice to mimic her. His voice cracked a little and it was adorable. "You're giving my little brother anxiety." He looked at Peter. "Isn't she?"

Peter giggled while he proceeded to strum the strings and mess with screws of the instrument to tune it. "Nope."

Jeremy laughed. "All right. No. He's not anxious and you're about to see why." He became serious. "We musical geniuses never get rattled."

"Are you going to shut up so I can play?" Peter complained. It struck Beau that he had all of his father's features, but none of his mother's. But when he opened his mouth, she could tell this was Elizabet's son.

"By all means, Mr. Mozart," Beau said. She reclined against the wall behind her and got comfortable. "Wow me."

JEREMY WATCHED IN FASCINATION AS Beau heard Peter play for the first time. Although Peter was not the best musician of the Tremaine children, he was still exceptional. There were adults worldwide who would be happy with a small measure of the talent the five-year-old possessed.

It was sharing these firsts with Beau that had him in knots. Seeing her face light up when she spotted Dover Castle, watching her run through the orchard pulling apples from the trees saying it was 'the best day ever,' and now, observing the pleasure on her face as she witnessed masterful music come from a babe. And the way she took to Gideon with such ease made his heart ache. She was his family—gratefully, not by blood, but by all that mattered. She was part of his soul. Being with her gave him a peace that he had never known before. So this was love.

He smiled when she looked up, her eyes wide with amazement as Peter played a full rendition of a song Jeremy had trouble playing competently. Of course, he had taught all the Tremaine children to play various instruments, but piano was his forte. Peter was a natural with the guitar, but he especially liked electric guitar and rock music.

"Brilliant!" Jeremy exclaimed when Peter sketched a lordly bow after completing the song. Jeremy cupped his hands around his mouth and cheered with the sounds of an enthusiastic audience.

Beau laughed. "I can't say I'm sorry enough." She reached over and touched Peter's shoulder. "That was amazing. You're as good as—"

"A Beatle?" Peter asked, hope shining in his eyes.

"I was thinking more on the lines of Mozart, Beethoven . . ."

Peter pulled a face. "They're boring." He set the guitar aside and then rose. He treated the instrument with great care, putting it back on its stand. He turned to Beau. "McCartney and Lennon *are* legendary. And they play guitar." He made his trademark disgruntled face—a mixture of cuteness with the promise of the Adonis he would become. "Mozart played piano mostly."

She looked to Jeremy for help.

He shrugged. "Peter is a bit fixated on the Beatles right now," he explained. "But if you ask Gideon, you may get what you're looking for."

Beau turned her attention to the boy in her lap. "You've got to be kidding me?" She frowned down at the downy dark blond baby hair beneath her nose. "Do you start them out from the crib?"

"She asked if we were kidding again," Peter pointed out.

Jeremy grinned and winked at Peter. "Pretty much," he said to Beau. He sat forward; the chair made a cracking noise as the legs struck the stone floor. "Gideon can play an assortment of wind instruments. He hasn't taken to strings."

"I've always wanted to play . . . something. I wish I could sing or play an instrument," she mused as she shook her head. "I envy you. You make it seem so easy. It's really amazing that the kids can play. I should have known they would be musicians like their mom."

"Playing an instrument is no big deal. Being a pastor's kid, or in their situation . . ." He pointed to the boys. "It's part of their lessons. It is added to their regular curriculum to enrich their studies. We could go as far as classing them as wealthy, like Caesar. He plays guitar—not well, but he plays. It's the way of things." He shrugged. "Most churches cannot afford to employ a music minister, so they teach the PKs." He grinned. "Be fruitful and multiply and all that. I was just a cut above the rest—an overachiever. There are two types of pastor's kids: the musicians, and those who wish they were. Joel can play bass and the clarinet, but hates it. Valerie teaches Sunday school. She doesn't have a musical bone in her body, but my parents did try to get her to take piano lessons. The Tremaines have all this at their disposal. Of course, their kids will flourish in creative venues. They have loads of time on their hands. You see where I'm going with this."

"Yeah, I see. You're trying to make it seem that musical talent is no big deal—"

"It's over romanticized," he cut in, still grinning. "All the heroes play piano like Beethoven, when true talent is merely work and a little bit of luck. And more work and practice, practice."

"I'll take some of that luck."

"Oh, you can play," Jeremy said. "Anything you want." He infused a level of challenge in his voice.

"I'm not a musical person, Jeremy. All I got was a mean curve ball. Elizabet's mom and mine were twins, but all the musical genes went to their side."

"Hey," he scolded. "I like your curve ball. And have you not been listening to me, woman?" He stood and held out his hand. "If you want to see what it's like, come with me. I'll show you."

"What do you mean?" She put Gideon aside and reached for his hand. "Like a music lesson?"

There was that pinch in his chest again—that abnormal gallop that let him know he was in trouble. So trustingly, she placed her hand in his whenever he asked. He didn't deserve the faith she offered after all he did to mess up her life. She lost years on account of him.

He helped her stand until they were mere inches apart. Gideon toddled to be with Peter near the fireplace. She tipped up her face, wearing an expectant expression on it. There was a level of excitement there, as well.

He grinned, brought her hand to his lips, and did the same to her other hand. "This is better than a music lesson. You're a natural and you don't even know it. You just need to feel the music."

"I'll *feel* stupid when you see that I can't be taught. Elizabet has tried."

Jeremy held her hand and led her to what seemed to be a common stone wall holding a bookshelf. When he tipped a burgundy leather bound volume the wall gave way, revolving open to reveal a piano on the other side.

"Impressed?" he asked as the piano rotated into the room.

She waved her hand dismissively. "Oh, no. I expect stuff like this now. I saw the mini hospital in the tunnels, remember?" She put her nose in the air and smiled. "Of course you have a grand piano behind your lair's wall. Why wouldn't you?"

Jeremy's head tipped back as he laughed. "Right-O. Of course I would have this." He beckoned her to step with him up to the piano. "It's to be expected."

"Naturally," she said. She gestured toward the instrument. "But how will you hide this? I mean, this can't stay here forever. Things like a hospital and electric guitars haven't been invented yet."

"We have to keep modern things a secret. There will come a time when all of this must be removed."

"But that's not today," she said. She ran her hand along the mahogany wood, lifted the case and exposed the ivories. The keys tinkled with shards of uneven melody when she fingered them. She regarded him over her shoulder. "I love it, Jeremy. It's gorgeous."

Jeremy's mouth went dry. He was unable to do anything but stand there and smolder. Everything that should shock and scare her, instead excited and fascinated her. Perhaps Gabriel was right: the women in her family were soft in the head.

"They're white," she murmured.

Jeremy nodded dumbly when she looked his way. There were times he forgot she knew most of his secrets. That she remembered he was once prone to bleeding all over piano keys was not lost on him. "I don't play to distraction any longer. I can start and stop when I please."

"No more obsessions?" she asked, her voice soft.

A smile curved his lips. He looked her over suggestively until she blushed. "I wouldn't say that." He was grateful to be able to change the direction of things with a joke.

He slid onto the piano bench and patted his lap. "Come. Have a seat."

"Your brothers—"

"Are playing a game and eating candied apples. They'll be content for an hour or so until they run out of food or patience." He patted his lap again. "Come on. I promise not to bite."

"I'm not worried about you biting," she teased. She glanced at the boys before she slid to sit on him.

He fidgeted to distribute her weight, ran his hands down her arms and led her hands to the keys. She was stiff as board. He grabbed her wrists and began rotating them. Alternating between flexing her wrists and shaking out her hands, he attempted to make her limber and submissive.

"Relax."

"I'm trying." She laughed.

"What do you want to play?" he asked to distract her as he continued to shake and rotate her hands. When she didn't answer the question, he placed a kiss where her neck and shoulder met.

Beau's shoulder hitched. "I know you know already. You're cheating."

"Say it. You have to ask for it," he said in a sing-song voice.

"Mozart."

"I knew it."

She elbowed him. A huff came from his lips. "If I could play anything, that's what I'd play. I know you think it's lame, but that's what I'd play. Don't ask if you're just gonna make fun of me."

"You do know how difficult it is to play Mozart, right?"

"I'm talking to you," she said. Her tone annoyed, but her hands were still pliant in his as he began moving them over the keys. "You're the self-professed musical genius. You can play anything."

"Oh, you think so?" he asked with a light chuckle.

"Can't you?" She turned to him, her hands stiffening.

He flipped her hands atop his and began strumming the keys with his long fingers. He had been told his hands were made for the piano. Long, slim digits—again, another part of his anatomy that he had no control over the way it was created, but it made him who he was.

Their eyes were locked on each other as he played a modern melody instead of Mozart. Softly at first, he began to sing the lyrics, but Beau's eyes widened and she smiled so adoringly that he wanted to fully serenade her like a callow fool.

"Sing louder," she begged. "I can barely hear you. I love it when you sing."

"I sing like a girl," he said with a snort. He only sang because he couldn't help himself. She was right—music just poured out of him. Even when he dissipated, he played music. It was a standing joke with the Amalgam: What tune would Jeremy take off to this time?

"It's perfect."

A rueful smile bent his lips. "The irony is that my voice sounds like this when I can do this," he switched tunes and played what she wanted, "with my hands." The melody started out slower, then built tempo until his fingers flew over the keys. His feet shifted on the pedals, causing Beau to jostle slightly in his lap. He used his thigh to bring her back to center; a smile tugged on his mouth. "Oh, no, you don't. Stay put, angel. This is what you wanted."

"I knew you could do it!" she exclaimed, her cheeks flushed and her eyes smiling. "What is it, Jeremy? Tell me what it is so I can put on my playlist and listen to it over and over. It's fabulous."

"'Sonata 16 in C major.'" He paused only to cage her hands under his again. Lining up her fingers with his, he closed his eyes and did something he had never done before.

He streamed his ability into her, using her fingers as if she were a puppet under his control. He gave her the ability to read the music he knew by heart. He allowed the melody to lull to its natural lazy notes rather than a faster tempo.

"I'm playing Mozart." Her voice held a tinge of awe.

"Yes, you are."

She watched her fingers move over the keys, a look of rapture on her face. He could not look away. Those who thought she was a tomboy and plain hadn't seen her the way he saw her now. And they never would, because she belonged to him. This innocent, enchanting girl owned him. For him alone did she open and become the girl he remembered. He had set her free again.

"Don't stop, Jeremy." She tipped her face back to smile her pleasure at him.

"Never," he murmured. He lowered his mouth over hers before she could turn away. The kiss was blistering because it had to be. Whether his little brothers tattled, he didn't care. He was enflamed. Consumed by a girl who had stolen his heart long ago just by being kind to a damaged boy. A measure of him was frightened by his loss of control; he never reverse siphoned—which was what he was doing. Allowing Beau to use his musical ability.

She was his first in so many ways. Even as he tried to slow his heart to a slow thunder, he knew she would not betray him. He tasted faithfulness and trust in her kiss, sincerity and forever. She was the kind of girl you kept eternally.

And yet, there was that small niggling voice in the back of his mind that whispered to him. Told him that when she truly saw the monster he was capable of becoming, she would leave him. She knew he had killed people. She understood what life in the Middle Ages entailed. Times were brutal. And in modern times, he would be hunted and killed if he was complacent and docile. What he was came with a measure of brute will and savagery. He was in part a violent force of nature. Unrestrained and prone to destroy whatever was in his way.

He broke the kiss on a gasp, his hands curled over hers. The melody ended abruptly with a discordant note. Beau's breath mingled with his, their mouths touching but no longer engaged in a kiss.

"Beau." Her name tumbled from his mouth of its own volition. He wrapped his arms around her body, clung to her, and brought her back closer to his chest. Her body was the perfect fit in the curve of his, molding to conform to it. His mouth left hers and he buried his face in her hair. "Please help me. Help me retain my humanity."

She did not know—not really—what he battled every single day. He had allowed her carte blanche entry to his tattered soul, but she did not see the beast lurking in the background, ready to pounce with little encouragement. And even though she returned his desperate embrace and matched his fervor with words of love and comfort, she could never be allowed to witness the real monster.

Or he would lose her.

"I can crush you if things get out of hand." The words fell from his mouth. "My right side is much stronger than my left. I can build momentum from my left, though. Like a storm. Hosts become the worst of what overtakes them. The furious acts of nature reside within us."

She pulled away, her eyes examining his. Her throat moved in an inaudible swallow. He sensed that she didn't know how to respond to his rapid and unexpected fire of confession, so he barreled forward. The information was pent up inside him and needed release.

"When I turned, it hurt so badly that I killed everything near me. That's why the animals were there—in the field that day. I couldn't help it. The power in me took over and my fear overrode any reason I had."

"Jeremy," she began.

"No," he insisted. "You've got to hear it from me. I can drop things into your mind, but I have to know that you can handle this. I want to know that you get it and I need to hear from you that you're in. Understand?" He wanted to shake her; make her see reason. His love for her was a painful circumstance that needed closure. He had to know she could accept him as he was. There was no going back.

Beau's mouth quivered. "I understand." He opened his mouth to begin, but she shook her head. "Wait." She pressed up and turned into his lap, her arms draping around his neck. Pressing a sweet kiss to his temple, she murmured her love in his ear. It was meant to be encouraging, but it broke him.

A sob left his lips. "I'm a monster, Beau. I can kill an entire nation in the bat of an eye. I can rob legions of their way of living by means of catastrophic devastation. I house a killer in my bones, Beau—do you really understand that? I can dissipate in seconds and take this castle down with me. I can annihilate the futures of everyone in medieval Dover in the blink of an eye."

"But you won't," she said, her voice rushed as well. "You're good, Jeremy. I know you."

"You know a boy who is buried. I have morphed into something else that humanity would want destroyed if they knew about me. There are hundreds of us and not all of them are like me. Most are out of control and hostile. The nature that invades us makes us rabid. It is a fight every day not to give in to the beast that rages inside of me. It screams to get out and destroy. If it weren't for Jareth, half of us would have destroyed the world by now."

"I don't believe that," Beau said, her voice soft. She pressed her forehead to his. "If that were true, I think that the world would have ended long ago. I have a feeling your kind has been around for a while."

"We don't know that," Jeremy said. His arms tightened around her. She was his life preserver at present, keeping him grounded and sane. "No one knows how far back the origins of hosts go. The earliest host in the Amalgam's employ is a man from China. He was turned in the Gansu earthquake of 1920."

"And he didn't destroy the world—did he?"

Jeremy released a short breath. "Are you listening to me? Have you heard what I've said? I'm dangerous, Beau. I lead a life that involves killing. The Amalgam uses me as a weapon of mass destruction because I'm considered one of the good guys. I'm an equalizer. I set the balance of things. I'm used to keeping hosts and humans from killing each other, and sometimes that means exterminating those who won't comply with the rules that govern the Amalgam."

"You are," she agreed. "The best. What you are describing is the life of a soldier. You're part of an incredible league that protects the world from nightmares no one even knows exist. You're a soldier, and soldiers face combat. There are casualties." Her face dipped down until their lips were together and she kissed him. "Tell me what is really bothering you, Jeremy, because I know it's not this—not what you're telling me now. I'm here. Just tell me. You won't lose me."

How very right she was.

Jeremy closed his eyes and kissed her, drawing her as close to his body as possible. "You're a fool," he whispered against her lips. "And I love you for it." He pulled back and smoothed back the hair that had fallen into her face. "You've forgiven me for leaving you to deal with things that were my fault and true all along. You've accepted that I am no longer a normal person . . ."

"You were never *normal*," she inserted, her lips twisting. "But you were always mine. And I love you for it. You saw me, Jeremy. You see what no one else sees. I want you as badly as you want me. You haven't changed so much that I don't know you. You're still my Jeremy. I see you, you know?"

"That's it," he said, his voice choking. "I'm still that boy even if he is buried deep. I'm still that non-verbal boy on the inside. I'll never be cured. It's who I am." He drew back and grabbed her hand from around his shoulders. "Inside is that boy and he will always be there." He placed her hands over his heart.

Beau's eyes traced to where her palms flattened on his chest, her eyes fluttering as a single tear rolled down her cheek and her mouth wobbled. "You mean to scare me, but you're not." She looked up at him. "That boy is who is keeping you a good guy. He's the best person I know. Always has been. That he is still you is amazing." Her face tipped up a notch, her chin jutting forward. "You don't scare me. I love the boy you were and the monster you've become. I'm still here and I'm not going anywhere. So stop trying to sell me something I'm not buying."

"You are soft in the head," he replied, but a smile tugged at half of his mouth despite the seriousness of the moment.

"I might be a little crazy, yes," she agreed. "But then, so are you. You were crazy to think I wouldn't accept all that you are. You're telling me these things as if you expect me to run away."

"Did I say how much I love you, Beau Angelle?"

"I love you right back." She smiled. "You wanted to hear that I'm in. Well, I'm in. Do I need to climb that fabulous tower I saw out there or will you believe me?"

"You could get hurt climbing that death trap. Gabriel accidently blew out the stone stairway during a training session last month. The northern parapet would be your best bet." A great burden lifted from his heart. His story was out now, and not just through a syphoning. He sensed the change in her. The change that comforted him that she understood his nature, both the good and the bad.

"Hm," she said, her expression grave. "Spartan warriors with means to blow things up, ancient soldiers able to time travel, and a league of hosts that can morph into my worst weather nightmares." Her nose crinkled. "Yeah, I'm still in. Sign me up. Call me crazy, but you had me way back when you bought out the entire fruit section at my store."

Jeremy sighed dramatically. "That easy, huh?"

Beau's eyes traveled to where his brothers were seated. Peter was reading to Gideon, but his gaze roamed to them. "Oh, yeah. You're practically a magnet for me. I never stood a chance with your new accent." She drew away a fraction. "We better go see to your little brothers. I think Peter is distracted. I don't want to be in trouble with Jareth. I really want to get on his good side, and sitting here on your lap, making out with you isn't likely to score any points. Know what I mean?"

Jeremy scooted her off his lap and turned to look over his

shoulder to where Peter smirked and then went back to reading to an intent Gideon. He kissed the tip of her nose as she slid away. "Stay with me while I finish up here? I'm almost done with the manuscript. I'll take you to the shoreline of the cliffs afterward. Deal?"

"Deal. But you don't have to barter with me. I'd stay anyway. I like watching you." She leaned forward and kissed him one more time. "I'll say it again. I'm in; all of me."

"You may regret that after you see the cliffs the way I have planned for you." His smile was mischievous. "Less than twenty-four hours, you're neck deep in the Amalgam, I've spilled my guts, and you're still here. You're pretty tough, angel. I'll give you that. You may be in, but you haven't seen all of my tricks yet. All I can say is that you asked for it and I'm going to deliver it."

Chapter 7

"Time jumping causes memories to haze. Sometimes, you might forget who is on our side or who is still alive. There is nothing like going back in time and seeing a dead man."
—Jeremy, while teaching Beau about the ancient time bands and travel stones.

"**B**RO," CAESAR SAID. HE TOSSED the Xbox remote across the sofa table. "I quit. You're cheating."

"Not so." Jeremy snickered. He annihilated Caesar's video game character before placing his remote next to him on the sofa.

It had been three months since he saved Beau's life, and in those three months, life had gotten good—and really good.

He had a girlfriend. A friend. Did he say how good life was? He and Caesar had gradually warmed up to each other again. Caesar's dad's oil company donated to the rebuilding of Benoit's Grocery. While FEMA provided temporary housing for Beau and her family, it was Randolph Enterprises that gave a cool eighty grand to rebuild a store that it considered an asset to the fishing and hunting industry of the area. Jeremy and Caesar offered their help to clean up the wreckage and begin basic production of the reconstruction process. They saw each other every day, grabbed lunch together, and eventually they were commuting and hanging out afterward to relax by shooting pool or playing video games.

When their part of clean up and construction was done, they kept up the daily interactions for fun. They developed a comfortable relationship that Jeremy never had before. While they had been friends when they were younger, this was different. Jeremy was a verbal participant now and that changed the dynamic.

"You're just a pansy." Jeremy scoffed.

"Gee, Jerm," Caesar drawled while tamping a pack of cigarettes against his palm. "You keep talking like that and I'll finally take you out in public." He lifted a brow. "Wanna go on a date?"

"Gad, no. You're not my type."

Caesar smiled. Jeremy liked how Caesar went with his little idiosyncrasies. He had so many of them that he forgot to use a filter around Caesar—like using the words gad, blimey, or pansy. He didn't want to mess up the comradery they shared, so he refused to siphon from Caesar and he didn't pry into his thoughts. It seemed wrong. He let Caesar be Caesar, and Caesar extended the same courtesy. Although Jareth pressed him to siphon for safety's sake, he refused. Friends should be able to trust one another.

"Want something to eat?" Caesar asked. "I heard my mom in the kitchen. Bet she brought sushi or some crap like that."

Jeremy grimaced. "Uh, no. Got anymore chips? Hummus?"

"You really need to explore the world of real food," Caesar advised. He stretched as he rose from the foot of the bed. Jeremy sat on the floor, leaning up against the bed. Caesar kicked the empty hummus container. "That stuff will *make* you a pansy. I'll go see what else she brought back." He wagged his eyebrows. "Spicy chicken burgers from Free-zo if we're lucky."

Jeremy's features pinched. "No, thank you." His stomach still remembered the burn of the last one he ate. Never again. Spicy food in a human hurricane's body was not a good combination.

"I'm bringing you sushi, then. No matter what you say— you know you like it. You're a doctor's kid. All rich kids like that kind of stuff."

Jeremy had rarely seen Caesar's mom. She was a socialite whose schedule was full all day, every day. But he knew a great deal about her. Like Caesar hated her and thought she was useless. While he idolized his absent father, his mother was nothing more than a meal ticket and landlord who gave free rent and big presents. Caesar talked about Jeremy's family having money, but made light of the fact that he had life pretty good, too. Jeremy guessed their families were about even on a financial level, but you couldn't tell with Caesar. In fact, he deliberately dressed like a bum rocker and drove a secondhand Jeep. Where Jeremy was the perpetual preppy, well-behaved obedient kid, Caesar was the rebellious rich kid who wanted to thumb his nose at his parents.

"I swear I'll vomit on your bedspread if you make me eat that stuff." Jeremy shivered at the thought of sushi. Just the smell would have his mouth watering, and not in a good way.

"Bro, you eat, like, five tons of food. What's a little fish and seaweed—"

Jeremy held up his hand. "Stop."

Caesar laughed. "You're serious." He placed a cigarette between his lips but did not light it. He never smoked indoors. "All right, then. Let's go to your house. What's for dinner? Veal culets? Filet mignon?"

"It's actually Mexican night at my house," Jeremy announced smugly.

"OMG." Caesar grabbed his heart; his cigarette bobbed between his lips. "You seriously have nights designated for special foods? I knew your family was weird, but Mexican night?"

Jeremy twisted his lips as he glowered.

"Oh, wait!" Caesar plucked the cigarette from his mouth. "I forgot. Your dad hates me. This might not be a good idea."

Jeremy appreciated how Caesar acknowledged Jareth as his dad. "He likes you." He smiled with half of his mouth. He wasn't lying. Jareth liked Caesar, he just didn't trust him. Jareth didn't trust anybody outside the tight family circle. It was nothing personal. "Maybe if you hadn't dropped the F bomb in the first conversation you had with him."

Caesar's face turned red. "That sucked."

"Yeah, well, it's all good. He doesn't hold grudges."

"Okay. Fine. Let's go to your house." He motioned to the TV. "My work is done here anyway." He thumbed over his shoulder. "I'm gonna go tell Mom I'll be back after dinner."

Jeremy snickered as he pulled his cell phone from his back pocket. "I'll just text Jareth and tell him to pick me up earlier than planned."

"Wait, he's coming here?" A look of horror filled his face. "Like, as in, Dr. Jareth Tremaine is coming to my house?"

"Last I checked . . . yeah, Dr. Jareth Tremaine is my dad." Jeremy chuckled. "Don't worry. Your house is twice as fancy as ours. Mr. GQ will approve, even if it's messy." He looked up from punching in his text. "If you tell him your bedroom was designed by Ralph Lauren, you're so in."

Caesar's lips spread over his teeth in what partly resembled a smile. "I'll just meet you over there so you don't have to drive me home later."

"It's no bother. I'll drive you back after dinner." The doorbell chimed at the same time Jeremy received a text from Jareth. He looked up at Caesar. "Well, that was quick." He shrugged. "He's here, so that settles it."

Looking back later, Jeremy wondered how he ever thought his life could be normal and he would have friends and a girlfriend, and life would be just grand. He should have known better. Uncomplicated lives were for everyone else *except* him. His middle name should have been Problematic. Jeremy Problematic Tremaine had a certain ring to it.

JARETH WAITED FOR SOMEONE TO open the door, only to be surprised that it was Jeremy. He peered inside the stellar home, and took in the perfect interior design. "Where is everyone?" It was an old establishment in the garden district section of the city, alarge, white Old-American style house with black shutters and a pool in the backyard.

Caesar's father was in the oil business; this kind of wealth came from corporate ownership. He had directed Ezra to dig into Randolph Enterprises, but he came up with a clean slate. It was a reputable business that employed hundreds of locals. Caesar Randolph, the original, however, was a bit more elusive. With corporate leadership being in Dallas, Texas, the man was never home. Jareth often wondered what kind of man left his wife and kid in a small town with no protection. Not that they needed protection in Gueydan, but what kind of person wanted to be away from his family? It was cold.

Of concern to him was that he could not get Jeremy to siphon information. His son could choose not to tap into peoples' minds, and he had a new personal code. He refused to 'spy' on his friends. He was loyal, honest, and extended trust to those whom he loved and to those who earned it. Obviously, Caesar had earned a level of Jeremy's trust. But that didn't mean that Jareth had to trust him, too.

"Caesar's coming. He's getting some money from his mom. Can you stop and get us something to eat?"

Jareth could not help it; he rolled his eyes. "You would rather eat garbage than Elizabet's cooking? It is Mexican night."

"We have tacos every Tuesday," Jeremy said. He pushed Jareth from the threshold and back into the enclosed entry. He held the door slightly ajar, his body in the opening. "Look. Can we get some fast food—just for Caesar and me? He's not a family kind of guy, that's all. I don't know how he'll take to sitting at the formal dining table making chitchat with freakish kids who sometimes speak Latin or Norman French when they forget to speak English. I want to give him a way out in case he's uncomfortable."

Jareth understood where this was going. He drew back and pulled his sunglasses off. "This is what peer pressure looks like. Let me get a good look at it." He frowned. What did one to say to a child who was embarrassed to have a functional home life? "It is ugly. Move aside so I can meet the parents who have obviously child-worshipped Caesar into an independent, self-important state of mind."

Jeremy kept a firm hold on the door. "No. I'll eat McDonald's and claim to love it."

"Today McDonald's, tomorrow your purity and your integrity. The compromises will go on and on."

"Really, Jareth?" Jeremy whispered. The voices of Caesar and his mother could be heard now. "I thought you wanted me to fit in? This is part of it. Fast food with a side of normalcy."

"Is he *regulated*?" Jareth hissed.

"No," Jeremy said, looking affronted. He peered over his shoulder. "He's Baptist. His family doesn't even attend Sunday services. They're unchurched."

"I like Baptist," Jareth said, not particularly to Jeremy, but as a matter of basic admission. As far as doctrine went, Baptists were the least of his worries. He pointed to Jeremy's chest. His sunglasses brushed the salmon colored cotton of his shirt. "You seem on edge. Have you refueled? From the blast I received when you opened the door, I would say they keep their thermostat rather low."

"I managed," Jeremy whispered. Caesar was coming up the hallway and into the foyer. "They have a cat," he added before stepping aside and grinning at Caesar. "We're all set?"

"Yeah," Caesar said, tucking his wallet into the front pocket of his flannel shirt. He tipped his chin toward Jareth. "What's up?"

Jareth lifted his chin and was about to say something utterly stupid and rude, but he settled for thrusting his hand out for a handshake. "I am well." They shook hands. "Jeremy says that your mother is home. We should be introduced. Jeremy spends a lot of time here and I would like to offer to pay a portion of the grocery bill he is causing." And he wanted to be sure there was not a cat that died from hypothermia laying around.

Jeremy rolled his eyes when he caught that thought.

Caesar laughed, but it sounded forced, as if Jareth surprised him. "She's on her way out." He thumbed over his shoulder. "Probably already in the car, backing out." He wore a look of conspiracy. "She's going to the beauty shop. I wouldn't want to be the one who stood between her and her "me time," you know what I mean?"

Jareth was perplexed, but he understood. Women of this day thought pampering was a God-given right. He put his sunglasses back on and smiled. "Shall we go, then?" he suggested. "Onward to McDonald's." He felt the urge to spit after he said it.

"Sweeeeet," Caesar said, and rushed past. As he retreated, Jareth wondered what was familiar about the boy. He had features that he had seen before, but could not place the likeness. It could be that he was related to a patient of his, but with that number in the hundreds, he was unlikely to figure it out without stressing about it. He looked back expectantly at Jeremy, certain Jeremy knew exactly what he was thinking because he had allowed it—twice today.

But Jeremy only mouthed, "Thank you."

Jareth twisted his lips. "You are very welcome." He caught Jeremy's arm when he went to pass. "You will have to pay for your food. I have a bet with Elizabet that I will not cave to modern conveniences. Fast food is at the top of the list. She checks my debits."

"She does understand your blatant dislike for food of a lesser nutritional value." Jeremy chuckled as they walked to the car side by side. He shook his head. "She'll lose this bet."

Jareth grinned. "It is so much fun to take her money and see her pout when she loses. But even that is not the best part."

"What is, then? Taking the mickey?"

"No." Jareth's smile grew a fraction.

"Gah!" Jeremy said, and pretended to gag. He narrowed his eyes. "Can you not do that around Caesar? Parents don't talk or act like that."

Jareth smirked. "No worries. I shall just avoid Elizabet altogether while your friend visits. That way he will never suspect that I am in love with my wife. I will totally ignore the mother of my four, almost five children."

"Great." Jeremy responded, despite the sarcasm in Jareth's voice. "I owe you," he added while opening the passenger door. Caesar had already climbed into the back seat and was inspecting the delicate craftsmanship of the truly divine car that was Jareth's joy.

Jareth waited for a beat to simmer down. The sarcasm in his voice had been meant to tip off Jeremy, yet he chose to ignore it. This new facet of parenting reeked. He could only hope that the values he had taught Jeremy would win over during this next stage of being a teenager.

Jeremy wasn't overly fond of fast food, but it was food and he *loved* food. Processed food had a tendency to slow him down, but that wasn't a bad thing when hanging out with someone who didn't have a heartbeat idly thumping in the midst of an eye of the storm.

Solomon watched longingly as Jeremy crammed five fries into his mouth.

"You'll choke yourself," Abigail warned as she passed, hugging a yoga mat.

Jeremy handed Solomon a fry. "Only if I talk and eat at the same time. So stop tempting me or you'll be the cause of my demise."

Abigail peered at him over her shoulder and stuck her tongue out.

Caesar watched Solomon reverently eat the fry handed him. "Homeschooled kids aren't allowed to eat fries?"

Jeremy instantly resented the jab at homeschooled kids. "Homeschooling has nothing to do with good eating choices and habits. Don't hate on homeschooled kids. It's not cool. We're not aliens, you know."

Caesar nodded, but still eyed Solomon, who practically had his eyes closed while savoring the food. "He's the oldest?" After the question left his mouth, he seemed to catch what he had said and a look of remorse passed his eyes. "I mean, you're the oldest. Then him, right?"

Jeremy was not offended. The technicalities of his birth were something he could not change. If anyone understood his family dynamics, it was Caesar. Caesar remembered his life as a Cameron. "Solomon and Abigail are the oldest. They're twins."

"That sucks," Caesar said, shaking his head. Jeremy looked confused, so he elaborated. "It would have been convenient if they had been both boys. The heir and spare in one try."

The back of Jeremy's neck prickled. What an odd thing to say. Combined with the tension he absently picked up, it took all he had not to reach out and siphon the meaning behind those casually spoken words. But he did not. Instead, he waited.

Caesar took a sip of soda, watching Jeremy all the while. "You look like I just said the F word in front of your brother. Dude, relax. I was just joking. You have a suit of armor in your foyer and speak like frickin' British royalty." He touched his chest with his fingertips. "Confession: I read. A lot." He shrugged. "It's not something I advertise, but I'm a lover of history. Sue me for the bad history jokes if they offend."

Jeremy relaxed. "And you pick on me for saying 'blimey'? Really, Caesar? Heir and spare? That went out centuries ago."

"But you know what I meant." Caesar grinned and Jeremy

shrugged. "Like I said, though. I love that stuff called history. Hell, light reading to me is an autobiography of Winston Churchill."

"He's brilliant, right?" Jeremy said, eyes wide.

"Wise man," Caesar agreed. He tossed the trash from his meal into the paper bag it arrived in. "So, are we gonna play Black Ops or music?"

"Music?" Jeremy said. More than half of his meal went back into his own bag. Like he would pick playing video games when Caesar had challenged him to a guitar duel. Caesar was under the misconception that Jeremy was only fluent on piano. He had no idea. Jeremy smiled. He had perhaps alluded to that misconceived notion. "You have to give me a ten minute warm up. You have an advantage over me in string instruments."

"String instruments . . ." Solomon began to say. Jeremy thrust his hand out and touched his little brother's knee. He sent a non-threatening electrical pulse into his body to silence him.

Caesar chuckled and did not notice Solomon's interruption. "Be prepared to eat crow, man. You're about to be dust."

Jeremy peeked at Solomon, who glared back at him. He squeezed his knee with no current this time, remorse in his expression. He had not hurt him, but he did not like using his abilities on his siblings. He saved that for life threatening events, like when he kept Peter from bawling when they were under siege by the French. The cry of the babe had almost given away their location. At the time, surprise was their strategy.

In the matter of a day, he had not siphoned from Caesar when he felt threatened, he lied about his musical abilities, Jareth had let him siphon thoughts three times, and he shocked his little brother. He was safer with Beau. Around her he could relax, siphon all he wanted, and be his true self.

"You sure you want to do this? I mean, we'll miss taco night. There's always room for tacos."

"Stop trying to avoid the inevitable butt whipping you're about to get," Caesar goaded as he stood. Jeremy stood as well, and grabbed Caesar's trash bag. "You're gonna be crying after that ten minute warm up, and I'm going to enjoy every moment. Facebook is going to blow up when I post the deets."

"Fire away," Jeremy said, and strode past him. They made their way through the den, leaving a brooding Solomon watching television in the media room. "I have like, twenty friends on Facebook, and most of them are family." He shrugged. "What do I care if Uncle Eddie thinks I suck at guitar?"

"I know for a fact that your profile has blown up with requests other than family."

"How would you know that?"

"Because I had to listen to Beau cry over it." He looked smug. "You do know she stalks you, right? And not just on Facebook. Your Instagram and Twitter too."

Jeremy grinned. "This I know. She has the passwords to all of my social media accounts. I made it easy for her to stalk. We have an open book policy—me being the open book."

On the far side of the room, in front of the windows, Minh and Abigail were seated on yoga mats in lotus position. Jeremy felt it necessary for introductions. "Caesar, this is Minh. He's a friend of the family and Abigail's godfather. Don't mind them—they're weird like this all the time."

Minh opened one eye. "Peace."

Caesar touched his bandanna with the side of his index finger in a small salute. "And I thought my mom was strange. She has a yoga group that meets every Wednesday at home. Talk about awkward, having a bunch of middle-aged ladies in downward dog all over your living room. I can't believe I'm not blind yet."

"We're praying," Abigail said, peeking through slatted eyes. "And you're disturbing us."

Jeremy jerked his head for Caesar to follow. "I just need to toss this in the garbage bin. Then, I can whip you." They turned into the kitchen and stopped short. His voice dwindled to nothing when they fumbled upon a private moment. Jareth had one hand on Elizabet's belly and the other on her shoulder while they kissed.

"*Te amo,*" Jareth said against her lips.

"*Di iterum sivis,*" she replied.

It was like a watching a love scene in a movie, but way more embarrassing. What a nightmare. Jeremy cleared his throat and they parted with a small peep of alarm from Elizabet. Jareth turned a thunderous expression to them, his hand curved protectively around his wife's stomach as he stepped forward so she could hide behind him.

They would never be considered normal. "*Etiam sit amet nunquam,*" Jeremy's words came out spontaneously in Latin. While catching Jareth and Elizabet making out and finding people in meditative prayer poses was typical for him, he was pretty sure Caesar would not think them ordinary at all.

Caesar laughed and posed as if he were bowing for the Queen of England. "Please, *rem gerunt,*" he told them in perfect Latin. Carry on.

Chapter 8

"He has a tendency to like artists like Buckethead. I've tried all the classics with him but he only wants to play rock. I've given up hoping he'll be the next Beethoven."
—Jeremy on his little brother, Peter's, musical aspirations.

FALLING IN LOVE IN AUTUMN was more than Jeremy had ever hoped for. The romantic evenings, the strolls in the falling leaves, listening to the wind whistle through the branches. Autumn had a smell, too. It smelled of hope, rain, and a lot like Beau. She was infused into every facet of his life, including his senses.

She rushed to his house each day after school to see what new adventure he had for her. Most days they traveled to medieval Dover. Benjamin was born in October; sometimes they stayed home and watched the children for Elizabet while she nursed the newest edition to the Tremaine family.

And then there were the days they just ran. Turning had not made Jeremy a runner. He had always been one. There was an art to it; nothing like a good run to give one a clean slate on life. It had the power to erase bad days and turn them into better ones. Running freed him and expended the excess energy that often threatened to consume him. When Beau struggled to match his stride, he slowed his pace and forced his internal winds to keep it leisurely.

But it was autumn, and winter beckoned. Running was becoming less of a liberty and more a fickle lover. Jeremy became weaker as the days turned colder, and often he was unable to leave the confines of home. It was in those times that he wondered what he was doing. Was he merely pretending that his life had a normal side to it? And while Beau claimed she did not mind, it killed him a little to watch her trail off with Caesar. Caesar, who had no trouble when practicing her pitch in the cold evenings. Caesar, who was sometimes her running buddy. Caesar, who could escort her when she was chosen for homecoming court.

Now that stuck with him, and he had to do something about it.

"Jeremy," Elizabet said. She tucked the blanket around Benjamin and shifted him in her arms. "I'm thrilled everything is going well with Beau—truly, I am—but you simply cannot do this."

"Nope. End of discussion," Jareth seconded. He reached for Benjamin when Elizabet lifted the bundle toward him. "I will not have you swooning in the middle of a football field because you have jealousy issues."

"Caesar is your best friend," Elizabet continued. "Surely you're not jealous that he's escorting Beau." Jareth grunted, and Elizabet frowned.

"What?" Jareth lifted a shoulder while he bounced their colicky baby. "Caesar does not have the same standards as Jeremy. While I am with you on this, it is for different reasons." He faced Jeremy. "Never trust another man with your woman. End of story."

"Well, surely Beau can be trusted." Elizabet frowned at Jareth. "After all they have been through, there should be a high level of trust here."

Jareth turned away, murmuring under his breath about misplaced trust. Benjamin took that opportunity to belch loudly.

"Look," Jeremy said. His surly tone of voice had Jareth returning his attention. "It is merely a courtesy that I am having this discussion with you. I have a plan and I plan to execute it regardless of whether you give consent. I'm eighteen, I'm responsible, and I've not asked for much. You can relent this one thing or not." He looked Jareth straight in the eye. "I'm escorting Beau even if it kills me."

"You fool! That just may be the case," Jareth steamed.

Jeremy squared his shoulders, his eyes glaring. "I'm doing this."

A sound of distress came from Elizabet as she looked to her husband.

"Elizabet," Jareth said. His voice had that deceptively calm tone that made Jeremy cringe. "Take Benjamin up to the nursery and see to the children. I would like a word alone with Jeremy."

Elizabet asked no questions, but jumped up and took her son. "Don't kill him," she murmured, then stood on her toes to place a peck on Jareth's cheek. She passed Jeremy a worried glance before she left the room and closed the door behind her.

"Here we are," Jareth stated, his arms spread open. "We have the ability to maintain two lives; we jump time." He flourished a hand toward Jeremy. "You are host for a hurricane, the strongest host in the world. *Category Jeremy.*" He bowed mockingly then and that made Jeremy's heart plummet. He could feel the animosity streaming across the room. There had been no warning or easing into the subject. Jareth was jumping into it with both feet. "You believe you are so clever that you can walk about in thirty-degree weather? Do you think Beau will want her escort carried away like a babe, nicely tucked away in an ambulance with paramedics who will have no idea what to do with you—*if* they can even get a proper set of vitals from you because you will be off the chart—and why?" He put his hand to his ear as if awaiting an answer.

Jeremy felt his eyes fill with tears. He knew he was grandstanding. He needed Jareth's blessing to go through with this or his life would be in grave danger. But Jareth would never listen to him unless he was passionate.

"What?" Jareth bellowed. "I am sorry; I cannot hear you. In fact, I will never hear you again because if you do something this stupid you will be *dead*."

"*Magister*," Jeremy pleaded, his voice sounding strained. "Please. This means a lot to her. You know her dad refused to escort her, and her brother is a bully. He'll make her miserable if she allows him this."

"There is Caesar."

Jeremy hated the way this was going. "He offered, but you said yourself that's a bad idea." It was a horrible idea. He had seen the looks Caesar gave Beau when he thought no one was looking. What he heard himself say was, "They're friends. What does it matter if you won't allow me to intervene?" He looked up with tapered anger in his eyes. "But it will be me. I'll say it again: No one is escorting my girlfriend but me."

Jareth's laugh was cutting. "Your little temper tantrums will not work on me."

That sobered Jeremy. He felt the urge to dissipate strong within him and fought it. Having base urges was normal to a host. The ability to control them and not act on them made a host human and redeemable. He was one of the only hosts who had complete mastery over his earthly nature. From almost crying like a baby to fully morphing in a matter of seconds, it humbled him. He remembered who he was and the code he was sworn to uphold.

Jeremy's shoulders dropped. "Jareth, I love her to a point where I don't know who I am without her any longer." He shrugged as he slipped his hands into the front pockets of his jeans. "If I can't do this, then I have failed her on a level I'm not comfortable with. I know the way Caesar eyes her. Like he's waiting for me to disappear again so they can take up wherever it was they left off." He grimaced. "I have no idea why he chose to rekindle our friendship. With the way he feels about

Beau, he should probably hate me." His shoulders lifted in a tight shrug, his arms held close to his body. "All I know is that I need a plan and I'd like your cooperation. I'm going to do this with or without you, yeah? So, please just cut the bull and let's formulate a strategy. I really don't want to die over something as trivial as homecoming."

"You do know that you are a role model for my offspring? You are setting the tone for Solomon and your little brothers."

"This I know," Jeremy smiled. "I'm paving a path of smooth transitions. They'll thank me one day."

Jareth shook his head. "They should be forced to stay in the nursery. Forever. I cannot imagine having to go through this each time one of you becomes a teenager. I do not recall giving Mrs. Wheatley this much trouble. I was docile. Compliant."

"They locked you up in the castle when you were three years old, Jareth."

"Not my nursemaid," Jareth said. "That was my uncle." He waved his hand. "Brother. Whatever he is."

"Brother," Jeremy said, his voice low. "My uncle."

"Precisely," Jareth snapped. "I was a biddable child. All I wanted to do was translate and please the king. And when I became older, I squired and learned to fight for my lands and country. There were no homecoming courts, silly football games and such. Growing children these days are senseless, vain creatures that only care for their pleasure. The vapid lives they lead are deceiving and dull."

"Your upbringing may have looked different, but there were jostling tourneys, the king's court, and Elizabet stealing through wormholes—we can't forget about her. She gave your life a dash of normalcy."

"What is this? I assure you, whatever you want to call it, I shall win. You shall never win an argument to convince me that modern society is anything but a decaying life built on the façade of a diluted pipe dream. They want unicorns and rainbows, castles and fair knights. They demand it, having no idea that knights who fight dragons are merely killers keeping war from the doors to their little dreams. That rainbows are a convenient promise written in the sky without romantic ideations, and unicorns do not exist. I am asking you to see reason, Jeremy. It is absurd that you would risk your life over this. It is a ridiculous tradition of man for the sake of vanity and sport."

"It means something to the people around here. Beau thinks she was chosen because of Rixby and his chances of getting a big scholarship."

"Clever girl," Jareth murmured.

Jeremy bristled. "It's my fault that people see her as daft. My fault. She *is* a clever girl. And beautiful, smart, and kind. The reason she was chosen for the court is pointless now. It's all about redemption and making things right for her. She will be redeemed and I'll be the one who sees to it. Everyone who ever laughed at her will recognize what she is worth. This modern society that you detest has my girl in pieces, Jareth, and I'll see her put back together. If I have to convince the world that unicorns are real—if I have to carry my sword up the middle of the Gueydan Bears' football field, waving it as a challenge to any bloke who has ever hurt her—then so be it. One thing about fair knights that you left out is that we are bold bastards. We take up a cause and fight for it, especially when our lady is being defamed."

Jareth's eyes widened a fraction. "Good heavens, you really are obsessed with this, aren't you? You will do this even though it may end in your death. Without my help, you will not have an out if you need one. It would be suicide to go it alone. You would risk your health for the love of this girl?"

Jeremy nodded briskly. "Is this concession I hear?"

Jareth let out a long breath and crammed his hands into the pockets of the lab coat he wore over his suit. "I do not know. Perhaps. There is much information I must sift through to see things clearly. You were never an easy one. Why can you not be like your brilliant father and I will lock you in the east tower till . . . let's say about twenty years old or so? I just need a couple of years to catch my breath."

"Ya big softie." Jeremy bumped his shoulder to Jareth's. "I knew you'd come around."

Jareth sneered. "I have my reason." He pointed to the doorway. "And she just walked out a minute ago with my literal future in her arms. When I think of all the things she lost to be with me, I remember her family. I remember the pain she felt leaving Beau behind, the guilt. She may never say it, but Elizabet wants you to redeem Beau. She bears the same scars of remorse and shame for abandoning her cousin." His stare hardened. "You have no idea what love is. It is sacrifice, pain—"

"I know what love is," Jeremy said, his voice rising. He sat on the arm of the chair behind him, his arms crossed. "I left Beau behind knowing that my actions were protecting her. When the government got involved, I was the one who breached the Pentagon and wiped *The Jeremy Files* from existence." His voice lowered and his nostrils flared. "I've killed people to protect her." He pointed an accusing finger at Jareth. "You've killed people to protect her. And she knows it, Jareth. She knows everything now. What's the point of not giving it all we've got to ensure I give it the best go I can? I won't die if you help me. You know that. It's your job to keep me alive."

"Being a father is not a job."

Jeremy's shoulders sagged. He pinched the bridge of his nose, closed his eyes, and let out a slow breath as his chest deflated. "I'm an emotional wreck. It's freaking thirty degrees outside and it's only October. How does this happen in Louisiana?"

He felt a warm hand on his shoulder. "It is not your request I have a problem with, it was the delivery," Jareth said softly. "Rebellion in a child of mine is an enigma. I will not tolerate it. You could have asked politely and worked on a delivery. I am not an ogre. I love all of my children and I want the best for them."

Jeremy opened his eyes a fraction, peeking. "I was going for passionate. Too much?" Jareth nodded. A grin tugged on half his mouth. "Look, *Dad.*" Jareth snickered, removed his hand, and turned away. "*Magister,* I need to do this."

"This I know," Jareth said to the floor.

"My delivery was that horrid?"

Jareth nodded again.

"Geez, I'm a mess when it's cold."

"Yes, you are," Jareth agreed. He motioned to Jeremy's feet. "Socks?" He *tsk*ed. "What are you, a little girl?"

Jeremy smiled; things were looking better. "If I ask with better delivery and tone, is there hope?"

Jareth's grin wobbled. "Perhaps."

"I have pointed out how easy you are, have I not?"

"You may have mentioned it from time to time."

"Step aside." Jeremy stood up. Using the back of his hand, he nudged Jareth from his path. "I have a plan to conjure and present. I'll keep you posted."

Jareth narrowed his eyes and refused to move. "Where are you going? We may settle this now. I have fifteen patients scheduled in the office this afternoon. It's now or who knows when."

Jeremy tilted his head. "You hear that?" he asked. "I have eager pupils. There are inquiring minds I must tend to."

The faint sounds of an electric guitar being tuned wafted into the room. Jareth's mouth thinned into a hard line. "Must every day be music day in this household? Has anyone ever heard of jousting? Fencing? Archery? My heir will be able to play a symphony but get shod over on the battlefield."

"And you were demeaning the tradition of homecoming," Jeremy said, his tone rueful. Jareth had the sense to look sheepish. "Have no fear, your grace. Your daughter is on the field with her godfather as we speak. Little bugger will be able to shoot me out of the sky before it's all over."

"She is rather good with an arrow." The pride in Jareth's tone was evident. He leveled Jeremy a concerned look. "Minh does take his mandate seriously. Do you think he will show her how to—"

"Yep. I saw her shoot a practical dust mote from a branch the other day. Minh has her firing three in rapid succession—you know how he loves to amaze people with his arrow machine gun tactics." Jeremy made a face. "His words, not mine."

"Perhaps you should fetch her from the field, then," Jareth suggested, his smile strained. "We cannot have her outshining her brother." He put his hand on Jeremy's chest to stay him. "And I will consider what you have asked. Work on your delivery, formulate a plan, and we will talk it over."

BEAU LOVED TO WATCH JEREMY with the children. He was patient, caring, and, quite frankly, hot. There was nothing like a man being sweet to kids that upped the sizzle factor. He was leaning over Peter, showing him a sheet of music. Solomon tinkered on the grand piano in the corner while Gideon sat at Elizabet's feet. Elizabet was reading a stack of sheet music.

That would take getting use to—Elizabet reading. She was dyslexic and had a slew of learning disabilities, yet Jareth had taught her. It was nothing short of awe inspiring. Beau could just cry with gratitude.

"Hey," Beau said as she sat on the floor next to Gideon. She pulled him into her lap and kissed the top of his head before looking up at Elizabet. "What's up?"

Elizabet shook the stack of papers she held. "It's overwhelming. I haven't a clue if people will pay for this."

The Tremaines were embarking on—and this term was used loosely—a musical career. Jareth announced they would be the next Von Trapp Family Singers. To raise money for church reform, they were forming a show that would draw an elite crowd. The tickets would be pricey and the music would be classical Gregorian chant. How appropriate for a medieval family. All proceeds would benefit the furthering of the divide between government regulations and the doctrine of the Church. While the Tremaine coffers were heavy, they were not bottomless, and flaunting their wealth was never an option. A trust would be set up to provide scholarships for young reformers, particularly those seeking entrance into reformation colleges. According to Jareth, it was all about informing and catechizing the next generation. It was not about a large following, but rather the right followers with a destiny to do what was right by informed doctrinal practices.

"I think if you open your mouth, they'll think they're hearing angels singing," Beau said. Elizabet smirked and rolled her eyes. "Just sayin'. I'm in awe of your voice and I've heard it all my life."

"That's what I'm saying," Jeremy said. He smiled a dopey grin when Beau looked at him and let her heart show in her eyes. It was always this way when they first set eyes on each other for a new day. "I think a hundred bucks a ticket is a steal."

Beau looked back to Elizabet. "You have another month or so to practice. What's bothering you?"

Elizabet looked uncomfortable, but shared anyway. "The weather." She glanced at Jeremy. "It's getting colder. Things will get . . ." She shook her head and tucked the papers into the folder lying on the table beside her. "Complicated."

"See," Jeremy said. "She's worried about me, not this new adventure." He shook his head. "It's not as if we are doing the concerts in extreme environments. We will control the venues."

"There's the issue of your plans." Elizabet frowned slightly. She crossed her arms and leaned back with a huff. "How can we know you'll be up to par when all of this takes shape?"

"He's not still harassing you about homecoming, is he?"

Beau asked, glaring at Jeremy. Jeremy's expression was guilty, but he smiled with charm. "He knows that I would rather walk myself than for him to risk it." She looked up at Elizabet. "Caesar is not an option. I don't know what he told you, but I never agreed to take him up on that. It's not like this is a life-changing event. I was chosen because I'm Rixby's sister and scouts are all crazy over him right now." She rolled her eyes when Jeremy sat straighter as if affronted she could think such a thing. She was not stupid. She was not popular. She was chosen by default of her relation to the prize quarterback for the Gueydan Bears. "Don't be so dramatic, Jeremy. Besides, Rixby said he'd behave and if I want him to walk me, he will." She shrugged. "I think it'll be okay. It'll make him look great to be out there at half time—like he cares and all that."

"What about you?" Elizabet asked, her voice soft.

Beau slumped a bit. "I'll live." She waved her hand in the air. "It's not like I wanted this. I just have to make it through the humiliation of standing in front a stadium of people who know I shouldn't be up there."

"It will look great on your college resumes," Elizabet inserted.

Beau cleared her throat. She did not know if there would be any college resumes for her. "Yeah, there's that too."

"You have just as much right to be up there as anyone else," Jeremy said with conviction. "You're the star pitcher for the parish league. That should count for something."

Beau lowered her gaze. Gideon's hair tickled her nose. They did not need to know the reason she never played for the high school was because she could not stand the snickers and jokes when she took the field. A person could only be called crazy so much before it infected one's soul. The parish team was different. Those from adjoining schools were forgiving and only cared that her pitch was clocked at lightning speed.

"Mummy," Solomon said, walking over to her holding out

a sheet of music. It broke Beau's concentration. She rubbed her cheek against Gideon's head as Elizabet accepted the paper with a raised brow. Solomon waved to the contents of the music. "It's jumbled. Can you help?"

Elizabet's lips trembled, but she smiled. "I'll call your daddy and he can help." She looked up at Jeremy, who shrugged as if he had done all he could.

"It's pretty basic," Jeremy murmured. His face pinked slightly and he shrugged one shoulder again. Beau felt a pain in her heart. Solomon was dyslexic like Elizabet; Jeremy often had to defer to Jareth when tutoring the boy. It was a struggle to keep him up with his siblings.

Elizabet scanned the music, her hand reaching to idly stroke Solomon's head. The touch was evidently soothing to the child. "Lennon and McCartney," she said, her voice low. "They'll get you every time."

"We could switch to something less complicated," Jeremy offered. He came to stand before Beau. His slipper socks were fluffy and had snowmen on them. "We don't have to do Eleanor Rigby." He sat beside Beau, his body stretching out beside her. His hand rested near her hip. "I chose it because of Abigail's newfound love of the violin. She'd rock that song."

Solomon gave a curt nod. "Let's keep it, then. I'll manage."

Beau leaned against Jeremy, his arm bracing her back. The children's ability to be so mature always amazed her. "Nice socks." She smirked. He had to be near freezing to wear anything on his feet. The boy practically went everywhere possible barefooted.

"Don't be a hater," Jeremy said, his toes curling.

"Hey!" Elizabet said, her voice raising a notch. She looked pointedly at the slipper socks. "Those are mine. Jareth gave me those last Christmas."

"Dover winters are brutal," Jeremy explained to Beau with a grin. "Thermal panels can only manage so much heat in an old, drafty castle."

Elizabet shook her head, a smile trembling on her mouth as she turned her attention back to Solomon. "We'll see what your dad says. He'll know what to do. I promise you'll be brilliant as always."

Solomon wrapped his arms around her, squeezing her and his eyes shut in evident adoration. Beau looked at Jeremy and found him watching her. Half of his mouth tugged upwards and his eyes crinkled.

"I love you," she could not help but mouth, a sigh tangling in the breath she used. It came out like a squeak and that made Jeremy flash a full smile.

"I know," he said.

Her heart flipped over. She loved him and this family. Times like these were precious memories she greedily gathered.

"Did you go the clinic yet? Did I miss it?" Beau asked.

Jeremy shook his head. "Practice was longer than I anticipated." The way his gaze avoided Solomon made her heart squeeze. "I pushed back the class until five. Wanna come?"

Beau nodded. "Definitely."

If seeing him with his siblings was smoking, then watching him with autistic kids was on fire. Jeremy volunteered his time weekly to a clinic Jareth set up for autistic children. Most of them were mildly afflicted and followed the lessons with ease. Jeremy took his time, allowing the kids to parallel play and learn at their own pace. He provided them with instruction on various musical instruments. Beau had a feeling it was more about building relationships and connecting with the kids that he did this. At best, a few of the children would pluck a few guitar strings and maybe sing a line or two. But it was vastly satisfying to Jeremy to be there and love on those kids. Even when it got out of hand and one of them acted out, he knew what to do and turned it into something positive.

"But you'll have to change those hideous socks. I won't be

seen in public with you like that," she added.

Jeremy smirked. "Weakling. I never took you as one to care for outward appearances." He wiggled his toes. "They'll love these. It will be a good ice breaker."

There was no answer that would do justice to what she was feeling. She felt again as though she was merely receiving while Jeremy kept giving and giving. It was impossible to keep up with all his life entailed. Being Jeremiah Cameron Tremaine must be exhausting.

Chapter 9

:The best thing about The Brac? That's easy. The food—definitely the food.:

—Jeremy Tremaine on why living in the Cayman Islands was essential

TWO WEEKS BEFORE HOMECOMING, THE fear became real. An ice storm rolled into South Louisiana. This was as odd as Louisiana having polar bears and penguins, but in classic southern style, the temperature could fluctuate twenty to thirty degrees on any given day. Desperate times called for desperate measures. All of the planning and calculating about homecoming and family concerts came to a screeching halt. Jeremy was sent home to the Cayman Islands to wait until the temperature consistently rose above fifty degrees. Not only was he banished as he called it, but he had to fly there . . . in an airplane. Jareth did not allow him to risk his health by dissipating. While Jeremy fought for his right to fly via his body, he was vetoed. Even though he could have taken to the atmosphere and been fine, the government was planting new satellites, and this concerned Jareth.

It was humiliating. He nearly hyperventilated on the plane multiple times. Not controlling the flying sucked. He likened the trip to being cooped up in a coffin for twelve hours. The insistent urge to throw a tantrum was keen. His body was more than capable of taking off and landing in extreme cold. What happened once he landed was what was important. Going from cold to warm was easy; he didn't see what the big deal was. It was those regulated satellites that had his travel arrangements jacked up.

"Eggs?" Eddie asked, holding the frying pan.

Eddie was Jeremy's uncle—his dad's birth brother. A Presbyterian minister by choice and trade, and a human volcano graciously bestowed via Mount St. Helens. Eddie was the only blood relative with whom Jeremy willfully remained in contact.

"Naw," Jeremy said, speaking through a mouth already full. "I ate a whole tube of bagels and an entire jar of peanut butter." He held up the banana he was devouring. "Dessert."

"Hmmm." Eddie frowned. He tipped his head to the side. "Do you hear that?" Jeremy stopped chewing and inclined his head. "That's the sound of my grocery bill going through the roof." Jeremy then blew a raspberry, and bits of banana flew everywhere.

Darian, the newest resident host, snickered and shoved his plate away. "I'm done." He looked at Eddie. "Can I go down to the beach? I'd like to have a swim."

A tornado by form, Darian was Minh's responsibility, but Minh's sister had gone into preterm labor. Both Gabriel and Minh would be out of commission for a while. Eddie was babysitting, as he so fondly called it.

"If Jeremy goes, sure." Eddie cast a glance at Jeremy, who merely shrugged his consent. He had nothing better to do. "I'm good with it. Lunch at noon sharp. Don't be late or I'll send out a search party." He shook his head and stared down at the frying pan he held. "Although I have no idea what to feed bottomless pits for lunch, or any other meal for that matter."

Jeremy grinned. He had missed his uncle. Standing a total of five feet, three inches, Uncle Eddie was the nicest guy he knew. Totally the granola type, Eddie had long brown hair that reached his waist. It was wavy and wild, just like his normal expression. He had a smile that made his cheeks round, and he rarely showed his teeth. His attire hardly ever changed: cargo shorts, a band T-shirt, and Vans. On cool nights, perhaps a flannel long-sleeved shirt served as a jacket, but never more. On Sundays, he wore the same to the pulpit. He was the most popular minister in the area.

"I just gotta grab some gear," Jeremy announced as he stood. He grabbed his shirt from the back of the chair and draped it over his shoulder. "I need to be reunited with *Kittiwake*." *Kittiwake* was the wreckage of an old rescue ship that sank offshore of Seven Mile Beach. There was something about floating among the wreckage that was peaceful. The scuba gear was in case he ran into another diver who found it odd that he was diving in his own skin and nothing else. The gear served solely as props.

It had been five minutes since Jeremy had thought of Beau and then his heart squeezed and he got brain freeze. It was painful even thinking of her, remembering the look on her face when he said goodbye after he promised never to leave her again. Even though it wasn't forever, stuff like this was bound to happen. His body simply could not live in the environment currently taking over Louisiana. It was the same with Dover and London. There were times past when the Brac, the smallest of the Cayman Islands where Dover's Amalgam headquarters was stationed, had been his refuge.

Jeremy rubbed the area where his heart beat. "Where's my phone?"

Eddie pointed to the counter. "Best leave it here. I'm not Jareth. I won't replace it if you get it wet."

"I'll just shoot Beau a text before I go."

Darian rose and took his dishes to the sink. "I'll meet you on the porch."

Jeremy nodded, punched a text out.

Going diving. Skype tonight?

Placing the phone in the back pocket of his shorts, he left

the room and went to get the scuba gear. He met Darian on the grand porch that surrounded the white plantation style rectory.

A female voice surprised him from the steps. "Can I go diving?"

Jeremy stopped in his tracks, the hair on his nape standing on end. Malia was the only reason he hated being here. "Uh, no." He snapped his shirt from his shoulder and pulled it over his head. "Hell no."

"Please don't dress on my behalf," Malia purred, ignoring the hostility in his voice. "I was enjoying the view. You have the finest happy trail I know."

Jeremy's mouth twisted, but he said nothing. He could feel the pheromones streaming off her. She was beautiful, he had to give it her. Native of Sri Lanka, she had long, shiny black hair, naturally tan skin, and green eyes. He should also remind himself that she was a lethal tsunami and a woman scorned and all that.

He motioned for Darian and they began the trek that led them to the beach. He rotated his shoulders as he walked, fighting off the tension Malia caused, enjoying the scenery and the perfect warm weather conditions. His cell phone vibrated in his back pocket.

Chemistry test tomorrow. Not as smart as you. 11pm good? It's gonna be a late night.

Jeremy smiled. Any time was good for him as long as he got to see Beau. He typed his reply.

"What's she like?" Darian nodded to his phone. Darian looked as if he should be a Californian. Blond, tall and lanky, the body of a surfer. It was hard to believe they grew them like that in Oklahoma. The guy played hockey and had been scouted by colleges before he was turned. It was hard imagining him in an ice sport.

"She's great," Jeremy said. They came to the clearing of the beach. He wedged his phone in the Y of a tree trunk and shucked his shirt again.

"Prettier than Malia?" Darian asked with a lopsided grin.

Jeremy frowned and grabbed Darian's wrist. He siphoned what he needed to know and thrust Darian's arm away.

Darian's face reddened in anger. "You really shouldn't have done that," he said, massaging his wrist. "It's none of your business. She's not your girlfriend anymore."

"Thank God for that," Jeremy said. "Literally. And she was never really my girlfriend. Check that little info I just gave you, bro. You'll need to know when to run."

"You know what it's like, living here. All the stupid rules."

"Malia isn't the answer for entertainment." He felt sorry for Darian, truly he did. Being a new host in training was brutal, especially with Minh as his guardian. It was hours of battle-field training and the rest of life was learning how to control the abilities you never asked for. Minh could be a jerk. As a former Minister of War, he expected perfection. "She's bad news." That was putting it mildly.

"She loves me, and you're jealous."

"Hardly," Jeremy replied, annoyance in his voice. It was moot to discuss this. Malia had toyed with Darian's emotions. He would be a Malia fan until she slammed a touch of reality into him, figuratively speaking. "Look, just forget it. I'm not going to say anything, but I want you to promise something."

Darian looked wary.

"Promise me you won't do anything stupid. If she dumps you, I want you to call me, okay?"

"Why would I call you?"

Emotions were high when physical relationships were concerned. He understood that. And Malia would break this guy's heart when he realized their link was not exclusive. "Because once Malia feeds you a giant spoonful of the bitter truth, you're gonna need someone to talk you down from going rogue."

JEREMY SET UP THE LAPTOP on the kitchen table after everyone else was in bed. After diving, he came home, showered, dressed, and went to meet Eddie at the church. They were replacing the church roof and he offered his assistance. It made the time go faster. Before he knew it, it was dinnertime and then nightly devotionals, then lights out. He was the only host not regulated to lights out here, because he was not a regular.

"Wow," Jeremy breathed when Beau's face became visible on the computer screen. He adjusted the laptop so the camera was centered. "You look amazing."

Beau's lips bent in sarcasm. "My hair is wet, I have no make-up on and I'm wearing your old shirt." She smiled then and lifted her shoulder, turning her head to sniff. "It smells like salt water taffy."

"Like I said, you look amazing. I love seeing you in my shirt. It's hot."

She giggled. "You're crazy."

"Crazy for you." It was a horrific pun, but he didn't care. It was true and he loved hearing her laugh. "How was the study session?"

"Caesar came over and helped," she said. "My brain does not get that type of math. Who combined science with math anyway?"

"You should see the equations it takes to prove time travel. Only Gideon of the future can explain it and make it sound logical." He lifted his glass of orange juice in salute. "Here's to science equations. May the people who understand them leave us alone."

"Aye-aye!" Beau laughed. "I'll probably use chemistry in everyday life . . . not." Her laughter tapered off as she watched him empty his glass. "How was diving?"

"Same old thing. I went to some wreckage off the coast. No big deal." He wiped his mouth with the back of his hand and set the glass away. "The weather is perfect, as always. I wish there were a way to harness it and carry it wherever I go."

"I love the pictures you sent me. The water is so clear. Nothing like Holly Beach."

Jeremy pulled a face. "Yeah, and we don't have e-coli in the water here."

"Hey, go chemistry! We just used it in everyday life."

"Naw, that's microbiology."

"Well, then, my case is closed," she said smugly. "I'll probably never use it, so what's the point in torturing myself on what will end up a C at best. I'm gonna rebel and refuse to study. That way I can Skype with you earlier and whenever I want."

The swinging door to the kitchen creaked and Jeremy looked up. Malia strolled in wearing the shortest hot pink shorts Jeremy had ever seen. The tank top she wore held no secrets either. A train wreck was about to happen and he didn't want to become a fatality.

"Yeah, uh, listen, I have to go." Jeremy put his hand on the laptop, ready to snap it closed if necessary.

"No need to end your chat on account of me," Malia's voice was loud and bold.

Jeremy ground his jaw as Beau's expression fell. Her hands went to her lap where he could imagine she clasped them, fidgeting. Her sudden change in demeanor let him know she heard the interruption. "Malia," he mouthed.

Beau's nod was small and pitiful. She ran her hands down the sides of her head to smooth her hair down and then rearranged her shirt. Jeremy felt her insecurities like a punch in the stomach. He knew how it would look if Malia came into view. He was shirtless, wearing shorts and barefooted and Malia was typical Malia.

Then his worst nightmare happened: Malia sauntered around the table. "Let me see what the big deal is," she said with a smile. She moved behind Jeremy and peeked at the screen.

Jeremy could see how they looked in the Skype box, him seated and her standing over him. They appeared cozy and intimately dressed for bed. It was awful.

"She's adorable, Jeremy," Malia exclaimed, a hand over her barely concealed chest. "Really, truly adorable." She put her hands on his shoulders and squeezed. "So natural. Just like a cute little country mouse."

Jeremy bucked her off. "Don't touch me," he warned.

Malia laughed and held her hands up in mock surrender. "No worries, Jeremy. I'll leave you two alone. I was just passing through for a snack." She wagged her fingers. "Bye-bye, country mouse. Pleasant dreams."

"Beau," Jeremy started when Malia went away. "It's lights out over here. Everyone is in bed. I didn't know she would come down. I have better Wi-Fi reception down here."

"You don't need to explain," Beau said, but her lips stiffened. "Lights out? So, you're like, alone with her?"

Jeremy ran his hand on the screen, over Beau's image, wanting so badly to touch her and make things better. If he could touch her, she would know that she had nothing to worry about. He clasped the laptop and stood up. "You can watch me go upstairs and lock myself in my room. Deal?"

"You don't have to do that on account of me." Beau muttered, but he saw the relief in her gaze. She sighed and threw herself back on the stack of pillows behind her. "Be quick about it. It's late and I have school in the morning. As it is, I'll spend the rest of the night crying into my pillow."

"If she's a country mouse," Malia wondered. "What does that make me?" Jeremy looked over his shoulder and gave Malia a stare that said he didn't care in the least. He was doing his best to get out of there before things went from bad to worse. She smiled over her coffee cup. "Oh, I know. A sleek she-panther." She made a claw like motion with her hand and swiped at him with a low, humming growl.

Jeremy kicked a chair between them as he passed. It tipped on its side legs and fell to the floor with a loud crash in the quiet kitchen. Malia roared with laughter. The sound of her voice became muffled as the swinging door closed after his exit.

He took the stairs two at time up to the third floor. His room was the conservatory at the top of the staircase, the warmest room in the house. Surrounded completely by windows, the heat was unbearable to some, but not Jeremy.

"Locking the door," he said as he fumbled with the doorknob.

"Can't she just bust through there? I mean, she's like you. Locks won't stop her."

Jeremy sat on the edge of the bed and balanced the laptop on his thighs. He tipped the screen back. Her forlorn expression made his heart hurt. "She wouldn't dare come up here. Believe me, she did that just to get a rise from me. I've been ignoring her since I've been home."

"She's beautiful, Jeremy. What are you doing with me?" Beau muttered.

"Loving you. Being ecstatic out of my mind that I won you." Jeremy fumbled with the computer as it slid off the slope of his lap. "You don't see yourself the way I see you."

"No one sees me the way you do," Beau said ruefully. Her mouth twisted. "I think you might be a little bit blind. I am a country mouse."

"I have perfect vision." He smiled. He ignored the nasty little nickname Malia had pinned. "I like you being my secret. If everyone knew how awesome you were, I wouldn't stand a chance."

A reluctant smile curved on Beau's lips.

"Are you mad at me?" Jeremy sighed, his shoulders drooping. He knew she wasn't angry with him, but the circumstances. "I wish I could touch you and make everything better. I don't like seeing you like this. You know, you've nothing to worry about. I'm all yours."

"You have no idea how much I want one of your mind si-phoning touches right about now," Beau admitted. "I want to trust what you say, but Malia isn't what I expected. She's more."

"You're more," Jeremy declared.

"Oh, Jeremy," Beau groaned. "I'm such a mess when you aren't here. The minute you were out of my sight, I turned into a complete ninny. I know I should trust you. You never gave me a reason not to. And I really want to be strong and all that, but then this happens. I look like this." She motioned to her face. "You look like that." She pointed to him. "And now I know what *she* looks like." Anger shadowed her face. "Beautiful Malia who is obviously still into you. How can I help being jealous? You're way over there. I don't know what's going on other than what I see over Skype and pictures you send me. You never post anything on social media. You've got hours and hours away from me with lots of free time. What do you do over there? I mean, you've been there less than a week and all I get is that you eat, dive, and play with exotic birds." She huffed. "Oh yeah, and you work at the church."

"That's pretty much it."

She huffed again.

"You have to trust me," Jeremy pleaded. "I'm with you. After all those years, it's you and me. Remember that. Remember everything I told you and passed to you."

"I do," she said. "I play it over and over, on repeat in my head. I keep telling myself that I'm being stupid to worry, but then Malia pops up on our Skype session and I'm a mess again."

"I really wish I could make it better," he said. "Do you want random posts? I thought you would rather I kept things just between us."

"I'm being stupid," she brooded. "I know you don't like posting stuff. You only like mine to humor me." She punched a stuffed animal on her bed. "Do whatever you want. We have thousands of miles and practically an ocean between us. It's not like I can make you or stop you from doing anything."

"Beau," he growled.

She flapped her hand. "Yeah, yeah, yeah. Let me have my tantrum. I'll be alright. Eventually."

"What's the temperature over there?"

Beau picked up her phone. "Thirty-one." She glared at him. "Stop trying to change the subject."

"Yikes."

She frowned as he made her realize he was done with bickering. "The highest prediction is forty at the end of the week."

"If it holds at forty and above, I'll be able to come back."

"There is another ice storm on this one's tail," Beau said with a sigh. "It will shoot up to forty for like—two hours on Friday and then rocket back down to the teens."

"Meteorologists make mistakes. We can hope," Jeremy replied.

"Homecoming will be a disaster. Even if you weren't escorting me, you would be there to hear me wail after it was over and done. I won't have anyone to vent to."

"Caesar loves when you wail," he teased, although it pained him to do so. He hated that Caesar was there and he was not. He had to be the example, however, and show the trust he was extending. "He thrives on that stuff."

"What a social butterfly, right?" She laughed tightly.

"He's 'naturally charismatic,'" Jeremy quoted what Caesar said over and over.

"So he says," she said and held up her phone, showing him the screen. "It's almost midnight." Her voice was grumbly and irate. He could sense she still wasn't ready to let everything go. It hurt that she would pull away instead of want to talk it through.

"Yeah, I know." He ran his hand over her image. He wished he could feel her, but he would allow her to run and lick her wounds. There was always tomorrow to make things better. "You better get on to bed. I don't want you falling asleep in chemistry tomorrow."

She pulled a face. "Why'd you have to remind me? Strike that word from your vocabulary. It annoys me. Add that to the list of things that causes me pain and suffering."

A half smile formed on Jeremy's mouth. "I love you."

Beau ran her fingers over his image. Her face softened when she heard the sincerity in his tone. "Same."

Once Beau's image was gone, Jeremy slid off the bed and onto the floor, and let the laptop fall aside. He thumped the back of his head on the bed behind him a few times in frustration. Jareth went on about how it was such a privilege to be who he was, what a great honor it was to have this mutation fall on him. There were times he knew Jareth said stuff like that to point to the bright side, to have Jeremy be appreciative that he had alternatives and he was free. And then there were time like these; the times that made him ache for the semblance of normal life he had long ago. A life where he would never have to leave Beau's side.

Beau tugged the switch to the bedside lamp and snuggled down under the covers. Tears swam in her eyes as she considered Jeremy, hundreds of miles away, with the goddess of beauty. She was being ridiculous, but she couldn't help it. It was the way of things: jealousy and the teenage life. They went hand in hand and she was walking with them whether she wanted to or not. She and jealousy were virtual BFFs.

The next morning, her phone lit up with a Facebook notification: Friend Request.

She skimmed to the app and pulled it up. Friend request from Malia Perera. Her thumb hovered over the delete button. Instead, she went to Malia's page and found it was a public page. She hit follow and saved the request for later. There was no way she wanted to accept the request, but she would stalk

her. She went through all of Malia's photos. There were ten total pictures taken with Jeremy from two years ago. She took
screenshots and saved them to her phone. It was evident she
was entering into self-harm. Inflicting pain by way of dwelling
on the past was her new hobby. Another teenage idiosyncrasy
she could add to her list of woes.

Caesar snuck up behind Beau and shouted in her ear. "What
are you looking at?"

She jumped, fumbling not to drop her phone. Wearing
gloves made her clumsy, and now she couldn't swipe the phone
and hide the picture she was moping over.

"What the heck, Julius?" she sneered. He hated his first
name. Who named their kid Julius Caesar? She balled up her
fist and struck him in the chest. It didn't do any good. He was
wearing three layers of clothing.

"You know you don't need to worry about that girl, right?"

"I don't know what you're talking about." She sniffed and
started walking away. She weaved between people to get to the
front of the line for her bus. She wanted a good seat up close to
the heater. "Go pick on somebody else."

Caesar caught her arm. "I'm talking about Malia."

Beau gaped. "How . . . ? What . . . ?

"Jeremy is my best friend." His eyebrows lifted, and then
disappeared beneath his red paisley bandanna. "We talk." He
glanced around at the crowd surrounding them. "Let's get out
of here. Come on, I'll drive you home, like old times. I know
you hate to ride the bus. Don't act like you're a liberal woman.
Unless you've taken a liking to being packed like a sardine."

Beau glanced around. She did hate riding the bus. It was
worse now that she had gotten used to *not* riding it. Whenever
Jeremy was here, he picked her up and they went for a run or
hung out.

"You'll run with me?" she asked tentatively.

"Uh, no?" he answered slowly, but she could see him

considering it. "You know what? Sure. Blow that junk away and live a little. Let's go." He tugged on her arm and led her out of the mangled line.

"I don't have any junk to blow away," she grumbled. "I just don't want to ride in a smelly bus today."

"Whatever. I'll take it." He glanced back, a grin on his face. "I promised Jerm I'd watch out for you. Now I get to say that I managed it at least a little." He fumbled in his pocket and pulled out his keys.

"I don't need anybody watching out for me."

Caesar grinned and unlocked the car doors with the remote. "Sure, princess. Whatever you say."

Caesar didn't get the door for her. He never did. That was the good thing about Caesar—or perhaps the bad. She wasn't sure anymore. Only Jeremy opened doors for her and treated her like she was fragile. Like she was loved beyond measure and adored.

Tears came from out of nowhere. She climbed into the Jeep and buckled up, her teeth chattering in the freezing interior.

"*Geez!*" Caesar shivered and slammed the door. He revved up the engine and put the heat on high. His breath made puffs of smoke. "Wish I had a cold intolerant condition and I could be on a tropical island somewhere."

Jeremy's family was telling everyone he had a medical condition that made him cold intolerant. This was a perfect excuse as to why they had a home in the Cayman Islands. No one asked any questions.

"Yeah, me, too." Or maybe she could become a human tsunami and things would start to look up. Caesar wiped the windshield with his gloved hand.

Until Jeremy came home, Beau thought Caesar was the best looking guy she had ever seen. Being a burnt ginger added to his allure. His hair was healthy, shiny, and long. It set him apart from everyone else, and he wore it with confidence. He had color to him, and blue eyes that sometimes looked green, depending on what he wore. His body was strong, but not bulky. She knew he worked out, but he didn't go overboard with the weights.

"Are you crying, Benoit?"

Beau closed her eyes and turned her head away. "Let's just go." She squeezed her eyes shut. "I failed that frickin' chemistry test today. I want to get home, change, and go for a run." She kicked the dashboard.

"Liar."

She let out a strangled sound. "Fine. Tell me what you know about her."

"Look at me."

Beau opened her eyes and rolled them. "Does it make a difference whether I look at you?"

He laughed. "No, I guess not. You're still gonna say you're not crying when you really are."

She looked at him, a smile tugging on her trembling mouth. "You're such a jerk."

"Yeah, I know." He tapped her cold nose with his gloved finger. The cold air that had been streaming from the A/C began to warm up. Caesar reached between them and put the Jeep in reverse. "So, where do you want me to start?"

"I don't know," she snapped. "Stop playing with me." She slapped his arm. "Start from the beginning. How do you know about the goddess of beauty?"

"Is that what you call her?" He sounded amused. She struck him again. "Okay, ouch. That's enough. It stings when you hit me. Wait 'til I warm up." She balled her fist. He palmed it and pushed it away. "This is all you need to know: Jeremy doesn't want her. End of story. She's a mean, clingy brat with jealousy issues."

Beau pressed her lips into a hard line. A burst of laughter left Caesar's mouth when he spotted her expression. "Seriously.

That's it. Did you expect some sordid story? This is Jeremy's life we're rehashing. Remember? Boring Jeremy would never have an ex who was actually interesting." He put the Jeep in drive and pulled out of the school parking lot. "They didn't really date even. The L word was never involved. Not according to Jeremy, at least. It was all one sided, and that was her side." He glanced down at her phone in her hand. "Why do you have pictures of her and Jeremy on your phone?" She looked up at him with wide, watery eyes. "It's kinda creepy, Beau, just sayin'."

"She sent me a friend request."

"So, you're stalking her instead of accepting the request? Yeah, that's normal and not stalker-like." He looked at her pointedly. "Like maybe you have clingy, jealousy issues."

Beau exhaled forcefully. "You don't understand."

"Oh, I get the picture. You're crazy over Jeremy and you're jealous. There's this hot girl on the island with him and you're stuck over here—with me, no less—and it's driving you insane with worry that he'll dump you when he realizes . . . What? Help me out here, what is he going to realize?"

"That he still loves beautiful Malia." She couldn't help but sound bitter.

"Well, that would be something, but newsflash: he *never loved Malia*. Were you listening while I was talking?" He frowned, peeking up at the red light as they approached. "She might be beautiful, but Jeremy knew that already."

"What do you mean?"

"Duh. Obvs, Beau." He rolled his eyes, mimicking her. "Jeremy knows what Malia looks like. He had, what? Two years just to stare at her and do what he wanted with her?"

Beau seethed with the thought of that. Of course, Caesar was right, but she was loath to admit it. This jealousy thing was hard to shake. It weighed on her shoulders as though she wore a heavy backpack. She wanted to wallow in it when she knew it was crazy.

"Truth." Caesar made a chopping motion with his hand to get her thoughts back on track. "Jerm had his chance with the goddess of beauty and still, he came back, found you, and swept you off your feet."

She absorbed what he said. There was truth in it. She swiped open her picture app and stared at what she liked to call 'the most hated' of the bunch. They were in the water near the beach, surrounded by clear aqua water and white sand. Tropical paradise. Jeremy had Malia on his shoulders. Both of their perfect bodies were in itty bitty swimming suits. It was the smile that got her. That smile Jeremy owned where all his sweet bashfulness was on display. His hands were wrapped around Malia's thin calves as if it were something he did everyday.

This picture seared her insides. The trouble with jealousy was that it had something like this to attach to. Living, breathing proof that something special had transpired between the love of her life and this beautiful girl.

Caesar grabbed her phone. Beau lunged for it, but he held out of her way, claimed she'd cause an accident if she didn't calm down. He looked at the picture and frowned.

"Give me my phone," she demanded.

He tossed it into her lap. "You're going to drive yourself crazy. You're digging up things that happened a long time ago. If Jeremy found out what you're doing, it wouldn't sit well with him. He'd be furious."

"Jeremy's never furious," she grumbled. She braced her feet on the dashboard. Caesar hated when she did that, but she did it anyway. She hugged her knees. "All he cares about is—"

"You," Caesar spat. He cursed and punched the gas pedal. The Jeep lurched forward. "He's obsessed with you, Beau. If I'm being honest here, sometimes it creeps me out how much he digs you. He's made a hobby out of dating you. We only hang out when you're tied up with work or practice."

Beau sat up. Although Caesar was saying this stuff like it was bad, it was music to her ears. Of course it wasn't true. Jeremy had a whole other life Caesar knew nothing about. There were times he went to medieval Dover without her, to work on a church reform project. He had the clinic meetings with autistic children once a week. And other times, he went to Amalgam meetings where she wasn't allowed. But he did spend a lot of time with her—that was true.

"He made me swear that I wouldn't let anyone touch you while he was gone, including me." He scoffed. "Made me promise to watch over you while you were at school, home, work . . . wherever you go, I'm supposed to be glued to you. Do you think I *wanted* to freeze my nuts off in the bus line earlier? Do you think I *want* to go for a run on icy roads where I'll probably slip and end up with a concussion?

"You're doing all of this because Jeremy asked you to?"

"Did I ever babysit you before?"

"No," she answered immediately. He turned to her with a smirk.

"Well, thanks, I guess." She glanced down at the image still on her phone screen.

"Delete that crap or I'll do it for you," he rumbled. "You're torturing yourself over something that doesn't even exist."

Beau's eyes roamed Jeremy's face on the image. The way his black hair molded to his head when it was damp, the way it curled at his tan neck. His wide mouth with that killer smile. The shy blue gaze that she loved so much.

She hit the delete button and watched the picture swipe into nothing.

Caesar released a long exhale as they pulled into the grocery store lot. The store was complete but they still lived in the full-size trailer FEMA had loaned out. It was next door to the store, so family visitors used the parking lot of the store, too. He parked but left the Jeep idling. "Now, that's settled. I guess you're going to make me freeze my bits off anyway. We still running?"

She didn't feel like smiling yet, but she forced one. "You know it, Randolph. Tuck 'em in, 'cause I'm going to smoke you. I have some tension to leave on the road."

They Skyped early that night. Beau set up the computer camera on the desk, pointed to where she could be seen while doing yoga poses. Caesar was lying on her bed, tossing a baseball up in the air. It hit the ceiling and then spun back down. He was driving her nuts with the repetition of it. The noise was breaking her concentration.

Jeremy appeared with a green bird walking around his desk. "Hey," he greeted.

Beau went from downward dog into cobra. "Hey."

Jeremy tilted his head like he was looking upside down. "Whoa. Trouble with your run today?"

Beau grimaced. "I strained my back."

Caesar snorted. "I strained my body."

"Caesar?" Jeremy asked, a smile on his face. "Is that you?"

Caesar sat up, leaned forward and made the peace sign.

"I texted you earlier. Are you having trouble with your reception?" Jeremy asked.

"It's dead. I left it charging at home. Can't use it at school anyway."

"Bummer," Jeremy said, and then passed a berry to the bird. "I was wondering how things were going." He tried to look nonchalant, but failed.

Beau grunted. "He's here, babysitting me. Does that answer your question?"

"We're busted, man. Bad day all around," Caesar said. "Don't ask—you don't want to know."

"Are you mad, angel? I only wanted to be sure you were all right. I knew there would be bad days. I've got them, as well. At least you have Caesar for comic relief."

Beau hovered in plank, doing a tricep push up. "You suck,

Jeremy," she breathed.

Caesar caved. "She had some pictures of you and Malia on her phone."

Beau went belly down with a huff. "Caesar!"

Jeremy grimaced. "Why?"

"Why not?" Beau groused. She sat up, smoothed her hair from her face and secured it with the rest of her contained ponytail. "I'm a basket case, all right?"

"Caesar, can I talk to Beau, alone?" Jeremy asked.

Caesar stood up and saluted. "She's all yours." He leaned down and kissed the top of Beau's head. "Just remember what we talked about," he murmured.

She nodded, swatting his legs as he stepped over her. The rooms were like closets in their temporary dwelling. He closed the door, the sound of his retreating footfalls echoing away.

"What was Caesar doing in your bedroom?"

Beau balked. That caught her off guard. "Are you serious?" she sputtered. "He was helping me study after we came back from running. I failed my chemistry test today. No thanks to you."

"Now your grades are my fault?"

Beau leaned forward and cupped her non-existent cleavage together. "She's adorable, Jeremy. A cute little country mouse," her voice mimicked Malia's accent perfectly. She flipped him off and crossed her arms. "She was practically naked. I'm supposed to understand how things are with you, but you freak out over Caesar? *Caesar?* Really?"

"You know how he feels about you," Jeremy said, his voice rough.

"We never dated, Jeremy! He's not my ex, just a friend. There is no comparison. And you're the one who asked him to follow me like I'm a baby. Don't get all stupid when you're only getting what you asked for."

"He was in your bedroom," he accused, his eyes flashing

with anger. "And you're dressed like that." His gaze dipped to her chest.

Beau looked down at her sports bra and yoga pants. "You've got to be kidding!" She glared at his image. "The boy who hates clothing is going to preach to me." She snapped her wrist his way. "You run around in your boxers half the time. Your Calvins are like what the red cape is to Superman."

"I'll be careful to remember that you feel so strongly about my dress code in the future," he sneered.

"Ugh!" Beau reached up and grabbed the camera. "I don't know why I bother." She yanked hard on the cord, and the laptop and a stack of homework flew to the floor in a scatter. The laptop broke into two pieces.

She blinked at the catastrophe she had caused. The camera's wires were exposed and the computer screen flashed as though it was having a seizure. *Damn it!* It had taken her a year's salary to save for that computer. Once again, her anger had destroyed something of value.

On shaky legs she rose and rummaged for her phone so she could text Jeremy and apologize. She shouldn't have blown up. She should have stayed calm and rational. That's how Jeremy was: calm, rational, sane.

But he had been jealous, too. Hadn't he?

Beau groaned and smacked her palm to her head. Her phone was in Caesar's Jeep. They used it as a GPS for their run and she left it charging when they went into the store for something to drink.

She dropped her face into her hands and began to cry. After a minute, she grabbed her pillow and screamed into it several times. *I don't know why I bother.* Why had she said that? It wasn't a bother. She loved Jeremy. They were just going through a rough time.

She showered and went to bed. She would text Jeremy first thing when she got her phone back. He would understand. He always did. It was the way he was wired.

Chapter 10

"I can travel faster than Continental Airlines and there
aren't any waiting times or delays. I can fly in any weather. If it's
cold, I just fly higher and then jackknife into the atmosphere. That
way, the cold barely has time to slow me down. Just have food ready
when I land—lots and lots of food."
—Jeremy bragging to Elizabet on his skills of flight, age eleven

JEREMY ENTERED THEIR HOME WHEN Beau's dad left the door open to go outside for a smoke. It was almost midnight, but he knew her parents kept late hours. They always had.

The warm interior of the trailer grected him, enveloped him like a warm glove. He allowed his body to take form, his boxers in his hand. Ducking into the laundry room, he slipped them on.

He had traveled at top speed, the weather slowing him somewhat when he reached Alabama. That was when he left the atmosphere. For some unexplainable reason, when he did that, temperature was no longer a factor, but he could only hold the course for short periods of time. He would be back in the Caymans by daybreak. Traveling this way was something he rarely did. Jareth would be furious if he found out. It was a risk he willingly took, but it was not smart. In fact, it was reckless.

The trailer was still new to him. He and Beau didn't hang out at her home often due to her family dynamics. Checking up and down the hall, he ventured out, keeping close to the wall until he reached Beau's room. He stole inside.

The only light came from the digital bedside clock. Closing his eyes, he adjusted to the dark. Her laptop was ruined on the desk and next to it was the remains of the camera, as well. Running his hands over the damage, he glanced at the bed. Beau was asleep on her side, hands splayed, her face sticky with dried tears.

He crouched next to the bed and ran his fingertips over the tracks her tears had made on her cheeks. "Beau," he whispered. Her lips twitched. He leaned forward and kissed her. "Wake up for me. Let me see your angel eyes." Dazedly, her eyelids fluttered. He placed his hand over her mouth when he saw the reality dawn on her. "Hush," he whispered. "It's me."

She grabbed his wrist and pulled his hand from her mouth. "What are you doing here? *How* did you get here?"

"I flew," he replied. Gently, he shoved her over. It was a twin bed, so the fit would be tight. "Make room, I'm freezing."

That made her move. She scampered as far as she could without falling out of the bed. She tossed the covers aside, allowing him to lie next to her. "Your skin is like ice," she said, and then pulled the covers over them. She ran her hands over his back and drew him close to her. She kissed him and her words rushed out unbridled. "I'm so sorry I got mad. I didn't mean to break the computer. When I realized I didn't have my phone, I freaked out. I cried myself to sleep, praying you'd forgive me. I don't know why I said what I did. I love you; it's not a bother to me. I was stupid. Please, say you forgive me. I. Love. You." Each word was said between kisses she rained over his face.

"Hush," he repeated. "There is nothing to forgive. I said harsh words as well. I'm here now." He pressed his lips to hers. "We shall never go to sleep angry at one another. It is not good to sleep with unresolved issues between us."

"You flew over here knowing you could die?" Jeremy nodded. "Are you crazy? Do you know what that would do to me if something happened to you? You came all the way over here because I had a stupid tantrum that we could have settled in the morning?"

"To put things right between us? Yes." His hands moved strands of hair that were caught on her sticky cheeks. "You cried yourself to sleep on my account. That should never happen. The only tears I want you shedding are ones that fall from unspeakable joy."

Beau strained to see his face in the dark. She ran her fingers through his damp, cold hair. "Why do I doubt you?" She brought his face to hers and kissed him deeply. "You did this for me. If something bad happens to you because of this, it's my fault. But I'm so glad you're here. I'm an idiot."

"Don't say such things about the girl I love," he murmured. He framed her face with his hands. "I've missed you. I've missed doing this." His lips captured hers in a searing kiss. His hands tangled in her hair.

A loud noise in the hallway startled them, and the door flew open without warning. Rixby poked his head in the room. "Beau . . . hey, you awake?" He sounded drunk. Beau gripped the air, the adrenaline from being caught made her heart feel as if it was lodged in her throat. But her arms, which had just been holding Jeremy, were now empty. She ran her hand over the empty space beside her, coming up on her elbow. Anxiety made her throat dry. Her eyes darted around the room.

"I'm awake." Light streamed in from the hallway, making her wince. She shielded her eyes with a shaky hand. "What's wrong?"

"They closed all the schools in the parish tomorrow 'cause of the heavy freeze. It busted the water pipes at the high school."

Beau glowered. "You woke me up to tell me that, bonehead?"

"Yep. Thought you might like to turn off your alarm and

sleep in. Ain't that sweet of me?"

"You're priceless," she drawled. Her fingers curled into the covers. She wondered if she dreamed it all. As far as she knew, Jeremy couldn't disappear, but he was gone. Vanished. Or her mind had fabricated the scenario. Being crazy blind in love in the throes of the teen years was turbulent stuff. She rubbed her tired, sensitive eyes. Her heart still beat a violent drum in her chest. "Now, close my door and let me sleep."

"Whatevs." He snickered, and then shut the door.

Beau pulled to her knees and crawled to the foot of the bed to lock the door. She didn't want a replay of someone barging in again. She didn't think her heart could take it. Sitting back on her heels, she listened to Rixby repeat his shenanigan at Aries' room, and then at Amos' and Andre's room. He was definitely drunk. The only time he displayed a sweet side was when he had a few drinks. Thankfully, alcohol affected him differently than their dad.

She glanced around her room. What the heck had happened? She had never experienced a dream so vivid, but it had to have been one. It seemed so real. Even now, she smelled saltwater and citrus, as if Jeremy had run through her room. Placing her hand over her heart, she fell back on her bed.

And jumped out of her skin when she spotted Jeremy hovering on her ceiling above the bed.

"At least you didn't scream," he teased, his voice low.

"Would you get down from there," she hissed.

"Yes, ma'am." He descended slowly toward the bed.

"Geez, you're going to make my heart explode or something." She pressed the heel of her hand over her chest. Her heart was beating so fast that it hurt.

Jeremy landed on the bed beside her. He turned to his side and propped up on his elbow. "I can help you with that," he offered, his eyes traveling to her heart. Apprehension and anxiety rolled off her in waves. He unfolded her hands, grasped her wrists together, and lifted them above her head. His face hovered over hers, their lips almost touching. "It's a little trick I know." His mouth pressed to the corner of hers in a whisper kiss. "Because I'm talented like that."

What was supposed to be a smart laugh but sounded like the grunt of a wounded animal left her mouth. "First, I'm going to kiss you senseless and absorb your anxiety. It's a buzzkill, angel. You really should trust me and learn to calm down." She made that noise again, incapable of articulating anything coherent. Already she could feel him releasing the unease pent up inside her. It was the sensation of twisting a soda cap open. The restless energy left her body wherever he touched her. His hands, his hips, his mouth. "Then we are going to spend the night in each other's arms—asleep. I'm not going to pretend this doesn't go against everything I believe in, but what's done is done. I'm here, and I can't leave now or let's face it—I'll die. And I don't fancy dying tonight." Beau nodded in agreement, too breathless for speech. He kissed her nose. "No, you wouldn't like that either." He placed a kiss on her mouth. "Trust me?"

He was asking for permission. His blue eyes sparkled when the outside security snuck in through the window. The outline of his face was visible for a second. He looked determined, like a man on a mission.

And he looked . . . she didn't want to contemplate how else he looked.

She nodded.

That was the last thing she remembered.

THE MORNING LIGHT FILTERED IN through a crack of the room darkening curtains that hung in her room. They were bright pink—a color her mom chose. It went with the comforter that someone had donated.

"Don't scream."

A smile curved on her mouth as she stretched her body out like a cat—long and lazily. There was a warm body next to her under the covers. She felt his stomach muscles contract at her movement. "You put me to sleep with your kisses last night." She turned onto her stomach and nuzzled his chest. This was the way she wanted to wake every morning. "Is there something you can do to wake me up?"

"All out of tricks, sorry." His hands skimmed through her hair. "I loved sleeping with you. It's the best sleep I've gotten in years." His eyes roved over her face that she was sure was creased and puffy from sleep. "I've never slept with anyone before. You've ruined me forever."

"Same."

"You're so soft," he continued in a whisper. The sounds of her parents beginning their day were evident in the trailer. It was terrible living in a tin can—there was even less privacy than when they lived behind the store. "And warm. With you around, who needs heat? You're like a furnace. And you smell so good—like Beau."

She giggled when his breath tickled her neck. Her shoulder automatically sandwiched his face, trapping him there for a beat. "Stay." What she asked sounded ridiculous to her ears, but the alternative was worse. Watching him leave again would stab her heart all over and she would bleed for days.

"I have to go." His voice was apologetic and soft. She tipped her face back to peer at him. He looked refreshed and not at all like someone who could perish if she were to lock him outside in the cold. "I have stayed too long, I fear. My core temperature has dropped significantly. I had trouble with my breathing an hour ago. Pneumonia can sneak up on me when I'm not vigilant, and showing up on Jareth's doorstep is not an option. You can't tell Elizabet I was here. I broke a slew of rules. Jareth is fair, but he will hold me to the law. No one can know I was here last night."

"All right," she agreed. She ran her hand over his chest, then turned to her side and snuggled up to him. His arms wrapped around her and he kissed the top of her head. "I won't say a word. How can I help? What do you need to go back?"

"I need a diversion. There's a spot in your backyard that is hidden by a low-lying tree. I need to get that spot in a hurry and dissipate. Can you go and check the perimeter for me? Make sure no one is about?"

"Of course. I'll do whatever I need to keep you safe." She pulled back and looked at him. "I'm sorry I acted like a baby and threw a tantrum. If I didn't have anger issues, none of this would have happened. You'd be safe. And warm."

His eyes tapered. "Seriously? This was my best idea in ages. My only regret is that it *was* an argument that brought me here last night. I don't like fighting with you. You don't have anger issues, you're passionate." His smile was bone curdling. "I like it when you're passionate about things that pertain to me. To us."

"Same." Her face heated. "I mean, I'm sorry I was so stupid and insecure. But it's sweet that you call it passionate. My craziness has never been called that before."

His face tipped off the pillow and he kissed her quickly. "Speaking of passion . . . any chance of you feeding me before I take off?"

Beau grunted and pushed his face away with the heel of her hand. "Geez, how romantic of you to bring food up right now."

They quietly enjoyed breakfast in her room. A pot of tea for him, coffee for her, and a dozen doughnuts she snatched from the store. They were hot and fresh. The local bakery had just dropped them off for sale. She slipped ten dollars into the till to make up for it. Jeremy insisted on paying; he ate eleven of them.

No one was about in the trailer. Her parents were running the store, which was slow due to the weather. The Pepsi vendor had just pulled out and the parking lot was empty. Her siblings were all sound asleep. The neighborhood was silent and icy. The roofs all glistened with ice.

"I love you," Jeremy said against her lips.

"I love you," she answered, tilting her head and forcing him to kiss her again.

He growled low in his throat, brought her closer, and lifted her body in his arms. A small, distressed cry left her lips when they parted.

"I'll be back soon. Another week or so. The weather is on the turnaround."

"I can't wait."

"Homecoming is this weekend?" he asked. She nodded. "I'll miss it."

"It doesn't matter. Take care of yourself. You've broken enough rules already because of me. I can handle this." She smiled. "I'll tag you in a post. Rixby is escorting me. Says it will help his image with the football scouts. I'll be the girl in the gigantic hat. Elizabet ordered it online. She says it's fabulous."

"Then it probably is. The duchess knows what's fashionable, no matter what time period. I can't wait to see it." He pulled away, pressing a kiss to her forehead.

Beau watched until he rounded the tree and waved, and then she shut the door.

A sonic boom shook the house, rattled the windows. Something in the kitchen crashed to the floor and the housecat hissed and jumped at the sound. It scampered out of the kitchen, all drawn claws and bushy tail.

Beau couldn't help but smile smugly. "My man."

Chapter 11

"I hated high school. Every time I get near a gym it makes me want to burst into a rendition of "Smells Like Teen Spirit." Nirvana knew what they were talking about when they pinned that. Teenagers' pheromones stink. I swear lust has an odor and it smells a lot like a basketball gym."

—*Elizabet Blackwell Tremaine on memories of high school.*

I T WAS HOMECOMING NIGHT AND things had changed. Elizabet was asked to sing the anthem for the game opening and Jareth was giving the opening speech. The news of their family's endeavor to become a singing troupe had spread. The Tremaines intrigued people. Church reform was a popular but sore subject in the area. Everyone wanted to know what was going on with the laws, but no one wanted a debate. Jareth was open on his views and this fascinated the public. They wanted more of him and what he had to say, even if he was not on the commonly accepted side. It was the manner in which he said things with no apology and with no offense to anyone in particular. He stated facts and didn't beg people to take his side, nor did he ostracize the opposition. The man had more charisma in this century than the one he was born for.

Beau reached up and fumbled with the ribbons of her hat. Elizabet had helped her choose her suit and it was lovely. A navy blue silk pencil skirt and jacket with a kicking hat that had been shipped from a store off Savile Row in London. It was where the Duchess of Cambridge shopped for hats. According to Elizabet, the hat was epic. What it was to Beau? Just *big*. The wide brim was twice the size of her head. It set her apart from all the other maids on the court, but Beau agreed that it was fabulous. Many people had said as much, and those who said nothing looked at it with unveiled longing.

She was thrilled. For the millionth time, she wished Jeremy were here to share this moment with her.

Rixby pursed his lips as he surveyed the line before them. There were three senior maids ahead of them. "Are you going to the dance after the game?" he asked.

Beau felt grateful that he was making an effort to be civil, even though it was because there were three scouts watching from the stands. Her eyes skimmed the seats but she had assessed all already. Jeremy was in tropical paradise, soaking up the heat he needed to survive. She just couldn't make her eyes understand that, nor her heart.

"No," she shook her head. The urge to be done with this was keen. She pictured Jeremy on the beach, and tried desperately not to picture someone next to him. She turned her gaze to her brother. It was an act of steel self-control for him to be polite. "I'll probably hitch a ride with Elizabet. I have no reason to go to the dance." Caesar had asked if she would like to go, but it didn't feel right. Knowing Jeremy was jealous of Caesar was reason enough to steer clear of any misconceptions.

"Almost done," Rixby murmured, noting movement in the line. He barely looked at Beau while he spoke. The announcer introduced another senior maid. "If you want, I can stall the parents." He glanced down at her, redness creeping up his neck despite the cold. "You can sneak out with Liz early. I know you Skype late at night. You can take off and call Jeremy early."

Beau's lips parted on a soft gasp. Not that her parents cared where she was, but homecoming would be a big liquor night for the store. Her mom had mentioned that she might be needed on the register. "I don't know what to say. You'll take my shift?"

Rixby's smile was lopsided as he nodded. "Say yes, little sister." He tipped his head to the side, his eyes roaming to where they often had since being at Beau's side. "I owe Caesar."

Beau frowned. "You're being nice to me 'cause Caesar is taking Natalie to homecoming?" She snorted. She wanted to thrash Rixby upside his head with the bouquet she was holding, but she refrained—barely. "I should have known."

It was not that Rixby disliked Caesar. No, it was not that easy. It was a case of the proverbial have versus the have-nots. Rich versus poor. Beau was sick of the double standard that was Rixby. He was giving her an out to call Jeremy only because it was to his benefit. He wanted to have something to smear under Caesar's nose to make things even tonight. It would hurt Caesar that Beau was giving up homecoming to go and Skype.

"What?" Rixby had the nerve to appear affronted. "You know how crazy it makes him that you're with the freak."

"Don't call him that," Beau said, her jaw clenched. Just when she thought Rixby could not make her any more mad, he brought up the reason her heart beat. She glanced around. People were thankfully more interested in the ceremony than their present conversation. Her voice dropped. "Jeremy's not a freak."

"Says little miss crazy herself," Rixby said, but chucked Beau under her chin. "Lighten up, Beau." She cringed, but could not go far without releasing her hold on his arm and calling attention. "You know I would never let just anyone call you crazy."

This was the Rixby she knew. The one who she so casually shared a womb with back in the day. Beau narrowed her eyes, but before she could retort, Rixby was roughly pushed aside. Her hand groped for him as he slipped away.

"What the—" Rixby said, his body tensing, ready for defense. He had to look up at the person who did the shoving, and when his eyes registered the tall guy standing over them, he sneered. "What are you doing here?" A trickle of blood leaked from the side of Rixby's mouth. His expression turned perplexed as he first touched the corner of his mouth with the tip of his tongue, then his fingers. He inspected the blood on his fingertips with a pinched face.

"Say another word and next time I won't be so quick," Jeremy said, his voice low. His hand gripped Beau's arm and he moved her closer to him, tucking her to his side.

Beau peered up into Jeremy's face and then at her brother. Something had happened in the blink of eye. Rixby's lip was beginning to swell and it was split.

But that wasn't it. Jeremy was here. He wasn't a made up fantasy in her mind. He was solid and standing right next to her with his arm around her, holding her close. The scent of beach and something spicy filled her senses. He had come for her. He was here. Again. He kept showing up and turning her world upside down when she least expected it.

"Jeremy," she gasped, gripping his arm. Her eyes took in his handsome face as he smiled at her, that small, shy smile that she liked to think was hers. "You're here." She stated the obvious and made him smile wider. "Why? How?"

Rixby's eyes bulged as his tongue flicked to where blood flowed again. "Frickin' freak," he hissed. He looked at Beau. "Did you see what he did?"

This time when the hit occurred, Beau caught the telltale sign. Jeremy's arm was as fast as lightening and Rixby's head jerked back with the force of it.

Rixby's hand covered his left eye. He grimaced. "What the—"

A quick slap across his mouth was delivered.

Jeremy took a deep breath. "It's a shame the wind is so strong this evening. Isn't it, Rixby? Like a slap to the face."

Beau heard the sound Jeremy's lungs made when he inhaled—a steady wheezing as if he was breathing through a straw. She steadied her bouquet, put her hand over his heart, and peered up at him. "You okay?"

"Never better," he said, but his face was pale. His lips were blood red, standing out in stark contrast to the rest of his gorgeous face. She noticed that there was a slight flare to his nostrils each time he inhaled as if he was drawing in as much oxygen as he could. He dipped down to whisper in her ear. "Did you think I would miss this?" She pulled back and saw his lips twist. "I can be passionate as well. No one escorts you on homecoming night but me."

"You're asking *him* if he's okay?" Rixby cried. His voice had an edge to it. He swiped his mouth with the back of his hand, leaving a smear of blood along his cheek. "He hit me." He pointed at Jeremy. "This isn't done, Cameron. I'm coming for you when this game is over."

"Good," Jeremy replied with a wicked smile. "I could do this all night."

"You're next," Mrs. Olivier's voice made Beau jump. She looked at Beau and then to the two escorts who flanked her sides. "Who's the lucky guy?"

Beau thumbed to Jeremy. "He is. Definitely." Her words were rushed, her face warmed with the excitement his words caused. "Jeremy, that is. He's my escort." She reached blindly for his hand and squeezed. It was gloved, but she felt his icy fingers through the leather and wondered what it cost him to strike her brother those three times. He must conserve his energy in this temperature. They stepped forward. "This is Jeremiah Cameron and he's my escort."

Mrs. Olivier eyes swept over Jeremy, the appreciation and surprise in her gaze seen before she could veil it. Not everyone had seen Jeremy since he returned, but when they did, it was met with wonderment at how time could transform a person. "I would never have recognized you. Good to have you back, Jeremiah."

"It's good to be back," he said, and flashed that all-American boy smile that made grown women weak as well as young ones. Even in his weakened state, the boy was lethal. Beau rolled her eyes despite the fact she was terrified for him. He was being charming even though he could go down any minute in this weather. His claim of being passionate was different than hers. When she was passionate, her stupid acts didn't normally risk lives.

Mrs. Olivier leaned forward, hovering near them with a slight smile on her lips. "Yes. Well, stand behind the line until your names are called." She gestured to the bright yellow line spray painted on the field. "Do you want to use your full name?" She was speaking to Jeremy.

"Just Jeremy will do." He looked down at Beau and squeezed her hand. *We are really going to do this.* Beau caught his wordless message as he turned his attention back to Mrs. Olivier. "Jeremy Tremaine. Please. If you will use my adoptive name, that would be better."

"I'll see you after the game," Jeremy said to Rixby before he stepped forward. "That is, if you still insist." He locked his gaze on her brother for several long seconds as though he may also be sharing an intent silent message with her twin.

Rixby swallowed roughly, his eyes staying on Jeremy. When he glanced at Beau, she realized her senses had served her correctly. A tidal wave of emotion passed between them.

"It would be wise to take this out, brother," Beau murmured. She gestured to where the team was gathered on the sidelines. "You'd better go before you find out exactly what else he can do."

"I disagree," Jeremy said, his voice also low. He looked at Rixby. "I would love to show you what I am capable of."

Rixby looked at Jeremy and nodded once—a stiff jerk. There was a wealth of rebellious submission in the gesture. He would comply with Jeremy's threat, but he didn't like it. "I wouldn't want to ruin homecoming." His chin tipped toward the bleachers. "Scouts are watching me." Jeremy gave him a mocking salute. "This isn't over," Rixby sneered, his bloody teeth showing. The inside of his lip was shredded from the blows. "I'm not scared of your little magic tricks."

"Then, by all means, stay after the game so I can show you more of my little tricks."

Beau put her hand on Rixby's chest and pushed him away. "Do you have a death wish?" She glanced up at the stands. "Say bye-bye to LSU. You'll never get in if you fight, Rixby. Don't be stupid. You'll lose your meal ticket and Jeremy will likely kill you."

"Like your little boyfriend could hurt me." Rixby's hard gaze passed overhead to where the scouts were seated. He used his index finger to poke Jeremy in the chest. "You're lucky tonight, but not forever."

Jeremy pushed Rixby's hand away. "Please, feel free to pick up where we left off anytime," he jeered.

"Name the time and the place." Rixby opened his arms wide. "I'll even let you bring Caesar. Two for one."

Jeremy stepped toward to Rixby, but Beau stopped him. "No, Jeremy. We're next." She glanced at Mrs. Olivier, who was watching with narrowed eyes as if she was about to call an intervention. "Please," she looked at Rixby. "Y'all stop it. I look stupid enough up here."

Beau witnessed a silent exchange between Jeremy and Rixby, her eyes bouncing between them. Suddenly a look of sheer terror passed over her brother's expression like a veil.

"You're sick, Cameron," Rixby spat, but he finally backed away. He glanced at the two of them with a sneer on his face, then turned and jogged to the sidelines. Most likely to jeer and brood and ruin her night anyway.

"Thank you," Beau whispered. She ran her hand up Jeremy's arm, silently encouraging him to steal heat from her. He was so cold. "You didn't have to do that."

"It's safe," he said. He stopped her roaming hand and clasped it again as he pulled her to the line. "He will never call you crazy again. I think he understands the way of things now."

"What did you tell him?"

"Nothing you need to worry about. He won't bother you again." Jeremy looked to the sidelines where Rixby was standing with his teammates. "And if he does, he knows it will be me he will reckon with."

"Thank you?" Beau asked. "I guess."

"Stop looking at me like that or I'll have to kiss you in front of this stadium full of people."

"How am I looking at you?" she asked, her eyes wide. Jeremy shrugged adorably and looked away. Beau gave her smile free reign. "Well, I would probably let you. I can't believe you just did that to Rixby. He was practically peeing in his pants when you did that siphon thingy." She shook her head, her grip on him tightening. "And I can't believe you're here. Standing in this cold. You showed up for me. Who does that?"

"I do," Jeremy said, his voice rough.

"Miss Beau Angelle Benoit, senior maid. Escorted by Jeremy Tremaine." The announcer said. What followed was her high school credentials, which Beau found utterly ridiculous. At this age, what sort of accomplishments did one boast about?

She stole a look at Jeremy as they walked up to the center field, wondering if he thought her list of accomplishments was foolish. Baseball. The choir. 4-H. Rally one year for home economics. His accomplishments of body and spirit made her look like chopped liver.

But here was the thing about Jeremy. He did not look for outward beauty or for high intellect. His condition was one that the outside did not really matter if one had an ugly heart. He had said as much when they were kids. The first time he called her beautiful angel, he was referring to her heart, her soul. She knew this, because at the tender age of nine, Jeremy

Cameron had told her he would love her forever because her heart was shiny. He claimed it had to be shiny because something so beautiful had to glimmer.

So, she—plain and obscure Beau—stood next to this epiphany of maleness in a public arena. Beside this guy who had lost his shyness and social introvert ways to a storm that he shared his body with. In his bespoke suit that was entirely black, he was breathtaking and commanded attention. His hair was adorably shaggy and his grin lopsided as the court giggled when they climbed the stairs up the bandstand. Normally, Beau would have been embarrassed to have so many eyes focused on her, but tonight she was not. It may have been that those eyes were trained on Jeremy, but it did not matter. He was looking at her and no one else. His blue eyes smoldered as he guided her to the chair designated for her and took his place behind her. His hands rested protectively on the back of the iron chair, and she felt some of the warmth seep from her as he used the chair as a conduit to share a measure of her body heat.

Jareth and Elizabet were still on the bandstand. Elizabet held a microphone, ready to sing the victory song when the homecoming queen was announced. Her mouth wobbled a smile as they passed, a look of concern on her face as her gaze remained on Jeremy. Jareth stood behind his wife, his hand on her elbow in quiet support. It was evident they had expected Jeremy. They weren't surprised, but apprehensive at the decision he made to be there. It seemed they were posed to pounce and intervene if necessary.

Of course, when the homecoming queen was announced, it was not Beau. And of course, it did not matter. What mattered was that she shared the night with Jeremy standing behind her, watching the rest of the game. Before leaving the podium, Jareth and Elizabet each passed next to Jeremy and inconspicuously touched him, allowing him to store heat from their bodies.

"How are you doing it?" Beau asked when Jeremy folded down in the chair beside her. He gripped the seat on both sides, hunkering down next to her. "You're so pale. I can see your struggle to breathe." She looked pointedly at the see-sawing motion of his barrel chest.

"I'm quite snuggly, actually. I have disposable warmers at all my pressure points." He grinned. "Do they make me look fat?"

Beau giggled. "Hardly. Don't think by being cute, I'll forget this can't be easy for you."

"You know I'll have to refuel as soon as possible?" he asked. He reached up and touched the corner of her mouth with the tip of his finger. "We can go to the dance, but I can only stay for one dance. It will be warm there, but I'll require extra measures other than artificial heat."

"We can skip the dance. Rixby will be there and I don't want you to get into trouble."

"I'm not worried about your brother. Didn't you hear what I said? He'll never bother you again," he said, his tone firm. "This night is for you. We'll make the most of it. You only have one chance for a senior homecoming and this is it. I came back to make this perfect for you." He shrugged. "You can look at it like this: it's a first and only for me as well. We'll muddle through it together. What doesn't kill you makes you stronger, right? Isn't that how the saying goes?"

Beau smiled and reached out to touch his face as he touched hers. "I'm so glad you're here." She knew she didn't need to worry about Rixby. There was something confident Jeremy passed to her, although he didn't give her the details. Whatever Jeremy did to Rixby had worked. It was another area of her life he had set her free.

"Me, too."

Beau did not look away when he turned his attention to the game. His eyes were shuttered, not focused on the game and she had the sense to realize it took all his concentration to stay alive. Tears came uninvited into her vision as the reality of his sacrifice dawned. When she said tonight did not matter, she had lied. To stand up in an arena surrounded by people who thought her crazy and simple would have been impossible if not for the boy next to her. She tried hard not to dwell on the fact it was because of him that people had that opinion of her, and perhaps it was penance on his part that he was present. But here he was and he belonged to her.

And now everyone knew that. There was a measure of redemption in that. He had released her from the cage society had forced upon her.

FOLLOWING THEIR ONE DANCE, JARETH got called back to the hospital, and Elizabet went with him. The kids had begged for Beau and Jeremy to babysit them. They missed making blanket forts in the den and eating s'mores in front of the fire. All of that had been done and now everyone was tucked in—even sweet baby Benjamin hadn't put up a fuss.

But there was always Peter.

Beau could hear water splashing in the bathroom. She pressed her ear to the door. "Jeremy, you okay?" she called.

No answer, but more splashing and the roar of the heater.

"Can I have a snack?" Peter asked from behind her.

"Can you wait right here and listen for Jeremy? He might need something. I don't want to leave him alone."

Peter nodded and slid against the door until he was seated. Beau listened for a beat before making the trek to the obscenely large kitchen. She opened the fridge, inspected the contents, and decided she knew why they were all brawny and vibrant. The pack of them were health nuts. It was a miracle they kept the s'mores ingredients she had stashed.

"I'll take herbal tea and a biscuit," Peter said from behind her.

Beau startled and slapped a hand over her heart as she turned to him. "You're supposed to be listening for Jeremy."

Peter shrugged. "He's finished." He looked at her pointedly. "Can I have a sweet biscuit instead of the plain?"

The corner of Beau's mouth turned downward as she closed the fridge. "What's the difference?" she muttered.

"It's scones," Jeremy said as he came into the kitchen. Beau faced him, bracing her back against the fridge. He was towel drying his hair briskly with one hand and motioned to the pantry with the other. "The sweet ones are in the red container. Jareth has everything color-coded. Red for things we should eat with caution."

Peter grinned. "I'll be sure to cautiously eat them all."

Jeremy smiled, snapping the towel at his brother as he passed. "S'mores weren't enough of a sugar rush?"

All the while, Beau was weakened by the view. Seeing Jeremy casually clothed in his pajamas never got old. He went over to the pantry and grabbed the red container that was almost out of his reach. Beau looked away when the hem of his cotton shirt rode up, showing the lower portion of his muscled back. She made eye contact with Peter and he lifted a black brow, a smile tugging on his mouth. The children were way too perceptive about all things love and relationships—with their parents being practical exhibitionists.

"Can you put the kettle on?" Jeremy asked as he rummaged through the cabinet.

"Sure," Beau muttered, her face warm at being busted by a five-year-old. She switched on the burner. Jeremy fixed three plates and arranged teacups on a tray. He placed tea bags into each cup. "I don't drink tea. I'll have some milk."

"You just haven't found the right one yet." Jeremy bussed Peter's hair as he passed, and came to stand in front of Beau. The towel he used to dry his hair was draped over his shoulders. "There is black, oolong, green, rooibos . . ." He made a turning motion with his hand. "The list is long. If you're going to be my girl, you must give tea the proper chance."

"You forget that you're American." Beau *tsked* and shook her head. "Americans don't take tea the way British people do. They practically thrive on that stuff. We Americans like baseball and apple pie." She smiled. "And Coca-Cola. I'm an all-American kinda girl. Got any Coke?"

Jeremy looked stricken as his fist struck the center of his chest. "This body is a temple. Of course we don't have Coke." He said Coke like the word tasted bad in his mouth. "And do I sound American?"

"Nope," Peter chimed.

Jeremy placed his hands on either side of Beau, grabbed hold of the stove, and caged her in. "I, my dear, sweet angel, am a British boy. Raised in Kent, London, and Dover. I forgot what it's like to be American long ago." Heat seeped through her; she was a conduit between Jeremy and the stove he was robbing heat from. "Why are you blushing?"

Beau scoffed. As if he did not know. She blushed further and tried to push him away. "Vanity, thy name is Jeremy."

Jeremy laughed, a low, dark rumble in his massive chest. "That's cute, but not accurate. I'm the most humble person I know. How many human hurricanes would go to a southern town homecoming dance? I should be given some sort of award. Did we really dance to a Rascal Flatts song?"

"You're so annoying."

"Yes. Very much so. I detest country music, but there I was." He smirked and made a twirling motion with his finger. "In all my awesome DNA glory . . . turning in circles to twang and whining."

"Oh, get over it," Beau said, her voice husky. "It was only one dance. I didn't make you stay for the line dancing. I'm sure that was only a matter of time."

"Is this going to be one of those moments Mum and Dad

call private?" Peter asked.

Jeremy put his face into the crook of her neck and she felt him smile against her skin. "Maybe." The sound of his voice vibrated through her, raising shivers along her arms and back. "And thank you for not making a ninny out of me in front of your friends. I'm a terrible dancer. I probably would have stumbled over the entire line."

Beau gazed over Jeremy's shoulder and saw Peter watching with interest. She cleared her throat and pushed him away. "Your brother is watching," she whispered. "Stop," she mouthed when he looked at her with a slow smile spreading on his face.

The kettle whistled. Beau had never been so grateful for tea in her life.

JEREMY PROPPED UP ON HIS elbow and stared into the fire. The best way to refuel was primitive means. Hot water worked well, and fire was even better. Any of the elements worked best as long as it was heated to maximum capacity.

"You're still cold," Beau said, tracing her hand over his bicep. She used both hands to roam over his body, spreading heat as she went. "It worries me when you're like this. What happens if you can't get warm? How long would it take for you to . . . for you to . . . ." She couldn't say it.

He gazed down at her. She was stretched out next to him on the pallet he had prepared in front of the fireplace in the living room. It was the room that was most open and while Jareth would probably not approve, it was the best place available. The children were asleep. Peter too, finally. It could not be helped that they were very much alone.

He fanned her hair out on the pillow, lightly traced her hairline and then down her nose. "You keep touching me like that and there will be a blackout."

"You need the heat," she murmured. She leaned up and pressed a kiss to his throat.

Jeremy gripped a handful of her hair and gently tugged her away. He stared down at her. "You test my control, Beau."

She smiled and kissed his chin. "You didn't answer my question."

He kissed her. A feathery, gentle kiss that had her melting against him. He smiled against her lips, and then reached out toward the fire. A single flame licked out when he drew it in. The heat radiated from his fingertips and spread throughout his body.

"You're cheating," she taunted against his lips.

"I've taken enough of your body heat." He pulled away and guided her to rest her back against the pillows. He drew his body partially over hers, pressing her into the downy blanket. "How long? Sometimes it can take hours, sometimes minutes or mere seconds. I can't be in medieval Dover during winter for long. There aren't enough heat resources. I've had to fly out of the atmosphere on occasion when it got particularly out of hand. It's a feeling I get; a sense of impending doom that I can't shake. Jareth calls it my internal thermometer. Says it's been divinely placed in my body to keep me alive. I've had to learn to live like this, so I know my limits and watch for cues from my body. I've been perfectly fine one minute and the next . . ." He snapped. "Out cold. Literally. We've been lucky that I've only required manual resuscitation on three occasions."

She watched his face in the firelight. He knew what she wanted. Over the past months that they had been together, he told her whatever she wanted to know, whenever she wanted it. But now she was holding back saying what was really on her mind, instead of asking outright. Since he returned, the topic of Malia had not been addressed. The sensitive subject had been invisibly injected into every conversation, though, since the fateful day on the island that Malia taunted Beau. Their conversations had focused on keeping it together, their days' activities, and the future—what they would do when he was able to return to the States. Neither dared to bring up the ill-welcomed matter of Malia while an expanse of land and water separated them. Not even on the one night he stole away to see Beau. It was a silent topic that begged to be set free.

Jeremy could hurt her emotionally. She understood that, but she still wanted to know their history. Most girls were this way, even if it upset him that she gave in to something so mundane and trivial. He believed her beyond that and wondered why she could not just let it go, see it for what it was. After all, he promised he trusted her where Caesar was concerned. He had a healthy level of jealousy, but he wasn't paranoid.

"I feel you reading me," she said, her voice soft. She ran her hands along his back, pulled him closer. "Don't be mad. I can't help it. I want to know. I feel that I can't go on until I know everything that passed between you." Her eyes lowered. "I know there are things you'd rather not tell me, but I want you to. Please." She looked up at him. "I can take it."

HE MADE A SOUND LOW in his throat, and glanced away into the fire. "No one compares with you. Isn't that enough?" He took her face in his hands and tipped her head back. He studied her face while his fingers flexed on her scalp. The silky strands of her hair flowed through his fingers. He was rough, but he was upset. It vexed him that she wanted this. He didn't like digging up the past. "Isn't it enough to know that you're the first and last for me? You said it yourself that you'll be the last girl I ever kiss and I heartily agree. Stop torturing yourself with things that mean nothing to me."

"I've always been curious, but since I saw her, I want to know. I can't help it. Call it morbid curiosity. I want to hear what that beautiful island girl did to turn your eye. I want to know what she did to chase you away. I want to know all of it. I want to know so I can put it behind me. It's like a wall between us."

"Well, it's a wall you built, because I don't see it as something between us." He let an annoyed huff escape his mouth. He barreled through it; it was what she wanted. "I didn't even consider Malia my girlfriend. She literally followed me around for a year pretending we were exclusive. She is brash, hot-tempered, and a little vulgar to be truthful. That was what intrigued me at first. She did things that shocked me. I wasn't used to anyone being so upfront and personal with their sexuality, but she was. Had it down to a bloody art."

"Jeremy—"

"Oh, no." He shook his head, yet even as he spoke harshly, he placed a kiss on her forehead. He pressed his lips firmly against her with a sigh. "There is no other way to do this but nasty. It's not a pleasant story. You want to know. Know you shall." She tensed, her hands flexing on his back and she nodded against his lips in a slight, jerky movement. "I didn't love her, if that's what this is about. I've never told another girl that before you." He pulled back and stared down at her. "But we were . . . involved. Is this what you're fishing for?" He asked the last part in a whisper.

Beau nodded again, even as her eyes narrowed. Her face was flushed with the close proximity of the fireplace. He was not sure if it was the heat that made her eyes water or emotion.

He could not help it, he looked away. Shame coursed through him as the memories fluttered in his mind. This would hurt him as well. "Host are physical. We can't help it. Our emotions, if left unchecked and unbridled, can rule us. Things can get carried away. But I've told you this before. It's why we have to be chaperoned and careful. I'm more inclined than normal boys to want things that . . . well, things that boys want. Do you follow me?" She nodded.

He did not care if it made him old-fashioned to adhere to moral ideals of early times. It grounded him. He thrived on rules. It was part of his old, obsessive nature that he embraced. Give him a list of regulations and he was ecstatic. It gave him goals and boundaries. But it was those strict boundaries that Malia used to lure him. To make him think he was missing out on all the fun life had to offer. "I have the propensity to seek to conquer in all primitive senses, but I have ground rules. Jareth doesn't give me rules pertaining to this. I've adopted them all on my own. Living in Dover in medieval times can do that to a person. It's a good thing, especially for someone like me."

Silence filled the small space between them as he let that sink in. He watched the fire with his head turned, listening to the crackle and occasional pop from the pecan wood logs he had thrown into the fireplace. The heat was perfect. The air was a flawless temperature and his core was properly warmed. He could easily dissipate if he was called to. The storm within was sated. Props that there was a girl partially beneath him. Human contact was best, especially when there were emotions involved. He had omitted that part earlier.

Emotions like love fueled him almost as much as fire. Beau had actually kept him alive tonight. It had been a risk, a proposal they decided to try. To see if his emotions were in direct correlation to the power of his core. He had never felt so strongly about another human being before Beau. Tonight, a huge step in the life he had as host had occurred. He would no longer be held back by weather as long as Beau was with him. Her love was a constant source of warmth for him—like a portable piece of the sun. And while he could grow weak and lose portions of his strength in dire circumstances, he had become more invincible than any other living host.

"We didn't . . . sleep together," he admitted. He did not miss the release of breath she had been holding, but he was not finished. "But it was close on numerous occasions. Malia does not have the standards I adhere to." He glanced at Beau. Her eyes swam in tears. So, it was emotions, not the sweltering warmth. At once, he hated that he was giving in to her silly demands and feminine curiosity, but she would have it no other way. She wanted it all, so she would have it all. The good, bad, and the ugly. "She wanted to. I wanted to. Not because I loved her, but because it was so hard *not* to. It's the way of things as I'm sure you know."

Jeremy pushed away from Beau, unable to bear the feelings that were churning within her. She must know that she was everything to him and all of this was vanity; a past he had left well alone. He sat next her, facing the fire, his legs drawn up. He rested his forearms on his knees and raked his hands through his hair. He would give her what she wanted, tell her things she thought she wanted to hear.

"She's beautiful, smart, and compelling. One of her abilities is that she can manipulate emotions. Make anyone feel whatever she wants. I can do it to, but don't. I was the only host we knew of who had other abilities besides the abnormal physical ones. Malia was confused that she couldn't get me to do whatever she wanted, because I am a siphon and trash like that doesn't work with me. I'm an unlabeled class. A different breed." He blew out a tight breath. "So is she. We were matched liked that, but only that. Our similarities end with our abilities. We are nothing alike. I can't stand her, Beau. She makes me feel dirty."

He twisted his body until he faced Beau. She tried to shutter the turbulent emotions she was feeling but failed. He reached out and grabbed her hand.

"I was with her a year because it was comfortable and quite frankly, because I was too lazy to get rid of her. I went through a time that I actually liked testing my limits and I took as much as I could without breaking my moral code. But then I grew sick of it, of her tagging along when I felt nothing for her, and every time I pointed out that we weren't dating she flew into hysterics." He paused, a smirk on his face.

"And then there was you." A curt, self-deprecating laugh came from his mouth. "You were nowhere around, but that didn't stop you from torturing my thoughts. Always. Always you. Always somewhere on the edge of my thoughts even when I shouldn't have been thinking of you. You had my heart in your hands and Malia knew that. She siphoned your name from me and used you against me. She said I could never have you. That I would put you in danger if I tied you to me. And that's true. Knowing what you know . . . you can never go back. You're stuck in this mess with me and what is my life. You've already been the target because of me."

Beau piled her other hand over their clasped ones. He felt the shift in her. "But that is what brought us together. If that hadn't happened, I would have never known the truth about you." That she would not be with him if she didn't know the truth went left unsaid. "I asked for this, you remember? I wanted this life . . . and you." She squeezed his hand. "And I wanted to know about Malia, whether it hurts or not. I needed to know." She leaned forward until her head rested on his shoulder. "She was awful, and I don't need to know any more details. Seeing you all over her is burned into my imagination forever."

"Would you like me to give you my memories with Malia?" He grimaced when her face fell. "You won't like them. I don't like them, but I'll give them to you if that's what you want. No more walls, and you'll believe me when I say it's been over for Malia and me for a while."

"You would do that for me?"

"I would do anything for you, Beau. You only have to ask. But you won't like them. I'm warning you. You asked for this. I would rather all of this stayed dead and buried. I'm not proud of my time with Malia. The only thing that kept me straight and narrow was the way I was trained. I couldn't break code. Being morally pure isn't addressed, but it is the atmosphere that surrounds us daily. We have a choice to make and staying focused is crucial. There is a time to mature into other spheres of life, but that time is not for me yet. It's more a code we adapt on our own. It's a higher way. A good way, but it's hard and some host never live up to it."

"The memories are that bad, huh?"

"Oh, yeah," he whispered. He closed his eyes briefly. "They will likely make you want to be done with me. Like I said, I'm not proud of it. But I will give you anything you ask so we can put this behind us."

"I don't think I'll ever be done with you, but I might want to get violent. Punch you maybe, or stab your heart out."

His eyes opened wide.

Beau laughed. "It's all right, Jeremy. Keep your nasty memories." Her face shadowed as her mouth became a blunt line. "I can only imagine what you looked like with her, and the images I've conjured on my own will keep me crying into my pillow for a very long time. I don't need your memories. You can keep them."

"Georgy Porgy made all the girls cry, remember? It sounds awful, but a lot of what I did was to forget you. It was always you. You quite ruined me when I was a lad. Made me mushy in the head, you did." He sighed. "But I am a boy and we boys follow a certain appendage of our anatomy on occasion."

She pulled away, her eyes narrowed, a twist to her lips. "You didn't see me kissing and feeling up all kinds of guys to forget about you."

Jeremy smirked. He wanted to remind her that her reputation as a crazy person probably saved her from that path, but self-preservation won. "I'm a cad and I'm playing the man card. We are beasts." She grinned and he felt instant relief. "But I'm reformed and the faithful sort. I've never been given to cheating. You've quite got me. I'm yours to do with whatever you'd like." He smiled. "Any ideas?"

Beau's bottom lip sucked into her mouth as she bounced her gaze away. "Are you really in a constant state of—"

"Arousal?" Jeremy offered.

Beau's head whipped back, her eyes wide. "Really? You just threw that out there?" She shook her head. "I wouldn't say it quite like that, but are you serious?"

Jeremy laughed—a full bellied laugh that shook his frame as he lounged back and tugged her hand as he reclined. "Don't look so scared, Beau. Jareth knows how to terminate me, and saying he's old school is like saying the earth is round. I told you I'm a class of my own when it comes to host. I've got a lot more control, as well. I didn't take as long to mature as the natural male species. I lost my youthful prowling—or most of it—a while back and I came out on the other side intact with my virtue. I promise I won't ravish you unless you ask it. But no, I don't walk around constantly ready to claim and conquer."

"So, you're a . . ." Her hand motion needed no interpretation.

Jeremy nodded and kissed her mouth. "All yours, angel. Forever. I promise."

"Promise?" she echoed, her expression shy and unsure.

"Absolutely, one hundred percent positive," Jeremy replied. "I was there. I think I would remember if I lost something as precious as that. I told you, it's the unspoken code I live by. It keeps me grounded. I don't have time nor the energy for complications."

"Good, because I was a little worried." Her reply was instant and stark in the quiet surroundings. Her relief was palatable.

It was a good time to take her mind off of Malia and his state of moral virtue. "You never have reason to worry," he said, and passed her the information he had withheld. Her eyes widened as he filtered to her the strength she carried to make or break him. *You are my portable sunshine. There isn't a place on earth I want to be if you aren't there by my side.*

"Does this mean you'll never have to go away again?"

"As long as you are with me and we feel this way, then no. I can stay with you in a blizzard and be relatively sure I won't kick my heels up and need to be buried six feet under. You've become a valuable asset in Dover's Amalgam and you didn't even have to ask for it."

"That sounds serious."

"It is. When I came to see you—during the ice storm, after we fought?" Beau nodded for him to go on. "I noticed that I refueled quickly and I stayed in a state of high power as long as I was near you. I told you I had trouble breathing, and I did that night. That was when I really felt what was happening. Your body fed mine, but it wasn't a temperature transfer. It was your heart, your mind. The way you feel about me fuels me. It made my internal regulator extremely happy. So when I went back to the island, I came clean with Uncle Eddie. He made me tell Jareth what happened and he ran some tests. There was something new in my DNA."

"I put it there?"

"It's the only thing that could've placed it there." He smirked. "This sounds incredibly cheesy, but it's your love. Your love can keep me alive. You think you can stick around so I don't need to jet off every time the wind changes? Perhaps love me for life?"

Beau chewed the side of her lip, gazed at him intently. She brushed the hair aside that had fallen into his eyes. "I'm up for the challenge. I think I can manage to stay in love with you for at least a couple of years. We can reassess things then. You might start to aggravate me. You know how dating superheroes goes—you'll always be off saving the world and stuff. I might start to feel you're using me for my ability to keep you hot."

Jeremy allowed his lips to creep into a crooked grin. "Brilliant. Don't think I didn't notice how you referenced my hotness. That's cute." He grasped her behind the neck and pulled her face to his. Beau half-heartedly batted him away, grumbling about his vanity. "Now that that is out of the way and we have our boundaries, we can kiss and touch all we want until I black out the entire neighborhood. I have to convince you that forever is a better plan than only two bloody years. I'm aiming for eternity with you, and nothing else will do."

Chapter 12

"Keeping up with everyone in Jareth's life is like taking part in a soap opera. You never know where these characters come from. "
—Jeremy Tremaine on having people pop up from
different time periods at odd times.

A NGELLE HALL ON THE CAMPUS of University of Louisiana in the city of Lafayette was typical for the type of concert the Tremaines would be performing. It was a small venue, quaint, expensive, and classy. Jeremy ran his fingers over the piano keys as Elizabet helped the children tune their instruments. Beau braided Abigail's hair in the dressing room. Caesar helped Jareth track down the person in charge of the sound. The music needed to be projected evenly through the hall. Proper acoustics were critical when Gregorian chants were performed. Power and presence were important aspects of the musical. It was crucial that the sound system was on point.

"Mummy," Peter said, a frown curving his mouth. "My tie is itchy."

"My suit is itchy," Solomon grumbled. He tugged on the collar of his tuxedo.

Jeremy smiled faintly as he resisted the urge to yank at his tie. "Man up, boys," he said, looking up at them. "You know how Dad is about us being gentlemen. We need to look sharp."

"I prefer a suit of armor to this," Solomon said, his face pinching. He looked at his mother. "Polyester? Cotton? What?" He shook his head before glancing down at the guitar he held. "It's torture, that's what. I'm here for the music. Not to resemble a penguin."

Elizabet smirked. "It's tailored for you, *your highness.*" A young girl dressed in her Sunday best passed near the stage and caught Peter's eye. She waved shyly before darting to the seats located at the front of the auditorium. For a beat, Elizabet observed as the girl met up with a friend and spoke animatedly. She tossed an amused look toward Jeremy. "What the heck was that about?"

Jeremy smiled. Peter was already a magnet for girls. "Thank goodness for itchy suits." He wagged his brows. "Otherwise we'd be swarmed by Peters' fans. Imagine if he was actually charming while standing there, instead of squirmy."

Peter scoffed, but his eyes traveled to the pretty girl who was desperately trying to seem uninterested. She appeared to be about ten years of age. It was ridiculous, but common. He really was a homing beacon for lovelorn girls. "Can I get some help with this?" He gripped the neck of his guitar. "It's a bloody nuisance to tune this thing in here. The acoustics are terrible."

"Watch your language," Jareth said as he climbed the steps onto the stage with Caesar at his heels. "Remember who you are."

"Yeah, Simba," Jeremy said. Peter stuck his tongue out at him, but looked contrite. Their dad would box his ears in public if he had to. Even carrying a baby around his body in a Snugli baby backpack, the Duke of Dover was not one to mess with. Jeremy motioned for Elizabet to wipe Benjamin's nose. There was snot precariously low on the babe's face and heading toward the custom made suit Jareth was wearing. Benjamin was strapped in front of Jareth, facing away so he could see the action and Jareth could better keep an eye on him.

"Do not pick at them, Jeremy," Jareth warned. He turned before Elizabet was able to wipe Benjamin's nose. She chased the arc he made, getting hold with a tissue before any damage was done. "We cannot have things escalating moments before the concert."

"Jareth, I can't find the special notes you made for Solomon. How will he follow along?" Elizabet grabbed Jareth's shoulder to still him and better clean Benjamin's face. Solomon was trying to be slick and not look to see if anyone had overheard. His face flushed as he doubled his efforts to tune his instrument. He didn't like when he was singled out as different. "I thought they were with the rest of them, but they're not."

"The file is in the car," Jareth said. He turned to Caesar; Elizabet's body flailed with the movement. "Can you fetch it? It is on the floorboard near the driver's seat." He smiled at Elizabet. "I made some last minute changes. Harrow knows a doctor who specializes in dyslexia. I had him look into sheet music and he came up with something new."

"Can you have them close the curtains? People are starting to arrive and we aren't ready." Her shoulders deflated as her hands balled up the tissue. "As if we could ever be ready for this."

He put his hands on her shoulders and squeezed. "Breathe, Elizabet. There is no luck in well-executed plans. You have practiced and refined this. The children are ready. You are ready."

She looked up at Jareth, eyes wide. "What was I thinking? One hundred dollars a ticket?"

"You are brilliant," Jareth said softly. His head tipped toward the general direction of the children. "They are brilliant." He motioned to Jeremy and mimed closing the stage curtains.

"I'll get it," Beau said. She came up the steps onto the stage and passed Jeremy a file. "Caesar said to give you this."

"See," Jareth said. "No worries, duchess." He said the word duchess as though it was an endearment. "I have seen you enchant many audiences with your voice. It bewitches the hearts of those who hear it. I, myself, am not immune. You have held court with the King of England, yet this frightens you?"

"Your father *likes* me," she said, scowling. "He knows me.

Likes the way I sing. And you would love me if I had the voice of braying mule. I can't trust you. You're blind where I'm concerned." She paused her tirade to touch his sleeve. "And I love you right back for it, but . . ." she motioned to the empty seats in the auditorium, her voice lowering. "But I charged admission for this. There will be a level of expectancy. They aren't the King of England by a long shot."

Jareth smiled and placed a kiss on her mouth just as the curtains closed. Benjamin giggled and grabbed hold of his mother, his little feet kicking in excitement to be sandwiched between his parents. "You are perfect and they will love you, same as my father, the King of England."

Jeremy passed Solomon a look. Solomon rolled his eyes, and Gideon snickered. Peter watched with unveiled amusement, the way he always did, as if he were cataloging facts for his own future relationships.

BEAU SAT IN THE WINGS backstage, watching the amazing talent. It was not a typical concert young people attended, but rather, it was more theatrical. She liked it. It was a chance to get all dressed up and feel that she touched culture. And seeing Jeremy in his element was always an extra thrill. A hurricane may have cured him of his idiosyncrasies, but it left this behind. The boy could really have a future in music if he wanted it.

They performed a total of ten songs as a family, three Gregorian chants and seven older hymns. The encores were a bonus—Eleanor Rigby first, and then the final song which Jeremy sang solo. The children were all removed except Peter, who remained to accompany on guitar from behind the curtain. Elizabet took over for Gideon on the drums, but they were hidden behind the stage so not to expose that a lady wearing an evening dress was rocking out on a drum set. She was a duchess, after all. Gideon's age hindered him from being more than the percussionist. What Jeremy was about to perform required a rhythm and beat that a four-year-old would struggle with—even a Tremaine youth.

"Did you catch where the loo is?" Solomon asked, his feet shuffling in place.

Beau looked around. Caesar had been missing since intermission. He was supposed to help her keep things running smoothly behind the scenes. "In the main dressing area where the girls changed."

He scampered off, the tails of his coat fanning out.

Abigail grabbed her hand and Gideon leaned against her legs as they watched the finale.

Beau gripped the hand of her small cousin, loving life. This glorious family that allowed her to share their space with them—and with such abandonment—made her happy beyond any of her dreams. The years of being lonely and forgotten were behind her.

Jeremy delivered as he always did, bringing down the house with a talent he didn't ask for, but nonetheless owned. He stood at the end, bowing singularly to where Elizabet and Peter were hidden and then to the crowd who gave him a standing ovation.

It was better than anyone expected. The number of the crowd, the performance, the whole setting and stage—it was perfect. This would usher in a new age for the Tremaines. They didn't just wow with their talent; their unity had also earned respect. People who respected would in turn be supportive and that was the take. This was for charity, after all, not for personal gain. Everyone wanted church reform, but didn't know how to fund it without being on the out of political awareness. They had just given hundreds of people an out. Lots could be conquered in the name of theatre and the arts. The Tremaines had chosen a clever medium to raise awareness for a movement close to their hearts.

Jareth signaled for the children to take the stage next to their mother when Elizabet stepped out with Peter. Beau released Abigail and Gideon, looking over her shoulder for Solomon.

"Where is Solomon?" Jareth asked, sidling up next to Beau. Benjamin reached out with a chubby hand.

Beau kissed the babe's fingers just to see him smile. "He went to the restroom."

Jareth looked peeved. "I told him not to drink two Icees before a performance. Elizabet dislikes curtain calls. We need to make this brief and painless for her." He let out a shallow breath. "Can you rap on the door and tell the fellow to hurry it up a bit? I cannot have his mother displaying her superpower for all to see."

Beau grimaced. It wasn't a superpower—it was a menace. However, it was sweet that Jareth called his wife's overactive stomach acid something kindred to greatness when quite frankly, it could get rather nasty in a heartbeat. "I'll be right back." She kissed Benjamin's hand again before making her way to the small dressing area.

She knocked on the door and found that it was not latched closed all the way. "Solomon," she called in warning as the door swung open. It was a tiny restroom, only big enough to fit a toilet and sink. The light was off. Strange.

Beau frowned and grappled for the light switch on the wall. As instantly as the light appeared, she saw the note taped to the square mirror over the sink.

She should have known that even fairy tale families had their thorns, and the ones where time traveling royalty were involved were a recipe for disaster. The best of kin can reveal that life is not perfect. Her proverbial rose-colored glasses were yanked from her face.

She read the note three times, each time the absurdity of it striking her more so than the last. It was a ransom letter. The most absurd part was that it was written in Caesar's hand. The heir of Dover would never have another curtain call unless Jeremy was forfeited in his place. Solomon had been kidnapped and the ransom was Jeremy and control of Dover's Amalgam.

"Jareth!" She raced the note back to where Jareth was still rounding up the children. "He's gone. Solomon is gone!" Her eyes narrowed on Jeremy as he sidled up beside Jareth, hearing her elevated tone. Shaking the letter in his direction, she addressed him, "This letter was written by Caesar. What the heck, Jeremy? Is there something you're not telling me?"

Jareth grabbed the paper from her hand and read what she had committed to memory. "We gave Caesar a place in my family and he has kidnapped my son?" His voice was low, a dull hum in her ears. He folded the note into his fist. He shot Jeremy a heated glare as though this catastrophe was entirely his fault. "The Huns have taken the heir of Dover's seat and your *comrade* is in on it."

Jeremy's mouth opened and snapped shut, his expression perplexed. "Caesar?"

"Did I stutter?" Jareth barked, tossing the note at Jeremy's chest. He barely caught it before it tumbled to the floor.

Jeremy read the messy scrawl of Caesar's print, chewing his bottom lip, shaking his head with the absurdity of it all. He looked up. "How was I supposed to know?"

"Oh, I do not know," Jareth's tone was condescending. "That ability you have to siphon, perhaps? Perhaps you could have discerned if your little friend could be trusted before you invited him into my home and into the lives of *my children*?" He looked over to where Elizabet stood, unaware of the devastating news. His shoulders slumped as he cradled Benjamin closer to him, running a hand idly over the babe's downy hair. "I must tell the duchess that one of her children is not within her care, but with a pack of lunatics bent on destroying all we stand for." His lip curled. "I will have retribution for this."

Jeremy passed Beau a look she could not interpret. It looked a bit like fear.

"I'll tell her," Jeremy offered.

Jareth shook his head, his feet already carrying him in his

wife's direction. "News such as this should come from me. She will need comfort you cannot provide."

Jeremy's eyes traveled to the note, tears filling his eyes. Beau approached him timidly, putting her hand on his arm. She did not need to be a siphon to know that he was devastated, because she was, too. This was unthinkable. The thought that Solomon was in captivity to a brutal league of men sent shivers down her spine.

"You couldn't have known. We both trusted him," she said. "We've known Caesar for years. He's hidden this—something—from us all this time."

Jeremy's expression was tortured. "My brother's kidnapping could have been prevented so simply." He balled the note and stuck it the inner pocket of his suit jacket. "I've failed my family. This is my fault. It's all me." He looked down at Beau. "I have to make this right."

Beau's heart skipped a beat; fear grabbing her with both hands and shaking her. From the information she gathered on the Huns, they were in for a bloody battle. The life of Solomon was in the graces of a gang of madmen. Her new life in this Amalgam was an unsure path that would be riddled with troubles.

Her hand squeezed Jeremy's arm and she laid her head against his shoulder. The place at his side was her destiny. She may not be aware of everything involved with the new twist of things, but she did know this: she would stand by Jeremy and defend him if necessary. Her place was here.

Medieval Dover, 1320

THE LEAGUE ASSEMBLED IN MEDIEVAL Dover. Seated at the massive banquet table in the great room of the castle was the Amalgam in its entirety. Hosts and guardians alike were accounted for. Their number was one hundred and seven. Warrior men and women who had been stolen from time to help protect the league of hosts. History had been combed and Jareth, Gabriel, and Minh had retrieved them and brought them together to protect vulnerable hosts. It was the prowess and proficiency of each that had gained them access into a life of service to Dover's Amalgam. Not one of them regretted the selection. They enforced the laws of the league with pride and excellence.

While the room was filled with bated anxiety, it was harnessed by the actuality that retribution was about to be served. Not so, however, with the duchess of the castle. It had taken Jareth hours to calm Elizabet, and finally he took the easy way and gave her a hefty dose of tranquilizers. He simply could not think while she was hysterical. His emotions volleyed between killing everyone involved and giving in and having a good cry himself.

His son had been kidnapped. The loss he felt was bone deep, rendering his heart open and bleeding as if it were in fact a physical wound. But he could not let Elizabet know how terrified and sick he was. His upbringing demanded he call the bluff of Gyula and let things fall where they may. He had a spare heir. It was the way of things. Let Solomon go and cut his losses. His son understood the drill. Jareth knew that Solomon was prepared to lay his life down for the seat of Dover. It was what he was bred to do.

But Solomon was a child . . . *his* child . . .

He envisioned the boy in his mind and tears swam in his eyes, blurring the scene before him. The Amalgam was seated at his table awaiting instructions. Those who were not seated stood at attention against the wall and surrounded the table. The large room was packed. It would be best that he not dampen the morale with healthy wailing and good old-fashioned cry.

"Didn't I tell you it would come to this?" Gabriel's voice taunted.

Jareth's hands formed fists on the table before him. The silver gauntlets that covered his forearms chafed, his silver armored gloves tossed casually next to his goblet. He was dressed in armor for battle, although they did not know precisely where that battle was to be fought.

"Wasn't I just saying the other day that the lives of our families were in jeopardy?" Gabriel demanded.

"Gabriel," Minh said, his voice low. "My brother." They looked at each other across the table, from the right and left sides of Jareth, flanking him. "You've said your peace."

"What if it was the duchess?" Gabriel snarled. "Or Liang? Perhaps if it were your sister you wouldn't be so smug."

"I can solve this," Jeremy said, his voice soft amid the grumbling taking place around the table. No one seemed to notice that he had spoken. Jareth was the only one who had heard him clearly.

"Now you want to offer your help?" Jareth sneered. He slammed his fist on the table, thereby silencing all of the rumbling. "This would have never happened if you had read the boy." Jeremy's eyes closed, his face pale against the candle and firelight. "If you had not decided that blind trust was so bloody important in friendship. They have my son. My son!" His fist slammed down again. The thick wood of the table shook.

"I was wrong. It won't happen again." Jeremy spoke quickly. He opened his eyes. "And I'll start my penance by surrendering. Find where the Huns reside and I will turn myself in. I'll make the trade only after I secure Solomon."

A caustic laugh left Jareth's mouth. "They don't want to bargain with you—they want to *kill* you. They will terminate you on sight and call it principle. Honestly? Do you think I'll willingly hand the strongest host known to mankind over to pack of lunatics?" He fanned his hand toward the far end of the table. "Ezra has ferreted one of their hosts. You are merely the beginning of this killing spree, not even the main course. They do not want an alliance with us, they want to exterminate the guardians and keep the host they can control with fear."

"Seriously?" Minh's voice cracked.

"A host was found near the Brac. A tsunami. Younger than Malia but was turned in the same incident." Jareth motioned for Ezra to continue.

Ezra's chair scraped against the stone floor as he pushed to a standing position. He was dressed in army fatigues. The symbol of the infantry he had served in during the Vietnam War was faded, but remained on his shoulder. On the opposite was the symbol of Dover: A Catherine wheel and Talbot dog. Its colors were bright and bold, a contrast to the rest of the well-worn uniform. He bowed to Jareth before he spoke. "Malia discovered the host on a routine run in Sri Lanka. She captured him and we detained—"

"Facts, Ezra," Jareth bit out. "Just the facts. The life of my son hangs in the balance. We have not the time for long-winded recounts."

"The Huns believe we stole the time bands, not that they were given to his grace as a gift. Gyula has used a lie as a premise to form this league of his." Ezra cleared his throat. "They aspire to be the only guardians in this world. They want exclusive rights to hosts."

"And there it is," Jareth said, and allowed the sarcasm to ride in his voice. "The age old battle of good versus evil. Blah, blah." He made an obscene gesture with his hand. Jeremy snickered inappropriately, but quickly fixed his face when Jareth passed him a glance. Minh bit his lip, but the corner of it twitched. "What I want to know is how we find these people so I can kill them. Suggestions? Anyone?"

"Crikey, Jareth," Simon Dare, the Duke of Margate, said. "Can't this be handled as gentlemen?" He appeared aghast at what he would perceive as Jareth's insolent behavior and speech.

Jareth leveled a stare at a man he had chosen as guardian based on his skill in the navy. There was no other like him on the seas. The Duke of Margate was legendary in the War of the Coalition of 1799, where his expertise in the sea hailed him nearly as great as Wellington. His level of skillfulness was an asset to the location of the Amalgam Headquarters. The English Channel was all that stood between England and an oftentimes an angry France. He was much needed, but came from Georgian England, when life was ruled by a polite society. The man was a stickler for things handled properly and with the least amount of blood possible. In short, he and Jareth were polar opposites.

"Do not 'crikey' me, Simon. Keep your benign little quips to yourself before I accidently run you through with my sword. As a blistering naval man, I somehow thought you would prefer to win this war rather than have our asses handed to us on a platter. I would think you would be on board with a plan that includes us killing them before they kill us."

Gabriel muttered something that sounded like "here we go" under his breath, while Minh sat up straighter, and with more interest on his face than before. Jeremy sank in his seat, a smirk on his face.

"So, all you little girls are having a moment of quiet solitude," he went on. "Or perhaps I could hope you are merely praying that God spares you, because I will not." His index finger rapped the wooden table like a gavel. "Either way, here is what I plan to do." He made a steeple with his fingers. "I am taking Jeremy with me and we are going back to Caesar's house to search for clues. Hopefully, the bastard left us something we can latch onto." He pointed at Gabriel. "Have all of the guardians round up their hosts and wait for us on the list. We are bringing the war here. It will be easier to wipe history's mind of hosts without the presence of television cameras and nasty reporters."

Gabriel saluted, his lips curved in a mocking smile.

Jareth's upper lip curled. "Feel free to allow the guardians their leisure on choice of weaponry."

"We live to serve, your majesty." Gabriel grinned.

Jareth turned to his right and Minh sat straight at attention, awaiting orders. "See to the women. If my duchess or daughter is assaulted, I shall blame you. Keep them underground if you have to. You know how Elizabet can be. When she fights her way out of that hefty Haldol dose I administered, there will be hell to be pay and she will be looking for me to take it from my skin." He tapped the table again. "Keep her under lock and key. I will not have my mind burdened with worry over her safety as well as getting Solomon home safe and secure."

Minh's face fell. "Oh, joy," he deadpanned. He gave double thumbs up. "Way to go, Jareth. Good call. Use the Minister of War as a babysitter. That's very clever."

"Once the women and children are secure, gather the remaining guardians and be ready on the northern list. We will drop the battle there," Jareth said. He pushed away from the table and stood. The discordant sound of chairs scraping and people scrambling to stand with their prince ricocheted in the room. "I will keep you all posted through Ezra. It is required that all of you stay in Dover until this is resolved. We do not know the magnitude of the situation, but we do know that we are stronger. We are better prepared. We are smarter." He looked at Jeremy. "And we have a legion of hosts at our disposal. May God have mercy on those who rise against us and may they be ready to meet their creator for we are taking no prisoners. *Dover enim rex Salomon.*"

The guardians chanted unanimously. "For Dover, King, and Solomon."

THE ENTIRE SCENE WAS SURREAL. Jareth had flashed them to modern Gueydan—the middle of town, no less—plus, he remained suited for battle in full silver plated battle armor. It was sight to behold, like something from the History Channel and HBO come together. A knight stalking up to a friendly, unsuspecting neighborhood. The saving grace was that it was nighttime. Most nosey folks would be on their way to bed instead of looking into the source of the bright light that flashed at the end of Third Street.

"If it helps to know," Jareth said as they walked up the driveway to Caesar's home. "I am not angry with you. This is not your fault. I blame Gyula or Caesar. Take your pick."

"Both," Jeremy said. He shook his head. "Although I'm at a loss at how Caesar fits. It doesn't make sense."

"Remember how I said there was something familiar about him?" Jareth asked. Jeremy nodded. "Yeah, well, I did my happy list making that drives everyone but me nuts and came up with something." He paused. The crunching of gravel beneath their feet punctuated the serenity of the neighborhood they were invading. "Gyula is a Hungarian name. It is a form of Julius."

Jeremy stopped short, the name tumbling out of his mouth like a curse word. "Caesar."

"Right-O," Jareth said with a shrug. "Caesar is Gyula's son. The child had red hair and I clearly remember his facial structure—the long face and the shape of his eyes. He must have traveled backward and planted him here to keep him close to you. To us."

"I'm gobsmacked."

"Yeah," Jareth breathed. "Me, too."

Jeremy could just imagine what this had cost Jareth. He was not a host with the privilege of being cured of his 'specialness.' Jareth had to live every day with a mild case of Asperger's. Those lists he spoke of had probably taken hours to decipher and a great deal of gray matter, which meant a loss of peace of mind. He would bet that the solar in Dover was riddled with papers hanging from the walls—all with neatly scrolled lists.

"So, what else do you have?" Jeremy asked.

Jareth shrugged. "It all depends on what we find in there." He tipped his chin toward the house. "I am guessing we are both about to be gobsmacked into the next century."

"Spidey senses are tingling?" Jeremy asked. His black brow winged upward suggestively.

Jareth scowled. "It is called discernment. You should try it sometimes." Jeremy's grin faltered. He sometimes forgot not to jest when Jareth was in the killing zone. "Now, get up there and ring the doorbell. If someone is home, I will wait here for you. Use your, uh, charm to disengage them. I do not want to cause any unnecessary scenes where Gabriel has to do damage control. If no one is there, we shall break and enter. Search the place and take what we must as clues."

By disengaging, Jareth meant for him to shock the person senseless—literally. An average, controlled shock could render a person unconscious for about thirty minutes. He rubbed his hands together. "Did I ever tell you that I love being in this family. Having my little brother kidnapped aside—we are pretty cool."

Jareth's face fell. "Yeah . . ."

"Jareth, I'm so sorry. I shouldn't have said that. Not now, at least." The raw expression had Jeremy uneasy. He was anxious over Solomon's capture; he couldn't imagine what Jareth was going through. Seeing Jareth vulnerable didn't look right.

"It is fine." Jareth wove it off. "If Solomon were here, he would heartily agree. Now get on with this. We have a war to bring to Dover. People are expecting it."

Jeremy marched the remainder of the way. He glanced back to see Jareth barely manage to hide behind a potted saga palm.

He rang the doorbell. The cat that resided in the home stared at him through the transit window on the side of the door. A second bell toll was not necessary.

"Jeremy," Caesar's mother answered the door. She was impeccably dressed as always in the evident yet not so evident yoga pants and polo to look as if she was the ultimate lady of leisure. "Can I . . . I mean to say—"

Jeremy was having trouble shuffling between the turmoil wafting from Caesar's perfectly coiffed mom before him and the anger streaming from Jareth at his back. He reacted quickly, reached out with his powers, and took what he needed to interpret the scene.

He wedged his foot in the door before she could slam it in his face, and at the same time, Jareth was there, pistol cocked and pointed at the lady's face.

"Where is my son?" Jareth demanded. He kicked the door completely open, his aim never wavering from between her eyes. A sputtering noise erupted from her as her eyes traveled the length of Jareth in battle attire. "Be quick about it, Catherine, and I may allow you to live."

"Catherine," Jeremy hissed. He pulled back to gape at the woman he had only heard of. Catherine of Torquay, once upon a time, had wanted Jareth for a husband. He had not returned the sentiment, however, and now there was bad blood between them—a massive understatement. Caesar's entire family was time hopping progenies. Catherine was a medieval maiden of high rank exiled to Scotland for the attempted murdered of the Duchess of Dover. "Caesar's mom is *Catherine of Torquay?*"

"Evidently," Jareth sneered, and nudged her with the nose of his pistol. She stumbled back into the foyer, gripping the door as to not fall over. They stepped into the house. "Give me one good reason not to blow your brains out."

"You arrogant pig," she ground out, teeth bared. "If you kill me, Gyula will never return your son alive."

"Where is your dear husband?" Jareth asked. His eyes roved but his aim remained steady.

"He is not my husband," she spat. "I hate him as much as you do. He stole from me. My innocence. My way of life. He left me here to fend for myself and my son. If you had married me, none of this would be happening. It's your fault. You were betrothed to me! When you broke the agreement, no one would have me—not after I was rejected by a bastard." The word rejected was laced with acid. "Women and minstrels may proclaim your beauty throughout all of England; you may be the best soldier in His Majesty's army, but you will always be a bastard. I could have saved you. Saved your name—made something of it. We would have had Torquay and Dover ports at our disposable. We could have owned the French and given them to the king on a platter. You would have been invincible. Instead you married that stupid, silly peasant girl."

Jareth made a *tsking* noise and shook his head. "My, my, what a mouthful. You have been waiting years to say that. I am sure of that, but you lost my sympathy long ago. Particularly when you endangered the life of my peasant wife." He glanced at Jeremy. "Find something to tie her hands together. We will remove her to Dover where she will be executed for treason."

Catherine screamed in outrage. "How dare you! You can't have me executed. I am no longer your subject. I am no longer a citizen of England." She straightened to her full height. "I'm an American and I have rights."

Jareth's eyes narrowed as he took her in from head to foot, and then a bark of laughter erupted from his mouth. "Where we are going, there is no America and you have no rights other than the ones I allow. I am taking you where I am lord, master, and judge." Catherine wriggled while Jeremy proceeded to tie her wrists behind her back. "It was bad form not to remember what I come from. I should have executed you when I had the chance. Banishment never works on your kind."

She spit in Jareth's face. "I hated it in Scotland. They're barbaric."

"And yet Gyula was your lover. That is barbaric, revolting, and I bet, rather nasty." Jareth wiped the spit from his face using the hem of her shirt. He smiled as he let her the fabric fall. "It sounds right up your alley."

"I hate you," Catherine scorned.

"And I hate you, too," Jareth said, making it sound like an endearment. "But look on the bright side. You only have a couple of hours left on this earth to hate me. When you took my wife, I sent you away instead of executing you because Elizabet asked it of me. Now you take my son?" He shook his head and *tsk*ed under his breath again. "This time you die."

"SHE HAD A CHILD?" MINH asked, his face a mask of confusion. He shook his head and returned to stringing a bow. "No wonder the termite wanted to marry Jareth so badly. She was knocked up. I guess it was better to marry a bastard than to birth one."

Jeremy grimaced, remembering the memories he had siphoned to fill in the gaps with the truth. Catherine and Gyula were the parents of Caesar—truth. The how that came to be was not pretty. He almost felt sorry for the girl she had once been. But she had set her sights on Jareth as a prospective husband to cover up her mistake, and that was nothing short of fraud. Still, he had to admit that a good portion of her remembered Jareth fondly. She had really thought she loved him; she believed that love was her motivation.

"It didn't go quite that way. She had already borne Caesar. Her sights were set on Jareth since they were children and she never gave up that hope, despite her unplanned pregnancy. She was thirteen when he was born," Jeremy said. "She gave birth in the orphanage in Portsmouth and left him there with the abbess, so no one was the wiser. Sir James, her father, paid a hearty sum to keep the officials quiet. Gyula retrieved him some years later." He passed Minh another wooden bow to string. "All the jumping back and forth through time was Gyula's choice. Confusing to me, and I'm the siphon."

"This is why time jumping is regulated," Jareth said as he strode into the room. "It is a travesty that anyone can think to take advantage of the privilege. It is blasphemous."

Jeremy took one look at him and grimaced again. He stood in the archway of the great room, drying his hands on a linen cloth. His expression was void of any emotion. His killing face. "Is it done then?" he asked.

Jareth nodded, one quick jerk. He walked into the room and tossed the cloth into the blaze that was roaring in the fireplace, but not before Jeremy spied the smudged blood covering it. "I trust that you filtered all the information we need to proceed with the next phase."

"Yes, *Magister*." Jeremy steeled his frame. He had taken the information he needed from Catherine before she was executed—an execution that Jareth felt was essential to perform himself. There would be no second exile when too many factors surfed about. Catherine would only have escaped again and come after them using a different approach. The Tremaines would not be safe as long she had breath in her body.

Jareth leaned forward onto the mantle, resting on his forearm as he stared into the fire. His hands curled into fists. "Please, do not 'yes, *Magister*' me." He thumped the stone; it made a dull thud that trembled the mantle. "I do not think I can bear that right now."

"Jareth, you just executed his friend's mother. Give him a break." Minh murmured.

"It's all right," Jeremy said, the fire of his words rapid, because he was more than all right. Jareth turned his neck to face him, his expression tortured. "She wouldn't have stopped. I saw the hate in her." He glanced at Minh. "I know how things work here. I'm not a weak link. I get it. Always have." He grumbled the last part, and then plucked the mass of arrows from the table. "I'm ready to go whenever you are. Just say the word."

"Now?" Jareth asked.

"I must see Beau before we go," he answered. "After that, I'm free. You?"

Jareth inclined his head as if all in the world was perfect and they were merely discussing teatime. "I will wait for you on the northern list. We have a wormhole to catch, so do not tarry."

"You're not going to the duchess?" Jeremy asked. It was irregular for Jareth to not pay a visit to the duchess before departing.

Jareth shook his head, his expression bleak. "I promised her the next time she saw me, I would have her son at my side. I fully intend to keep my word or I shall die trying." He turned to Minh. "Walk with me to the abbey?"

Minh's chair scraped across the floor as he stood. "Of course, your grace." He bowed, and then eyed Jeremy expectantly.

Jeremy pressed his mouth into a hard line, but he went down on his knee, genuflecting. The angle allowed him to spot the specks of blood that randomly peppered the metal plates of Jareth's armor. "Your majesty. I offer my allegiance. My services belong to Dover, the crown of his majesty, King Edward, and to Almighty God. *Soli Deo gloria.*"

"To the glory of God alone," Jareth repeated in English, his head tilting a fraction. "For Solomon. Let the flag be raised. Our enemies will rue the day they tempted the dragon bastard of Dover." He passed Minh a hard look. "We will not relent until the sea runs red with the blood of Huns."

JEREMY PRESSED HIS LIPS TO Beau's once, then twice, and perhaps even more. He lost count because he never wanted to leave her. Being with her had become a safe place for him.

And she sensed it.

"You have to go," she whispered against his lips.

Jeremy ran his hand up her spine and rested it on the nape of her neck. "I know. Just a little longer."

"Are you really going to the year 1802?" she asked. "Do you

know what the weather will be like? Do you need me to come along in case?"

Jeremy sighed. "I'll be fine. It's autumn where we're headed. Nothing I can't handle." She wouldn't let him have this peaceful moment. He could sense the anxiety coursing within her. "There is a school for deaf children in the district of Thanet. Gyula is using it as cover for hiding hosts. To think this was taking place under our noses." He kissed her twice more, quickly, before she could fuss. "Or rather under Margate's notice. This marks the beginning of the opening of Pandora's Box—mark my words. History is riddled with dealings of Gyula. We just haven't discovered the breaches yet. This will change everything."

"Be careful." Beau's hands traveled from his waist to his shoulders. "What about Caesar? What will y'all do about him?"

"I can't answer that. It depends on how much of a fight he puts up. We don't know his involvement with Gyula's league. We know that they are father and son, but the depth of that alliance remains to be seen." His eyes darted from hers briefly. "If only I'd read him, none of this would be happening." He made a short growl at the back of his throat. "This would've been avoided. It's all my fault. My brother was kidnapped because I valued a friendship more than my family."

"You know that's not true," Beau barked. She softened her tone when he winced. "He was our friend. We both trusted him, Jeremy. I did too. It wasn't you alone who made this mistake."

"I don't want to kill him, but I also don't want this to end in the death of my little brother. I can't help but feel partly responsible."

"I know, I know," she chanted. She made it sound as though she was praying. "Please, be careful. Come back to me."

"I will," he said. He lifted her from the ground and hugged her tightly. He loved the way she wrapped around him when her feet left the floor and he twirled her in his arms. "Promise me you'll stay close to Minh and Liang." Liang had the training fit for a ninja princess, a precarious master of the martial arts, like her brother. "Jareth said he would have you home before anyone notices you're gone. If we need you, for any reason, I will send for you."

"I'll be right here, on this side of the wormhole, waiting for you." She crossed her heart. "I promise. We're in this together. Always."

"Always."

Chapter 13

"A host is trained with ultimate justice in mind. Without a measure of goodness, we are lost. It is up to Dover to provide the instruction. Who is Dover? The presiding duke is Dover; the Duke of Dover is Magister."

—Liang Morton to Beau Benoit when asked about how the Amalgam was governed

The District of Thanet, near Margate, England 1802

THE ROYAL SCHOOL FOR DEAF Children stood in the distance. It was an imposing building, beautiful and castle-like in size. Built for obvious reasons, it also housed a mass of hosts being disguised as deaf subjects. It angered Jareth that Gyula risked the lives of innocent children. Housing unstable hosts close to children was a recipe for disaster. After rescuing Solomon, he would take control of the school and make sure Simon, the Duke of Margate, was given rightful guardianship over the school. Simon knew how to handle hosts and children. It would be one more time period under the ultimate protection of Dover's Amalgam.

Once they rounded the red brick building, Jeremy proceeded to rip his clothes off, starting with his shirt.

"There are at least twenty hosts in different ranges of strength. Most are young and won't pose a problem, so I say we leave them here and deal with them later. I'll send the five strong ones to you. Fifty or so Huns." Jeremy toed off his slip-on shoes and reached for the drawstring on his flannel pants.

"Gyula is there."

"Perfect," Jareth replied. He turned to Gabriel. "Ferret them out. Margate and I will wait here with the wormholes ready."

"Fire in the hole," Jeremy quipped just before he dissipated. His form shot upward into the sky.

A dark cloud appeared and thunder rumbled.

Gabriel's head tilted. "Do I hear . . . ?"

Jareth's mouth twisted. "Right-O. My son is in love, all right. Singing love songs is what he does now. Perhaps we can hope for a better exit. Preferably a tune that doesn't make me feel like hugging my targets before I kill them."

CAESAR'S HANDS PAUSED ON THE zipper to Malia's dress. "Did you hear that?"

Malia stepped away, batting his hands off of her. "He's here." She listened for a beat, the confident expression she always wore was slipping. "With Dover's army."

She was always like this after sex—like she wanted nothing to do with him. It was something he was getting used to, but he didn't like it. Malia was beautiful and she liked using the fact she was attractive to get her way. He was a slave to her charm and could not resist her anything she asked of him.

Caesar shrugged to appear unaffected by her rudeness. "Let them come. We're ready."

"Don't be an idiot," Malia sneered. "I told you this wouldn't be easy." She grabbed her backpack and removed the time band from her wrist.

"Where are you going?" He hated the neediness he heard in his voice, and the hurt. "I thought you were staying to help us fight." She was, after all, the spy who had made all of this possible. It was Malia who found Dover's Amalgam's weak points. She told them about Jeremy's power to siphon being weak when he was emotionally involved—although she had been wrong about that. Jeremy had dismembered Silas easily enough the night they sent him to destroy Beau. The Hungarian League hadn't expected that. Some of her information had not been correct, but nonetheless, they couldn't have gotten this far without her.

And she hadn't been wrong about how easy it was to abduct Solomon on the night of the concert. That had been a flawless execution. She was still needed. The Huns did not know the magnitude of Dover's Amalgam's army. Being that she was a strong host, they needed her in this fight.

"I can't. I have to get back before Ezra realizes I swiped his time band."

"Did you sleep with him to get it?" The jealous accusation popped into his head and out of his mouth. He grabbed her arm before she could activate the wormhole.

She glared at her arm where he held her. "Let. Me. Go."

"Answer the question." He bit out. Now that he had asked, he knew it was true. She was faithful to no one but herself.

Her chin jutted out. "He's old. Gross. What do you think I am? I don't go around sleeping with just anyone."

"You're lying," he accused. He didn't know why he hadn't seen through her before. She had used him to get back at Jeremy. He could feel it. He looked to where his hand wrapped around her wrist, and felt the memories and thoughts leak from her into him. "You're an emotion sucker like Jeremy."

She shook her arm free. "It's called a siphon, you moron."

He lunged for her, but she tossed the time band and leaped through so quickly that he knew she used her powers.

He sat there staring at the place she disappeared, feeling like an idiot for believing that she loved him. The worst part was that she allowed him to discover her nasty little secret of being a siphon so she could give him the lowdown of her plan.

It had nothing to do with helping his father's league and everything to do with getting back at Jeremy. She never intended to help the fight. Again, he wanted a girl who had Jeremy issues. This time, however, his life was at risk. Malia had just let him know that Dover's army was more lethal than an atom bomb.

He cursed under his breath and went to look for his father.

It was their way to fight in the manner they had been trained in their respective time periods. Jareth had learned that the hard way. The guardians fought better in their natural form, and no amount of contra-training could change them. So he let them be. Unhampered by his heavy bronze breastplate, Gabriel proceeded to scale the front of the building where they suspected the Huns were congregated in the great room. He swung his shield over his plumed helmet so it lay slung low on his back over his red cloak as he employed his massive arms to lever his way up.

"You must know that I had no idea they were here," Simon said. Jareth averted his attention from watching Jeremy become a wicked act of nature and glanced back at him, seeing that he was seriously going to do this now—here. The man had social issues. Social issues being he was a prig—a stickler for doing things the gentlemanly way. "If I had known—"

Jareth held up his hand. "It is all good, Margate. We regulate time jumps. This could not have been foreseen unless we breached time."

"Will the rules change?" Simon asked.

A loud noise and hollering rent the air around them. Gabriel emerged from the building by leaping through a window. Glass shattered and fell to the ground. He landed on his feet and crouched low, cloak fluttering behind him, his body bent over the form he held in his arms.

That was exceedingly quick. Gabriel's own time record for claim and conquer had just been trumped by Gabriel himself. It was awe-inspiring. Jareth made a mental note to give him a raise.

"He's got the boy," Jareth announced. He tossed the band from his right wrist into the air and a wormhole expanded open with a burst of light. Simon did the same; the two wormholes gaped open side by side.

Jeremy swooped low, forming a cloud to camouflage Gabriel as he ran with Solomon toward the wormholes. A legion of Huns was at his back. Arrows rained from the sky like a firestorm plague of biblical proportions. Two arrows were lodged in Gabriel's thighs and three in each arm. Mentally, Jareth considered the damage from his wounds. Gabriel would not be able to fight. The chance that the arrows were poisoned was high.

"Dad!" Solomon cried when they reached him. His eyes were wide with fear as he latched onto Gabriel's neck.

A sob nearly escaped Jareth's mouth before he stopped it. "Put him behind me," he barked to Gabriel even as his gaze searched for any damage on his son's body. "Remove those arrows at once, Gabriel. Once we are in Dover, go to the infirmary and wait there."

Gabriel set Solomon on his feet. The boy immediately threw himself at Jareth, hugging his legs even though they were covered in heavy armor. "Hell no. I'm not sitting this one out," he sneered. "Bastards tried to use a host on me." He thumped his breastplate with his fist. Ice crackled there. "They have one who can manipulate water—some sort of blizzard or something. They had him on ice so he could blast me. Popped out of a frozen casket like some kind of sick Disneyland ride."

Jareth passed his hand over Solomon's head and smiled briefly into his son's face. "They cannot tote an ice casket down through the wormhole." He looked at Gabriel. "He will be as weak as a newborn babe without the right environment."

"My sentiments exactly." Gabriel drew his spear and sword. "He's mine."

"Tally-ho, men!" Simon yelled. He drew his pistol and sabre.

"Here they come. Look alive!"

Jareth unsheathed a smaller sword and handed it to Solomon before he shielded him with his body. Bringing the eye shield down on his helmet, he raised his sword in a defensive pose and assessed the situation.

Jeremy steered the unwilling hosts and Huns into the awaiting wormholes. He ignored the wailing as his body wove between and through them as he forced them through. If Jareth was a wrangler, Jeremy was the enforcer. No one got away on his watch. The winds gave the enemy no choice but to comply and go wherever he desired. Two of Dover's own guardians leapt into the wormholes to guide the traffic into the proper time conduit. Under the guidance of Simon, Ezra and a French commander of Napoleon's army pressed the streams of Huns down the correct pathway of the open wormhole. Their aid was not necessary, but Jeremy welcomed it. He didn't like when one of his siblings was involved in battle. It divided his attention. Jareth didn't need a babysitter host, but Solomon was barely out from under his mother's wing. And he had just been kidnapped. That made him vulnerable; the child would not be in top form when fear was a factor.

And he had to keep his eye on the five hosts he gathered with the Huns. They had tacked them on with their number, which was fine with Jeremy. They were weak and easily driven like cattle among the herd he was prodding into the proper time channel. There were others left behind in Thanet, but he would deal with them later. Those still had a chance to pledge their allegiance to Dover, while these five had made their loyalties known.

"Ready?" Jareth asked Solomon as the last Hun host was wrangled into the wormhole.

Solomon sidestepped to take his position next to his father. He lifted his sword. "Not how many, but where!" The Spartan maxim tumbled from his mouth like an oath. One side of

Jareth's mouth tipped upward—he had wisely chosen the boy's godfather.

"That's it, young Padawan." Gabriel grinned and flexed his neck side to side. "I'd say the boy's ready, Jareth. Let's go. Minh is on the other side, getting a head start. I want to be sure there are plenty of big ones left for me."

Jareth led the way through the wormhole, choosing the amethyst path that led to medieval Dover. A legion of Dover's guardians followed in his wake, each bearing arms and ready for the battle that would be unleashed on the other side. Jeremy ditched them again, dissipating as soon as they breached the far side of the wormhole. His form became a dark cloud as it disintegrated the five enemy hosts straight through the heart before anyone could blink.

The boneless forms of the slain hosts appeared as their lives were stolen from them by one more powerful. On their knees, shock on their faces, their bodies sank and folded to the ground in death. They went down like deflated balloons, their bodies fileted by the mighty winds of an impossible hurricane. All bone and sinew was stripped and became nothing as Jeremy went in for the kill.

Minh was in position at the top of the list, sniping Huns one by one with deadly arrows. Abigail stood next to him with an arrow drawn, doing the same.

Jareth did a double take and his mouth fell open.

"Close your mouth and fight, dear," Elizabet said as she pushed passed him. She aimed and fired her pistol at the Hun he'd been too distracted to notice approaching his back. "We need a little help here."

"Abigail is on the list, *dear*," he growled, running a Hun through with his sword. He shoved the body off his blade and turned back to her.

"Impressive," Elizabet commented, a brow cocked upward. "So efficient and smooth." She turned her attention to

Solomon, who was in a sword fight. "Would you like to worry about the heir rather than your daughter, who is in the capable hands of her godfather?"

Jareth turned and sliced down the man opposite his son. "Get them off the field, Elizabet," he bellowed.

She smirked and wiped a smudge from her face with the back of her hand. "Chauvinist."

"Whatever," Jareth grumbled, and then stalked away. He spotted dark hair bobbing, occasionally peeking above the stone embankment as the subject ran across the list toward the archers. He turned back to Elizabet. "Peter?" An untenable notion seized him. "Woman, where are Gideon and Benjamin?"

She had the decency to look ashamed. "Peter's reloading the arrow stock for Minh. Gideon and Benjamin are in the nursery with Beau, of course." She flung her arms wide. "We had to use them! You know we can't use Dover's real army. Only the Amalgam for issues of hosts and time travel." She pointed to him. "Your words, not mine. Your army—," she bowed low, "—your majesty, is locked in the tunnels, drugged with a sleeping draught as ordered. That leaves about one hundred guardians and hosts at your current disposal. That's a small number when I didn't know how many Huns you would drop on us. I wanted to be prepared."

Jareth grimaced, and turned back to the battle. It was his rules, but his children and wife were not part of the battle plan. They had improvised that part. It was definitely time to change the rule system. Lots and lots of revisions were needed.

"Get your children, wife," he called over his shoulder. "And do it now, before I haul you off, give you the spanking you deserve, and lock you in the nursery." He grinned when he heard her little indignant snort, knowing full well she was, at the same time, hurrying her chicks to safety like the mother hen she was.

Jeremy materialized in front of him. "Caesar isn't here. Neither is Gyula. I'm requesting to travel back to Thanet and find them."

"Granted," Jareth said. An arrow whizzed past his ear. He balked and swung his head toward the list.

"Sorry, Daddy," Abigail called, her hand cupped by her mouth so her voice would travel. She used the same hand to wag her fingers in a girly wave.

Jareth automatically waved back, and then frowned at his hand when he realized what he was doing. "Any suggestions for a rebellious duchess?" He removed a time band from his wrist and handed it to Jeremy.

"Did you threaten to spank her?" Jeremy asked.

"Always do. It never works."

"Then my suggestion is that you put a little action to your words." Jeremy smiled. "But wait until I get home. I want to watch when she turns the spanking to you."

Chapter 14

"The age of Dover's Amalgam has begun. The age where host and man live together with purpose. We will defeat—nay, we will smash and destroy any league who threatens this treaty."
—Simon Dare, the Duke of Margate, addressing Dover's Amalgam after the first battle against the Huns

JEREMY QUICKLY LOCATED THE HOSTS hidden in the dormitories, where they had been kept separate from the students housed there. Ranging from ten years old to twenty, they each greeted him with humble hearts and attitudes once he siphoned the truth into them. Now they understood what had happened to their bodies and that there was a league formed to protect them rather than exploit them. They allowed him to rummage through the armoires in search of clothing that fit. Understanding his dilemma and dissipating problems, they agreed he should be dressed when he faced the enemy. Walking around in public wearing only a pair of white boxer briefs was something he did—occasionally—but would rather not. Especially in a time where there was a proper way to do everything. Margate didn't get to be a pompous prig by default of his lofty title. He was a product of his time. Wearing the proper attire in 1802 was serious business.

Jeremy promised to return for them once he found Gyula, and then slipped through the wing that housed the sleeping quarters and crept down the staircase. He knew where Gyula was—and Gyula knew that he knew where he was—so there was no hiding what was about to happen.

He entered the large solar on the third floor, his spine steeled as he closed the door. Gyula was not about, but Caesar was there. And dressed stylishly for the current era, although Jeremy was pretty sure that was a pair of jeans he had adapted. Pants in these days were rather itchy. "Your majesty," Caesar mocked, and then bowed. A leather cord held his long red hair back. "How good of you to come. Welcome to our headquarters. I'm sure it isn't as accommodating as Dover Castle, but once we clear out the vagrants, it will be most acceptable."

"Everyone is dead," Jeremy said, his voice a low drone in the still room. A log popped in the fireplace as Jeremy reached out to grab fuel from it. The fire conduit rode the air as he sucked it into his core. There was a crisp sting to the air, but nothing a little flame wouldn't help. "It's just you and Gyula. I killed the hosts who refused to surrender. The others will be taken into Dover's Amalgam. You've lost, Caesar."

Caesar watched, wide-eyed, as Jeremy fed from the fire. "I wondered how you did it," he said. He pointed to the stream of fire. "Malia uses water currents." He shrugged one shoulder, a look of indifference on his face. "I thought she was cool, but this is better."

Jeremy stopped the streaming at once, his hands gripped into fists at his sides. "What do you know of Malia? Where is she? Is she here?"

Caesar laughed, and then lifted his hands, as if surrendering. "Dude, relax. She hates me." He pressed his fingers to his chest. "I personally think she hates all men—just saying. But whatever. We're done. You can have her back."

Jeremy did what he should have done from the beginning. He strode to Caesar, gripped his arm, and began streaming memories from him. Part of him felt remorse for stealing so much, so he gave a measure back. He let Caesar know his mother was dead.

"You used Malia," Jeremy snarled. He pushed away, his

upper lip curled. "How dare you take advantage of her! She's under the protection of the Amalgam now." He stood straight. "I demand you fight for her honor. If you will not, then I shall. Name your weapon. I'll fight you man to man."

Caesar rubbed the spot Jeremy had gripped. "I don't care about her honor," he spat. "Go fight yourself for her honor!" He shook his head. "Your father killed my mother!"

"You should note that she was exiled from Britain and she broke the parameters of her sentencing. What she did was a criminal act. She left Scotland and she had the heir to Dover kidnapped. She was never supposed to leave the confines of the Isle of Skye."

"Oh, please do forgive her for loving the almighty Jareth Tremaine." Caesar stepped back, his gaze becoming hard. "Do you know she used to cry when she caught a glimpse of him? She peeked through the curtains when he dropped you off. Made me sick when I saw it. She never did pay my old man the time of day."

"Caesar, your father is a killer." Jeremy understood that Caesar was motivated by misplaced information and trust. Gyula had lied to him, too. He had siphoned that information to Caesar as well, and hoped it helped. "He wants to see the world amuck and wild. There are no systematic plans with him, only anarchy and mayhem. He believes hosts are animals that should be controlled. That we are no longer even considered human when we are. It's another form of racism in the making if we allow it. If he gains control of the Amalgam, there is no telling how history could be rescripted. He wants subjects, not an allegiance."

"He's a strong man, Jerm. I've seen him kill a toddler host who wouldn't stand down for the cause. He will rule better than a knight tangled up in church issues. He's a real warrior, not some misguided religious zealot."

"He actually calls it a cause? I'll say it again: it's anarchy.

Look at what you've become with a lack of boundaries. You defrauded a fellow host of mine; you lied to me—your closest friend; you bartered the life of my little brother for a man you don't even like."

"I love my father," Caesar claimed, his voice rising. "He's always been there for me. As for Malia, the little slut, she took from me as much as I did from her, so I consider us about even. Believe me, she wanted what she got."

"Hosts are sensual creatures," Jeremy replied. "We tend to be governed by our base emotions and needs. You knew that and you took advantage of her anyway."

"So, I guess that appeases my curiosity about you. Did you enjoy it when you shagged Beau, because I sure—"

Jeremy's hands went instantly around Caesar's throat. "Leave Beau out of this," he growled.

Caesar's surprised expression transformed to bug-eyed panic as Jeremy increased the pressure on his windpipe. Caesar might have believed he was safe due to the cold weather here, but he didn't realize that Jeremy's core hadn't dropped enough to cause his abilities to wane. He was still at ninety percent of peak strength, and the insult to Beau caused an energy spike. The left chambers of his heart swelled and fueled his core as he gained strength.

"You think you love her, but you don't," Caesar taunted. "You think you know her, but you don't. You've done nothing other than cause her pain. The host who dropped on her house—your fault." Caesar continued to goad Jeremy even as his eyes bulged. "Oh, yeah. I'm that good. Malia may be a siphon, but she's a poor one on her best days. She wasn't able to extract that info from you, but I can."

Jeremy felt a prick over his heart, and he grimaced as the pressure increased. The pain felt like the sting of a bee, but the burn of it was spreading. He looked down and immediately shoved Caesar away. The force he used lifted him into the air, where he flew until his body hit the wall and slid down.

He ripped open his shirt and touched the trickle of blood that flowed from his chest. The knife had barely broken the skin; he would heal. He regarded the knife in Caesar's hand.

"You have no idea what you are doing," he warned.

"Black onyx." Caesar held the dagger aloft. From the blade to handle, the knife was fashioned entirely from onyx. It was the only weapon that could terminate any host. He struggled to his feet with a grimace, favoring his right leg. "Oh, I think I know what I'm about." He pointed it at Jeremy. "You told me to choose my weapon. Well, here it is." He motioned him forward. "Let's duel for the honor of a girl who has none. How does it feel to die for a remorseless whore? Please, tell me so I can pass this on to Beau while I comfort her."

"Like I said, you have no idea what you're doing," Jeremy shouted. He wiped his hand down his chest; blood smeared over the newly healed wound. "You don't know everything about that blade." That he held it in his bare hand was a testament that he didn't know half the secrets of onyx.

"I know it's one of the only weapons that can kill you when you're at top strength." One of his shoulders lifted. "What else is there to know?" He tapped the blade to his lips as he mockingly pondered. "Oh, yeah. It's my ace in the hole. I'll win and get the girl after all."

Jeremy's mood instantly shifted from distress to anger. "Beau will never have you, even if I'm not in the picture. She knows about you."

"Well, then, my friend Malia will pay her a visit." Caesar grinned. "Since we are done with each other anyway, she'll have no problem helping a guy out. One touch is all it will take." He saluted with the knife. "Bye-bye to Jeremy. Forever. Hello, Caesar. Seriously, I really do hope you took care of that nasty detail called virginity, because I hate when they cry and get all emotional."

Jeremy lunged for him against his better judgement, against what his mind advised. Caesar wielded a blade that could end him, but he stayed and fought on behalf of Beau, a girl worthy of honor.

He grappled for the knife's handle above Caesar's head, trying to wrangle it from his grip. Jeremy hooked his foot around Caesar's ankle and brought them both down. They rolled over and over on the floor as they struggled for control. Jeremy was afraid if he dissipated, it would be easy for Caesar to bring the knife to his core. So he stayed in his skin and fought like a man.

"Caesar! No!" A voice shouted from nearby.

Malia appeared in the doorway, a backpack on her shoulder and a time band dangling from her fingertips. Jeremy saw the moment she realized Caesar had onyx.

"Get out of here," Jeremy told her through clenched teeth, and held Caesar at bay. He was stronger than Jeremy had allowed for. Training in the Hun army had been of benefit. He was tactful and smooth in his movements, which made it difficult to predict his next move. He was so focused that Jeremy was sure he hadn't noticed Malia's arrival.

Caesar rolled them again. This time he was on top, the blade poised over Jeremy's heart. Jeremy wrapped his hands around Caesar's and struggled. The knife trembled.

A rush of water coursed between them and covered Jeremy's body like a glove.

"Run, Jeremy!"

Jeremy's body was forced from beneath Caesar and went spinning and slamming against the wall. He scurried to stand just as the knife fell into the blanket of water.

"Don't!" Jeremy bellowed. He ran forward, but it was too late.

The form of Malia reappeared. She gasped when she spotted the blade protruding from her chest, and grabbed at it.

Jeremy dropped to his knees by her side while Caesar rolled

to a standing position, bouncing on his feet, his eyes darting around as if coming out of a daze. Malia had been at top form; there was probably three hundred joules pulsing through his body. The current would put him out of sorts for a while, but he was lucky to be alive. Caesar hopped from foot to foot, the charge making it impossible for him to stand still.

Jeremy searched her face. "Malia, why? I had him. You didn't—"

"My fault." She gasped, closed her eyes, and yanked on the knife. "I provided the information they needed to take the heir of Dover." The blade slowly slid out, stained with blood. "You have to take this. Don't leave it here—with them."

"It's not your fault. I trusted Caesar. He was with my family because of me."

"But I knew when to take him. When your family's guard would be down and distracted. I stole Ezra's band and searched for a time."

Jeremy accepted the blade. Malia curled her hand around his and the blade. She stared into his eyes, reading the emotions that their bodies housed. Their memories, their thoughts, their hearts. They had nothing in common, but they were both hosts.

Jeremy saw the confrontation she had with Ezra just minutes before she arrived. She realized her allegiance was with Dover, and Ezra had threatened to turn her in, make her see reason. She had seen Jeremy's death, and it had almost been too late for her to correct her wrongs, but she made it. Made it in time to save his life. Now she was in a natural state, no longer a host. He felt the freedom flow through her soul. It was what she wanted.

"Forgive me, Jeremy." Malia smiled with trembling lips. A tear fell from her eye. "I hope she knows how lucky she is. I would have given *anything* for you to love me like that."

Jeremy held her hand until she passed.

"You can take that blade, man, but we have others." Caesar

hit the side of his head with the heel of his hand and gave his head a shake. His equilibrium would be off for a while.

Jeremy flipped the knife and caught its handle. He rose, his lip curling as he took in Caesar's trembling form. He hoped the electrical currents gave Caesar nightmares for the rest of his life. "Stay away from my family. If you come near any of them again, I will kill you. And that includes Beau. She's off limits to you." He pointed at him. "I'm letting you live because it was Malia's dying request, and because I know ending your life is too easy. You need to live to regret what you've done." He lifted Malia's army green backpack from the floor. "Tell your dad I've got his blade."

"He'll never stop. He'll hunt you—your kind—until you're dead. Extinct." Caesar's teeth clattered together, making it difficult to speak. He clenched them together to stop the rattling. "You can't share a world with us. Eventually, one of your kind will get ideas and we'll all be screwed."

"You trust me," Jeremy snarled. He took two long strides forward and bumped his chest to Caesar's. "I was your friend. Don't try to sell me your dad's story because I'm not buying it. Somewhere in there, you know I'm right. You trust me."

Caesar shivered, closed his eyes as the currents wracked his body. Jeremy felt remorse, but from the corner of his eye, he saw the prone body of Malia.

He shoved Caesar's chest with his index finger. "You tell your dad I've got his blade and I'm coming back for the others." He tipped his head to access Caesar's memories. "Ten. Thank you very much." He held the blade between them, flashing it before Caesar's eyes. "This is ten, so I have nine to go."

"I'm going to kill you," Caesar bit out.

"I highly doubt that," Jeremy retorted. He cuffed Caesar's face with the back of his hand, then stepped back. "I allowed you the opportunity to fight me this time because I know what you're hiding. I see the struggle and I get it." He shrugged, lifted the backpack higher onto his shoulder. "After all my father has done to me, there is still a part of me that wants his acceptance. That needs him to acknowledge that I'm his son and I'm as good as Joel." He held Caesar's gaze. "You have to let it go. All the screwed up mess that your life is—the hate, being forgotten, ignored. Just let it go. It's not worth it. Until you do that, you'll be doing the bidding of a madman you don't even like." Caesar opened his mouth, but Jeremy silenced him with a tilt of his head. He arched a brow. "I'm a siphon, Caesar. You can't lie to me." He blew out a breath, and then peered around the room. "Listen, I have to go." He motioned between them. "Don't think this here was a bonding session, because it wasn't. The day you kidnapped my little brother, we became enemies. You took advantage of a member of Dover's Amalgam and then slaughtered her. Lastly, but most important to me, you threatened the life and honor of the girl I love. You don't get to come back from that one."

JEREMY PUT HIS HANDS ON his hips and peered up at the ceiling. Gabriel and Minh were bickering about the authenticity of the blade while Jareth turned it over in his hands, staring at it as if it was piece of dung. Simon Dare merely listened while he kicked back in a cushioned armchair, nursing a strong brandy and a shoulder wound. Ezra was there too, but he remained quiet. Jeremy had confronted him about his affair with Malia. Jareth would have to be told, but he was leaving that up to Ezra. They had sent for Malia's body. She deserved a proper burial.

"Did it pierce the skin?"

Jeremy took a deep breath and counted the beams above. Someone jostled him—it was Minh.

"Did it pierce the skin?" Minh repeated, his words slow and deliberate as if speaking to a sensitive child.

Jeremy bristled. "I bled. Is that good enough?" Minh leaned

forward, studying Jeremy's chest. Jeremy pushed him away. "Are we done here?" He directed the question to Jareth. "I'd like to go put some clothes on—for the third time today. And then I would like to have a nice dinner with my girlfriend . . . away from all of you. No offense, but I want nothing more than a good steak, a soft girl, and a nice fire." He looked at each of them. "You lot clearly do not fit the bill."

Jareth's mouth was stern. "You will see the duchess after you dress. She is worried sick over this." He put the offending weapon down and pushed it to the edge of the desk. Jeremy didn't know why this blade bothered Jareth so much when every guardian kept one in case a host went rogue. "And stop by the nursery to say hello to Solomon. He asked to wait up for your return and I granted him permission."

Minh's nose brushed Jeremy's pecs. Jeremy frowned and pushed him away. "Really? Don't you have someone else to bother?" He pointed to Simon. "Go cozy up to Margate. There's a wound you can sink your teeth into. It's real and everything."

"I was merely searching for an entry mark." Minh sniffed, looking offended. "Not that I don't believe you, but it is odd that the Mongolians can master something as complex as a flawless onyx blade. They must have stolen it."

"It is evident that we must move in a different course." Jareth brought his hands together in a light prayer pose, fingertips touching. He spread his fingers wide. "Gabriel, you will have to travel to the future and alert Gideon. He is our best physicist. Give him the blade so he can test it. He will be able to properly date it and find the source."

"The craftsmanship is Asian," Minh muttered. He glanced at the blade, then eyed Jeremy's chest again. Jeremy scoffed and turned away. "I think it's the work of my people. Perhaps Liang can help. She was friends with the town's gemstone keeper's daughter. If it's one thing my sister knows, it's fine gems and jewels. It would have been mined during the reign of our dynasty."

Jareth inclined his head to Gabriel. "See that your wife looks it over before you take it to Gideon. Keep accurate data. We want nothing missed this time. The life of Jeremy depends upon it."

Gabriel bowed. "Yes, your majesty."

Jareth's brow rose, Minh pulled a face, and Jeremy said, "Huh?" They all gaped at Gabriel as if he had grown a horn on his head.

Gabriel sneered, "What? I can be sincere." He stood straighter; the shield on his back fell lower. "I know when respect is needed. We kicked some Hun—"

Minh coughed loudly into his fist, drowning out the word Gabriel loved to use liberally.

"Fine." Gabriel smirked at Minh's antics. "Since I'm surrounded by little girls, we kicked some Hunny buns today—how's that?"

A pop of laughter left Minh's mouth. "Oh, that's a good one. I love that cartoon. It's my favorite." His laughter rang louder. "Hunny buns. It's the best line."

A look of disgust passed over Gabriel's expression. "Saying that tasted bad in my mouth," he said without humor. "If it's your favorite, why do you cry every time you watch it?"

"It's so real," Minh explained, his expression stark. "You do realize they research that stuff. The accuracy is uncanny . . . you have no idea."

"I have an idea," Gabriel retorted dryly.

"That's right," Minh said. "The models posturing like a pack of bulls pretending to be Spartans."

"They're actors," Gabriel pointed out. Minh shrugged one shoulder. "Are you finished?"

Minh sniffed. "For now."

Gabriel turned back to Jareth. "Bad puns aside, you fought well today, my friend." His gaze became fierce as he struck his forearm over his chest. "*i Et serviant tibi meus princeps.* I'm proud to bear the mark of Dover."

"We did kick some Hun ass, did we not?" Jareth asked.

"Jareth!" Minh hooted, his face pinched.

"I like your version much better," Gabriel beamed at Jareth. His hand sliced through the air. "No stupid cartoon puns needed."

Jeremy laughed. "What happened to our home being PG?"

"It was just upgraded to a firm PG-13," Minh said. "Or R. Depends if it's charismatic or reformed brethren doing the rating." It wasn't that Minh was offended. He was merely accustomed to being around the girls all the time and had taken to monitoring their language like a nursemaid. Jeremy smiled wider just to annoy him.

"What?" Jareth asked, leaning back, putting his feet up on his desk. He folded his hands over his stomach and tipped his chair back. "We are all adult men here. This is my personal solar, my castle."

"I could smell the testosterone clear across the moor," Elizabet complained as she entered through the small door normally used by the servants. "Better open a window or I'll probably suffocate."

The clunk of Jareth's chair legs striking the floor vibrated in the room. "Darling?" He sat up. "Is everything all right? The children?"

"Are all safe in the nursery. Does someone have to be in distress for me visit . . . what did you call it? Your personal solar?"

"Love," Jareth started, the word slowly rolling off his tongue. "We are in the middle of a meeting of great importance."

"Mmm," she hummed. "I listened at the door for the last ten minutes and all I got from it is that you come in here to drink." She looked pointedly at Simon. "Curse," She turned back to her husband. "And pose like a bunch of boars in heat." She struck her chest as Gabriel had, rolling her eyes.

"You call me a jackass all of the time," Jareth pointed out.

"And the brandy is strictly for medicinal purposes," Simon said, raising his glass to her. "Jareth won't allow me any laudanum."

"For the last time, Margate," Jareth bit out. "Laudanum has opium in it. I did offer to provide you a scrip for Demerol, but you refused. It is not as addictive when used under the direction of your physician. The last thing I need is to add an addict to my menagerie."

"What's a scrip?" Simon asked, his face scrunched up.

"For your information, husband, he kind of ass I call you is an obstinate animal that has to be prodded and yanked to be moved. They have unrelenting stubbornness." She looked at Simon. "You may carry on with your brandy, your grace. I completely understand your dilemma. You are quite forgiven."

Simon lifted his glass to her again and then drained the contents.

"Anything else?" Jareth asked.

"Actually, yes. The reason I came." She motioned to Jeremy. "Haven't you noticed that one of our children is standing here in his underwear? Not that it isn't normal for the males in this household to have no regard for feminine sensibilities. And not to mention a lack of discretion, but he is no longer a child. Either he'll give Mrs. Wheatley a heart attack or I'll have young maids swooning everywhere if they catch a glimpse of him. He needs a bath, clothes, and food. You know how depleted his calorie reserve is after he dissipates. What were you thinking?"

"Bless you, Mum," Jeremy piped in.

"Kissing up to me won't work," she told him. "You risked your life going back for Caesar and Gyula and I'm not happy about it, but we'll talk about that later." Her gaze softened. "I had Mrs. Wheatley prepare a tray to be brought to your room. It should be there by now."

"Yes, ma'am," Jeremy quipped, his mouth struggling not

to smirk at his fellow menfolk. He bowed to her and then to Jareth, knowing full well how ridiculous he looked in his undies—as the duchess pointed out.

Jareth waved him off. "Anything else?"

Elizabet smiled. "No." She lifted the hem of her velvet dress and curtsied. "I thank you for your time, your grace."

"Do not mention it," Jareth murmured as she floated from the room. He waited until the door closed behind her.

"Jareth—" Minh began.

"No one say a word." Jareth held up his finger. "Not a word, not a sound, not one syllable." He looked at Jeremy. "What are you still doing here? Did you not hear what the duchess said?"

"I was scared to leave, actually," Jeremy replied. "Do you think the maids are still awake, roaming the castle? I'd hate to make anyone swoon." He flexed his biceps.

"And I was on the verge of asking for your man card. I must revoke it after watching that delicious scene unfold," Minh said while inspecting his nailbeds.

Jareth sneered.

Gabriel clapped his hands together. "Well, I'm going out back to the northern list to scream cuss words for about ten minutes," he announced. "After I find myself a good strong ale in the kitchen, that is. A nice dark, manly brew." He cast a glance at Jareth. "You coming?"

Jareth stood. "No ale for me, but I'll join you. I can always tell Elizabet I have been plagued with a rapid onset of Tourette syndrome if she hears me."

"What about me?" Minh whined. "I have cigars."

"You stay here and babysit Simon," Gabriel grumbled.

"Why do you always leave me out, Gabriel? It isn't nice," Minh grumped.

"Because you say things like 'delicious scene.'" Gabriel's voice mimicked a high-pitched female. He glowered. "You shouldn't be revoking man cards. You should be trying to rescue what's left of Jareth's gonads, like me."

"Calm down," Jareth directed. He held up his hand. "I do believe my man card is safe. I have encountered far worse than one of Elizabet's blistering set downs, I assure you." He grinned. "My gonads are in safe hands with my wife."

"Ugh," Jeremy said, and covered his ears. "If only I could unhear that."

Chapter 15

"Rules-schmules."
—Gabriel Morton on Jareth's updated Laws of Dover's Amalgam

"YOUR MAJESTY," THE SERVANT GIRL said as she bowed over the polished salver she held.

"Thank you," Jeremy replied in Norman French. He waited for her to leave before he opened the seal of the letter that he had plucked from her tray. He was in the main hall, waiting for Beau to come down so they could have dinner. Although he had already devoured everything from the tray Elizabet had sent to him, he could always eat more.

He walked over to the chair by the great fireplace, unfolding the letter. It was from Caesar. His back stiffened and he glanced around even though he knew Caesar was long gone. It made him aware that they weren't truly safe until the last of the Huns were destroyed. As long as they possessed any of the travel stones, there would be trouble.

When you least expect it, I will be there. Time will pass, but my grudge will not. I will never forget what you have stolen from me. CR

What had he stolen? It was a question that Jeremy had difficulty with. Did he steal a portion of his life? The life of his mother? Did he damage the well-being of Caesar's future?

"Your hair is still damp," Beau said, her hand passing over his head.

He tipped his head back and smiled at her. "Hey."

"Hi." She smiled, then came around and curled up in his lap. "What is this?" She took the letter, her eyes skimming it.

"A warning."

She peered at him over the paper. "I feel sorry for him. Can you imagine having parents like that? All this time I thought his mom was just a selfish, rich narcissist. She was the witch who bargained with Gyula to kidnap Lizabet and hide her in the underwater cave before she learned to swim. Lizabet could have drowned!" She shook her head. "Talk about nefarious characters! Caesar's life is more screwed up than both of ours put together. No wonder he is the way he is."

Jeremy mouth dropped open. "I've got one of the world's worst fathers," he pointed out. "But I don't go around abducting people and ravishing girls. I've been abandoned and forgotten, but I still managed to turn out all right. Your father isn't any better than his, either. Should I feel sorry for you?"

"I was trying to be fair." She put the letter on the round table next to the chair. She draped her arms around his neck, and leaned forward in an embrace. "I can't shake the notion that I would have felt an evil or something in him, you know? I don't feel he's all-bad. He hung out in my room. We ran together. He helped me pitch." She shook her head. "How can someone act that convincing? It seemed as though he cared and wanted to be my friend."

"Yeah," Jeremy rumbled. He reluctantly had to agree that there was good in Caesar. It was the reason he let him live. As long as there was a thread of hope, he would allow it. "I know what you mean."

"What do you think? I may not be a siphon, but I see the wheels in your mind churning."

"Misguided." Jeremy shrugged. "Misplaced trust. I siphoned the truth to him. What he does with it is on him. I can't make him see the light. He has to choose it now. He believes what his dad says; that hosts must be tamed and conquered. That we should be caged until we are needed or necessary. That we serve a purpose only to please our masters, and the Monglians believe they should bear that title: masters."

"So, there's a chance he can redeem himself?"

"Did you hear what I just said? They want to rule over us. Kill the ones who won't bow to them. Caesar believes all that garbage. It would take something profound to change his mind and turn him against his dad. And let's not forget that he killed Malia. I don't care what she did; she was a member of the Amalgam. We have a code, and we protect what is ours. He needs to be punished for what he did."

"Then why did you let him go?"

That was a good question. He could have detained Caesar, brought him to Dover for a trial. It was only partially true that he allowed Caesar to live because Malia willed it and he wanted Caesar to live to reap the consequences for the deeds he had sown. Jeremy wasn't weak as Gabriel had alluded; he was more than willing and capable of ending things when necessary. But there was something else. Something he couldn't shake.

"You sensed the good in him," Beau said. She put her hand over Jeremy's heart and felt the rhythm pick up a notch. "I can hear you, you know. You're filtering straight to me."

"There's a chance, all right? I'll admit it. He didn't mean to kill Malia. I felt the remorse in him, and he didn't want to kill me, either. It was meant to scare and distract me so his dad could make his escape. He'd never wielded an onyx blade before. He didn't know they have a homing thread in them to destroy. I tried to warn him. He was brandishing it like a regular knife, the fool. I cautioned him that he didn't know everything there was no know, but he wouldn't listen. I think Gyula deliberately keeps him the dark."

"What will you do with that information?"

"Tell Jareth," he grumbled. "I'll have to tell him that Huns don't care about the agenda of protecting hosts, nor finding them. They're in it for the glory of the fight, the battle. Go fig-ure. The Huns are *acting* like Huns. Like the barbarians they are."

"I knew you'd make the right decision."

Jeremy growled in his throat. "That doesn't mean I have to like this." He rested his head on the back of the chair, then tipped his chin to look at her. With one hand, he brushed her hair over her shoulder. "What I do know is that you have noth-ing to worry about. I will protect you. No one will hurt you. And I will protect my family. Dover must be secure for future generations. The Amalgam will ensure a safe haven for my kind."

Beau used her finger to trace the crease between his eye-brows. "You get this look when you're worried. You're talking like you're so sure of everything, but your face tells me a differ-ent story. What's bothering you?"

"History repeating itself. This time, my kind will be the fo-cus of extermination. When I ended the lives of the Mongolian host, I heard what they were planning. They will not relent un-til all compliant hosts are subdued. They are only interested in those of us who will comply."

"Are there many who will?"

"We aren't designed to comply, no. Jareth says we are still intricately created and have a nature that is geared to do wrong. The heart is desperately wicked, you know? But with us, we can become vain and think we are more. Use our powers to force things. We have the propensity to be worse than the nor-mal person. Having the powers of nature will do that—make us think we are invincible when in fact, everyone has an expi-ration date. This looks to be a war that will span the centuries. Gyula is using the time bands without thought of the repercus-sions. He has no rules. He is simply a dictator with a god com-plex—and his legion is growing."

ON A SUNNY AFTERNOON SOON afterward, Beau stood next to Elizabet on the cliffs' edge, watching the children. They were playing tag, and careful to stay clear of the precipice. It was a beautiful day, sunny but cool. There was no snow, which was good for Jeremy. Not that it mattered anymore. All he needed was Beau and a moment alone to refuel. She was always up for that.

Elizabet shifted Benjamin in her arms and secured the blanket around him. "So, you don't mind being Jeremy's Wi-Fi hot spot?"

"I like that," Beau said, her lips quirking. "Wi-Fi hotspot. I'll be sure to tell Jeremy that one. He's always going on and on about how hot he is. It's my turn now. He can only be as hot as I allow him."

"Mummy, Mummy!" Solomon called, running up to his mother. He skidded to a halt at her feet. "I need the loo." His voice dropped an octave, his face flushed from exertion.

A bubble of laughter popped out of Elizabet's mouth. "The world is your loo." She motioned to the general area around them. "Choose your tree, bush or just take a patch of grass if you don't feel like lumbering for the tree line. We girls will look away."

"Dad says I shouldn't do that. He says that young dukes should set the precedence for proper behavior. Peeing outside is not considered dukely behavior."

"Um," Elizabet hummed, and passed Beau a look. She fumbled in her pocket. "Your dad said that, did he?"

Solomon nodded, all seriousness. Beau bit her lip to keep from laughing. Jareth was sure to turn his heir into a little soldier, a total rule follower. There was nothing wrong with a kid being a kid and using a tree trunk, for goodness' sake.

Elizabet produced a small, carved wooden animal from her pocket. She held it out to Solomon. "Go up to the castle, then." She jerked her head toward home. "Take this to your daddy on your way to the loo. Last I saw *his lordship,* he was in his solar. Tell him that your exercise was interrupted because he won't let you pee on a tree."

Solomon took the toy and stuffed it in his pocket. "Is there a message that goes with the little animal? You know he will ask me why I'm bringing him a jackass."

Elizabet smiled and this time, Beau did laugh. Her cousin's smile was diabolical. "He'll know the message. Just tell him that the jackass is from me."

Solomon shot off, his little legs pumping as he ran up the incline to the castle.

"I would love to witness that delivery," Beau said, laughter in her words.

"We'll hear from his majesty, don't you worry," Elizabet said. The title dripped from her lips with heavy sarcasm. "We won't miss a thing. He'll be sure everyone knows his displeasure—bellowing from the list, calling my name as if it's a curse word." Elizabet's smile wobbled on her lips, her eyes tapered as she shielded Benjamin. "Incoming," she muttered. She tipped her head to the shaft of light that burst into the already bright day.

Beau looked over her shoulder and then sidestepped to stand next to Elizabet as the wormhole contracted and opened only a few feet from them. This was a normal occurrence. It reminded Beau how different her life had become in the span of four short months.

A boy of thirteen or so with a mop of curly brown hair stepped out. His blue eyes darted left and then right until he spotted them, and then a beam spread over his face. He had two perfect dimples in his cheeks. "Mum!" he cried, and threw himself at Elizabet. His arms wrapped around her and the baby.

"Benjamin," Elizabet greeted. The greeting caused Beau to balk. She looked between the baby in Elizabet's arms and the boy who was wrapped around her like an octopus. "What are you doing here?"

Time jumping had recently been re-vamped, and Jareth was allowing more of it. It was to be expected that they would see an increase in weirdness like this.

"Oh, Mum! You're alive!"

"Geez, Ben," Jeremy said as he emerged from the worm-hole. "You couldn't wait for me?" A much older Jeremy took note of who was present. His gaze stopped on Beau, a brilliant smile curving his mouth. "Wife."

Beau's mouth sprang open. "Wife?"

"Too soon?" Jeremy asked with a tilt to his head. He smiled broader when he spied her discomfort. "How old are you?"

"Seventeen."

"Underage," Jeremy muttered, his head shaking. "Kissing you senseless is out of the question, then."

"Jeremy," she warned.

"Mum is dying," Benjamin interrupted, and brought every-one's attention back. "Honor was born and you . . . abrupted?"

Jeremy nodded. "Precisely." He turned to face Elizabet. "Your placenta detached. We have you partially stabilized, but you need blood. Jareth has us fetching him from five different time periods. He's the only match for your blood type, and we'll need enough pints to drop them in rapidly."

A second wormhole opened next to the first and a grown up Peter stalked out, his jaw tense. He tipped his head in greeting. "What's up?" He looked at Jeremy. "I have Dad. I just took him from the future. Honor's a teenager and Mom is fine. She'll make it. Solomon sent me to hurry you along. We still need more blood. Stat. The three Jareths we brought can't give any more. We need two more."

A sob left Benjamin's mouth. Elizabet's hand ran through his hair in a soothing motion. "See, I'm fine. It will be fine," she murmured.

"Geez, runt," Peter said. He motioned to the castle. "Stop

your crying and go get Dad."

Benjamin pressed a kiss to Elizabet's cheek. His eyes brimmed with unshed tears. He bussed the baby's cheek and was off, taking the same route young Solomon had gone moments before.

"You look well, cousin," Peter said with a lopsided grin.

"Remove your lady killing smiles from my wife, Peter," Jeremy warned. He put his body between Beau and Peter, thereby obstructing her view. "Don't you have someplace to go? Like back to saving Mum's life? Aren't you the anesthesiologist?"

"I have Abigail watching the monitors." Peter shrugged. "I did the hard part already. Mum won't need to be extubated for some time. I have her under quite well. Dad says the surgery will last a while. Total hysterectomy. She blew out the posterior wall of her uterus. Besides, I have to go fetch another dad from another time."

"I'm standing right here," Elizabet muttered.

"Sorry, Mum," Peter said. "You did hear me say that you're fine, right? I just saw you in the future." He smiled. "And let me add that you look fabulous."

"I don't see how all of this time jumping can be good," Elizabet said, her voice pensive. "What was Jareth thinking when he allowed all of this?"

"Saving lives," Jareth said as he ran up with Benjamin at his heels. He was half presentable with his black jeans barely tucked into Hoby hessians and his white shirt billowing. He had no coat. "It's what we do. Your life, above all, I will protect, my love." He paused to take a breath and tucked the small wooden animal into Elizabet's pocket. "Keep it safe for me, will you?"

"You're so not a jackass right now," Elizabet said. She stood on tippy toes and kissed Jareth's cheek. Her eyes swam with tears.

Jareth turned his face and kissed her mouth, taking her into a fierce kiss.

"Gah!" Jeremy said, and turned away. "Some things never change, regardless of the century."

"I like it," Peter grinned. The teenage Benjamin threw his arms around the bundle of his parents and baby. "Looks like the runt's timing doesn't change either. Always throwing himself into the fray of passion."

Jeremy tugged Benjamin away. "Come on. Let's get back. I'll need to scrub back into surgery. Solomon will need a break. We've been gone long enough."

"Mum," Benjamin said. She reached out and clasped his hand before Jeremy tugged him further away. "I love you!"

"And I, you, Benjamin," Elizabet answered. She looked away, tears brimming full in her eyes.

"We have this in hand, Benjamin," Jareth promised. He put his hand on Benjamin's shoulder and led him to the wormhole. "We have a good report, so let there be no worrying. Your mum will live."

"Aye, she will," Peter agreed. He placed two fingers to his brow in a mini salute. "I'll see you guys shortly back at Dover Castle." He bowed to Elizabet and then to Beau. "Your majesties—lovely as always. Always a pleasure to be seen by you." He winked at Beau. "Looking young and hot, cousin."

Jeremy shoved Peter back into the wormhole. He stepped toward her. "He's not wrong, though. You do look young and hot."

"Really, Jeremiah?" Jareth asked. He stood in the wormhole with a bawling Benjamin in his arms. "You would cause a delay in the duchess's recovery by flirting with your girlfriend?"

Jeremy kept his eyes on her. The intensity in his stare made her squirm, as she knew others were observing the exchange.

"Wife," he mouthed and grinned. He kissed the tip of her nose, his hand skimming down her arm and to her chest in gossamer whisper. "I have forever, Beau. Know that. I win you in the end, as I promised." He kissed the corner of her mouth. His voice dropped to a whisper. "Our daughter looks just like you."

Beau's eyes widened and her heart kicked up at the secret he shared with her. He pressed another kiss to the corner of her mouth before he stepped back with a cheeky grin on his gorgeous face. He turned to Elizabet and bowed.

BEAU WATCHED AS JEREMY BACKED away and into the wormhole. He lifted his hand in a small wave as the opening contracted and closed. She gave herself a hug to chase off the goosebumps that rose on her skin.

"Will I ever get used to this?"

"No," Elizabet sobbed. She wiped her cheek on her shoulder and shifted the baby in her arms. "Benjamin gets to me every time. He's all dimples and heart." She cuddled baby Benjamin, her mouth wobbling as tears ran down her face. "Mummy's sweetheart."

"He's pretty cute," Beau admitted. She gave Elizabet a pointed look. "But did you see Peter? Geez, girl! What are you feeding him?"

"I know, right? A Lothario in the making." Elizabet sniffed. She laughed through her tears. "He is the spitting image of his father, but he obviously has my mouth—or rather what comes out of it."

"Obvs." Beau snorted. "I say we lock that one up. Save us some heartache."

"Mum," Solomon said, breathless from the long trek. Jeremy was with him. "We just saw Benjamin leave with Dad. Will everything be all right?"

Jeremy threaded his fingers with Beau's, his expression concerned.

"Peter said it will go well," Elizabet reported, her eyes on Jeremy. She schooled her face to appear undaunted. "But not before he spewed all kind of medical jargon." She paled a bit.

"I almost die in childbirth. Then I lose my girl stuff. Just great. I hope I don't have to take hormones. I can barely stand all of y'all with all my girly stuff working properly."

"TMI, Mum," Jeremy said.

"Tell me about it," Elizabet agreed. "Jareth's new rules for time jumping will give me nightmares. You think I wanted to know I'm bleeding to death somewhere in time?"

"But you'll live," Solomon said, his voice firm. He reached for his mother's hand. "Benjamin said it would all be well. He promised."

"All will be well," Beau inserted. "Peter saw her in the future. She's fine and your baby sister is, too."

Jeremy's fingers tightened and Beau felt the beginning of siphoning.

Elizabet called for the children. "I'm going back inside. I find myself in need of a restorative nap. I feel a swoon coming on."

"I'll bring them in," Beau said. "You go up. We'll be right behind you."

Solomon followed his mother while Abigail began to gather the cricket game they had set up. Peter continued to chase Gideon, but they were running toward the castle.

"Help your sister!" Beau hollered. She shook her head when they performed a drastic turn and flipped over one another—taking a tumble down the grassy slope. They ended up crashing into the cricket balls and mallets that Abigail was trying to put away.

"Something you want to tell me?" Jeremy asked.

Beau untangled their fingers and turned away. "I think you know."

Jeremy grabbed her arm. A smile curved on her mouth as she faced him. "I told you I'd get forever." It distinctly sounded like he was bragging.

"Did you really ever doubt?" she asked. She grabbed his hand and laid it over her heart. "If you say yes, I swear, I'll punch you."

He leered. "Oh, I'm not thinking of punching you. I promise."

Beau rolled her eyes. "You're impossible." She recovered his hand and smirked when his fingers squeezed where they weren't supposed to. "Feel that? That is a doubtless heart."

Jeremy shook his head; his Adam's apple bobbed on a rough swallow. There was no hint of jesting on his face any longer. "I never doubted. I've always known it would be you. Just you."

"Just us," she whispered, and pressed his hand to her heartbeat. "I give you forever, Jeremy."

His fingertips shifted slightly as he followed the rhythm strumming there. His eyes caught hers and held. "The day I walked into your family's grocery store, I was lost. I took forever that day. You say you gave it to me, but I took it, Beau. I would never have stopped until you were mine."

"You're not so scary that you can force me, Jeremy."

"Have it your way." He smiled. "You offered it to me and I took it. Gladly."

"Jeremy . . ."

He placed his fingertips over her lips. "Shut up, Beau." He *tsk*ed her as his hands traveled to her upturned face. He leaned toward her. "There are such better things to do with your mouth than quibble with me."

He kissed her then, and it didn't matter how they came to forever, only that they had arrived and it was wonderful.

About the Author

ELIZABETTA HOLCOMB LIVES IN SOUTH Louisiana with her husband, children, and cats. When she is not working nights as an RN, she is in her writing room creating more stories of Dover's Amalgam. Mother to 5. Marmee to 1. She enjoys hearing from readers who love Jareth and Dover's Amalgam. Connect with her on social media or send an email via her website.

www.elizabettaholcomb.com
www.facebook.com/ElizabettaHolcomb
www.instagram.com/elizabettaholcomb
https://twitter.com/DuchessofDover
www.pinterest.com/elizabettaholco

More by Elizabetta Holcomb

The Guardian: Chronicles of Dover's Amalgam
The Heir: Chronicles of Dover's Amalgam
(Coming Fall 2016)
The Spare: Chronicles of Dover's Amalgam
(Coming Winter 2016)

Want more right now?
Turn the page for an unedited/working back cover blurb of
The Heir due for release in September 2016

The Heir:

Chronicles of Dover's Amalgam Book 3

Solomon Tremaine

Heir to all that comes with Dover's Castle: Dukedom, lands, and an Amalgam of hosts in which he will gain guardianship. When a group of bandits begin stealing biblical manuscripts from the castle vault for public distribution, Solomon must prove to his father that he is worthy of his to-be title by catching the thieves. With a range of learning disabilities, he feels that his approval is conditional and this is a way he can gain the Duke of Dover's permanent approval. But when studying for medical school and an obscure girl come into the picture, being worthy and jumping between time periods cannot hold a candle to his world turning upside down. She isn't what he expected . . .

Shelby Adams

Shelby is building a college portfolio that will guarantee her way out of the small town she lives in. Her life is filled with 4H showmanship, work, and keeping up her GPA, when she sees an opportunity she cannot refuse. After meeting Solomon Tremaine at a Beta Convention, she becomes obsessed with getting to know a boy who is more enigma than real. Seeing him as the key to an adventure of a lifetime, she has no idea the secrets he keeps when she is swept into a life of hosts and wormholes. It was more than she bargained for . . .

Two are better than one . . .

As Solomon and Shelby form an unlikely bond of friendship, they realize that common relationships aren't for those with a pack of Hun's and angry medieval Church officials chasing their every move. Struggling to keep their relationship private, they begin to work together in more ways than just tutor and student. But when Shelby becomes wounded in a time she isn't a part of, things change and Solomon fights to keep her alive. He must keep her safe from the Hun's who seek to erase his life, when all the while, all he desires is to make her a part of his life that can only mean never ending danger if she agrees to stay.

99136957R00167

Made in the USA
Lexington, KY
14 September 2018